Praise for
The Kindred Spirits Supper Club

"I am absolutely smitten with *The Kindred Spirits Supper Club*. Amy E. Reichert has created a heart-squeezing love story, with a perfect sprinkling of mystery and magic. A deliciously sweet tale about ghosts, growing up, and going home. Reichert has hit her stride in this one!"

—Emily Henry, #1 *New York Times*
bestselling author of *Beach Read*

"A sweet, fun read. It's warm, cozy, and full of hometown charm—and there's a brilliantly quirky cast of ghosts, too!"

—Beth O'Leary, *Sunday Times*
bestselling author of *The Switch*

"Delicious, heartwarming, and a ghost who wears Chanel? Unsurprisingly, I found *The Kindred Spirits Supper Club* utterly unputdownable!"

—Evie Dunmore, *USA Today*
bestselling author of *A Rogue of One's Own*

The Optimist's Guide to Letting Go

"Delightful and heartfelt."

—Karma Brown, international
bestselling author of *Recipe for a Perfect Wife*

"A delightful treat—Amy's writing gets under the skin of family: how they drive you crazy, but you love them just the same. An absolute joy I am sure readers will take to their hearts."

—Veronica Henry, author of *How to Find Love in a Bookshop*

"Reichert has created wonderful true-to-life characters in a novel of secrets and regrets, loss and hope."   —*Library Journal*

"With charmingly developed characters who are thoughtfully crafted, this story will cling to readers through the final pages."

—RT Book Reviews

"A delicious read full of family and food."   —*Kirkus Reviews*

"Written with Reichert's hallmark humor and heart. . . . Lose yourself in this rich and rewarding read!"

—Pam Jenoff, *New York Times*
bestselling author of *The Ambassador's Daughter*

"With characters that are as complicated as they are original and a voice that is warmhearted and wise, you will hug this book when you're done."

—Taylor Jenkins Reid,
bestselling author of *Daisy Jones & the Six*

"The characters are wonderfully imperfect, and their relationships are recognizably flawed, making their journey around and around—and finally back to—each other immeasurably satisfying. Bravo!"

—Christina Lauren, *New York Times*
bestselling author of *The Honey-Don't List*

The Simplicity of Cider

"Reichert captures the food, relationships, and unique settings of the Midwest at their best. I was absolutely charmed by *The Simplicity of Cider*."

—J. Ryan Stradal, *New York Times*
bestselling author of *The Lager Queen of Minnesota*

"The perfect blend of sweet, smart, and immensely satisfying. If foodie fiction is a thing, Amy Reichert is the grand master."

—Colleen Oakley, author of *You Were There Too*

"It's charming, heartwarming, and magical."

—Nina Bocci, *USA Today*
bestselling author of *Meet Me on Love Lane*

"A novel as delicious as cider and as enchanting as magic.... This is a lovely book, meant to be savored."

—Karen White, *New York Times*
bestselling author of *The Christmas Spirits on Tradd Street*

"A lot charming and a little bit magical, Reichert's latest is warm and poignant and romantic."

—RT Book Reviews (4-star review)

"The ultimate ode to celebrating the dazzling splendor in small things. This will give you more fuzzy feelings than you can count."

—*Redbook*

Once Upon a December

Amy E. Reichert

BERKLEY ROMANCE

New York

BERKLEY ROMANCE
Published by Berkley
An imprint of Penguin Random House LLC
penguinrandomhouse.com

Copyright © 2022 by Amy E. Reichert
Excerpt from *The Kindred Spirits Supper Club*
copyright © 2021 by Amy E. Reichert
"Readers guide" copyright © 2022 by Amy E. Reichert
Penguin Random House supports copyright. Copyright fuels creativity,
encourages diverse voices, promotes free speech, and creates a vibrant culture.
Thank you for buying an authorized edition of this book and for complying with
copyright laws by not reproducing, scanning, or distributing any part of it in
any form without permission. You are supporting writers and allowing
Penguin Random House to continue to publish books for every reader.

BERKLEY is a registered trademark and Berkley Romance with
B colophon is a trademark of Penguin Random House LLC.

Library of Congress Cataloging-in-Publication Data

Names: Reichert, Amy E., 1974– author.
Title: Once upon a December / Amy E. Reichert.
Description: First edition. | New York: Berkley Romance, 2022.
Identifiers: LCCN 2022025330 (print) | LCCN 2022025331 (ebook) |
ISBN 9780593197790 (trade paperback) | ISBN 9780593197806 (ebook)
Subjects: LCGFT: Romance fiction. | Christmas fiction.
Classification: LCC PS3618.E52385 O53 2022 (print) | LCC PS3618.E52385
(ebook) | DDC 813/.6—dc23/eng/20220527
LC record available at https://lccn.loc.gov/2022025330
LC ebook record available at https://lccn.loc.gov/2022025331

First Edition: October 2022

Printed in the United States of America
1st Printing

Book design by Elke Sigal

To the ladies of 320 Jacobs Court.

For the Present is the point at which time touches eternity.

  —C. S. Lewis, *The Screwtape Letters*

Treat every day like Christmas.

  —Buddy the Elf

Once Upon a December

Once upon a December, a girl met a boy,
but she didn't remember.

Chapter One

IN A PLACE OUTSIDE OF TIME, EVERY DAY WAS DECEMBER.

As a resident, Jack Clausen treasured all of the Christmas trimmings that came with living in the Julemarked: the sparkling lights, fresh-cut pine branches, crunchy snow, joyous music, and abundant holiday cheer. The festive alley contained several shops selling handmade goods like sweaters, toys, ornaments, and so much more. His family's bakery, Kringle All the Way, was one of many shops run by the Julemarked residents, a tight-knit community that never stayed in one place for long.

Too early in the day for customers, Jack's hands carried multiple white bags containing freshly baked kringle slices he would deliver to his neighbors, the smell of cinnamon and almond wafting to his nose as he pulled open the door to A Stitch in Time, the knitwear store near the bakery.

Tables and shelves were stacked with every possible item that could be created with knitting needles, from sweaters and blankets to hats and scarves to stuffed animals and flowers. Behind the counter, Mrs. Pedersen already waited for customers, the soft clack of her knitting needles buried under the jangle of entrance bells. A pale green knit hat covered her soft blond curls, which brushed the shoulders of a matching Nordic sweater. Everyone in the Julemarked had similar sweaters and hats, just like everyone grew up with toys made by the Hagens at Time to Play, or drank coffee from mugs the Estradas made in their store, Kiln Time, or devoured kringle made at Kringle All the Way. The Julemarked residents provided what one another needed, when they needed it, always watching out for one another.

"Set them on the counter, dear," Mrs. Pedersen said, nodding at the bags in Jack's hands. "Anika will be out soon if you want to stick around."

Since birth, Jack's mom and Mrs. Pedersen had maneuvered Anika and him toward each other—it wasn't going to happen, but moms will be moms and he didn't blame them for wanting their children to find happiness with people they had known all their lives. Thankfully, Anika agreed with Jack and was equally amused by their maternal machinations.

"I need to finish deliveries before it gets busy, but tell Ani I say hi." Jack pointed to the bag on the counter. "There's an extra pecan slice for you." Since he still held more bags to deliver, Jack pushed the door open with his backside.

"Always so thoughtful. Tell your mother to stop over later. The new batch of peppermint schnapps is ready," Mrs. Pedersen said.

"Will do." Jack stepped out into the alley. A few beams of sunlight streaked across the red brick of the Julemarked's walls, a reliable sign that customers were soon to follow. He completed his deliveries to the rest of the alley and headed back to the bakery to get ready for a day of slicing and selling kringle to a long stream of hungry customers.

As Jack turned the last corner next to the bakery, he saw the large black wrought-iron arch that marked the entrance to the Julemarked, the line between his world and the Outside. Next to it hung a large black clock that counted from one to twenty-five with only one moving hand—a constant reminder that time worked differently here. To any Outsider, the single hand didn't seem to move, but to the residents it made perfect sense. It marked the days until Christmas. Currently, the hand pointed to the space below the three, indicating it was December 3—the third day into the current Yule. The clock would stay silent except for the last minute before midnight on Christmas Eve, when it would ring twelve times to let the residents know the Nulstil was about to begin—the seven days from Christmas to New Year's Eve, when the Julemarked was cut off from the Outside, giving residents time to rest and prepare for the next Yule. When the Outside celebrated New Year's Day, the Julemarked opened in a new location and it was December 1 again.

Looking at the watch on his wrist that told actual time, Jack picked up his pace. Customers were already starting to wander into the alley from the Christmas market on the other side of the entrance, one of many around the globe that the Julemarked would connect to each year. There were locations, like Copenhagen, Paris, New York, and Milwaukee, that they connected to almost every year, but it was never a guarantee. As far as Jack could tell, no pattern existed. This Yule they were in Milwaukee, the previous Yule was Seoul, the next one might be Paris or

Buenos Aires or one of a thousand Christmas markets in between.

Living in a magical alley was like that, and you just had to go with it.

While he loved everything about the Julemarked and each Christmas market they visited, Jack had a soft spot for Yules in Milwaukee. Maybe it was the locals' fierce and loyal adoration for all things kringle or their enthusiasm for winter weather. Maybe it was the way they embraced public drinking from the many mulled-wine stands or how they fundamentally understood that cheese and butter made everything better. But while all of those were reasons why Jack loved Milwaukee, none were the top reason. That spot was reserved for Her.

He remembered when they first met fourteen years ago.

Jack had looked up to help the next customer who stood in front of him at the bakery counter, and it was a young woman accompanied by three friends, all four of them wearing identical red knit hats. Her eyes sparkled with laughter at whatever her friend had just said, her cheeks almost as pink as her lips. A charming dimple on her right cheek deepened the more she laughed. Sparkly ornaments dangled from her ears and she wore a bright red winter coat and green scarf—the embodiment of Christmas spirit. Jack loved to see it.

"What can I get you?" Jack said.

Without looking up, she pointed to the cherry kringle. "That one, please." She blinked as her blond friend whispered something in her ear. "Shut up," she said to her friend. She turned back to Jack.

Her friend whispered in her ear again as he picked up the kringle slice and a bag to slide it into.

"Fine," she whispered, louder than she meant to, given the pink flush to her cheeks. Directing her comment to him, she said, "I bought a pack of five hats." She pointed to her head. "And I have an extra one. Would you like it?"

The two friends behind her giggled and elbowed each other.

The dimple-cheeked girl held up the hat. Jack looked down at his hands, which were full of kringle and sticky with frosting, and leaned his head over the bakery case so she could reach him. She slid the hat over his dark blond hair, making sure to pull it down far enough in the back so it wouldn't fall off. Her hands were gentle yet confident enough to make sure it fit snugly. When she pulled her hands back, he straightened and smiled.

"How do I look?" Jack said.

Her eyes twinkled.

"Like Santa's younger brother."

"If I'm going to accept this, then you need to accept something from me." Jack looked around the bakery for something he could give her. On shelves around the bakery stood dozens of nisse figurines wearing red pointy hats, small elves that were a part of Scandinavian Christmas traditions. He liked to carve them at night after completing the bakery work. It kept his hands busy. Using a piece of parchment paper so he wouldn't transfer any of the sticky frosting from his hands to the figure, he picked out a small wooden one with a large nose and fluffy white beard sticking out from the bottom of a bright red hat that covered his eyes. "Here's a nisse."

Even with the parchment paper barrier, Jack felt a tiny spark when he set the gnome in her outstretched hand, like a tiny static electricity jolt, most likely from the dry winter air, but enough for him to *pause and look into her eyes to see if she felt it, too, but her facial expression did not change. She stayed focused on what he had said.*

"Knees—oo?" she said, sounding out the word.

"Yep. Spelled n-i-s-s-e. Or with an R at the end if there are more than one; that's pronounced knees-ah. They are the Danish Christmas elves. We have to give them rice pudding on Christmas Eve or they cause all sorts of mischief."

"Nisse." She said the word with more confidence, holding the small figurine in the palm of her hand. "Thank you. I'll make sure he gets his rice pudding."

"Jack," Orn growled at him, a warning to get back to work. She paid for her kringle and her friends filed out of the store. When she turned back one last time, Jack nodded his head, then turned his attention to the next customer.

"Jack's got a girlfriend," Mads said, speaking in Danish so the customers didn't understand what they were talking about.

"You mean that barely adult child who just left?" Jack asked.

"She said you look like Santa's younger brother," Mads said.

"Yeah—that means I look old to her, at least twice her age. Santa is ancient. Old Johan could look like Santa's younger brother."

He straightened the hat on his head, noticed how nice it felt, and returned to work.

She had just been a friendly customer on a busy day who gave him a lovely hat he still owned.

He hated that he still didn't know her name after meeting her so many Yules ago—fourteen years in Outside time. Each time he'd learned a little more about her. Each time she had forgotten him and the Julemarked completely, just like the rest of the customers. Somewhere over those fourteen years, he'd started anticipating their next encounter, dreaming about what he'd discover next.

This year, he knew what he wanted to learn—what he had to learn. Her name.

Chapter Two

WITH A NAME LIKE ASTRA NOEL SNOW, OF COURSE ASTRA loved Christmas. The twinkly lights, the smell of pine and cinnamon and fresh-baked cookies, picking out the perfect wrapping paper for each present. Unlike any other holiday, Christmas was a season—nay, a state of mind—and Astra embraced it fully. With a closet stuffed full of Christmas sweaters, she also possessed earrings depicting every form of Christmas iconography from sparkly stars to wise men to jolly Santa heads, and no less than a dozen Santa hats in varying states of holiday bedazzlement. She began decorating her house the day after Halloween, culminating with cutting down and decorating a Christmas tree the day after Thanksgiving—a Fraser fir, of course—preferably a not-quite-perfect one.

A decorated tree marked the true beginning of the holiday season from Thanksgiving all the way through the New Year. Everyone was jollier, sparkling lights on every house made the long winter nights more beautiful, and every morsel of food evolved from mere sustenance to celebration. Cookies, turkey, stuffing, homemade candies. Leftovers become special treats. And so many cheese-and-sausage platters—it wasn't a holiday party in Wisconsin without one. For the hard-core Wisconsinites, there were the cannibal sandwiches—raw ground beef on rye bread topped with raw onion. Astra preferred throwing one on the grill, but her dad loved them as is.

Yes, Astra was made for the holidays, with the highlight being the annual getaway weekend with her college roommates at the Milwaukee Christmas market. Sure, they could stay at one of their houses in the metro Milwaukee area, but part of the fun was staying up all night in the hotel, sharing beds, and reminiscing just like in their college days. Over the years, the hotel rooms had gotten nicer, and the booze more expensive, but they still shared one room and two beds and all the giggles.

And she was meeting her beloved college roommates downtown tomorrow morning if she could ever get out of work. At the Milwaukee Northeast branch where Astra worked as the library director, chaos had taken over. In the ladies' restroom, the toilet next to an exterior wall had frozen solid, but no one had noticed until after someone tried to flush and the water didn't go anywhere. A plumber was on his way, and in the meantime, she had set up a space heater to thaw the water. All the cookbooks in the library stacks on how to grill meat had gone missing. Again. She had Chloe, a circulation desk clerk, scanning the library to find them. Ever since radio frequency ID tags had been added to the books, it made finding mis-shelved (or hidden) books easier. And now she had to kick Mr. Whitney off the computer for looking at inappropriate images. She stood behind him, his screen full of male genitalia, most of it medical illustrations, but a few shocking photos were in the mix. While they weren't any more graphic than what played on TV most days, it was still inappropriate in the middle of the library, where a kindergarten class would soon be walking by on their way to story time. So engrossed in his screen, he hadn't noticed her hovering behind him.

"Mr. Whitney." Astra tapped him on his shoulder. He turned slowly, his watery gray eyes blinking up at her as he registered her sequined red sweater, sparkling reindeer necklace, and Rudolph earrings, which glowed. He didn't even minimize the screen. "Mr. Whitney, you can't do that here and you know that."

"I can search the internet. My tax dollars pay for this."

"Yes, you can search the internet for what you want to view, but you need to be sensitive to what other people, especially young children, can see. They have a right to be at the public library and not be exposed to inappropriate images. Our policy clearly states that improper use of library resources may result in being asked to leave. I don't want to have to do that."

"I have a condition." His eyes didn't meet hers and Astra was sympathetic to having to look up sensitive topics in public spaces. Alas, most of her job lately seemed to be finding the least offensive solution to the majority of patrons.

"I'm sorry to hear that, but I'm sure we can find some books that will have the same information, and you can bring that home."

"You know, if I were looking at dismembered bodies, you wouldn't be kicking me out."

"Actually, I would. Young children don't need to see that either." She gave him a smile and waved over Adam, the research desk librarian. "Adam will help you find what you need."

After a bit more grumbling, he got up and followed Adam into the stacks. Astra closed the tabs, deleted the history, and rebooted the computer to be extra cautious. He always tested the boundaries but never acted belligerent or truly disruptive—and more importantly, he didn't seem to have anywhere else to go. Generally a model patron, it was only every few months that he did anything that crossed the line.

That taken care of, she surveyed the library. Kids and their moms filed in for preschool story hour; the Gal Squad, four gray-haired ladies, worked on a puzzle near the large bay windows where you could almost see Lake Michigan if the foliage didn't block the view. With the lovely sun streaming in, they met there every morning, like cats who sought out the sunbeams. Sometimes they played mahjong, sometimes bridge, sometimes they did a puzzle. Janice at the reference desk listened to a mom who flailed her hands as she spoke but kept her words quiet enough that Astra couldn't tell the topic. Janice would let her know if she needed backup.

"Found them." Chloe walked toward her carrying a tall, teetering stack.

"Where were they?" Astra asked, taking the top half of the stack and setting the books on a nearby rolling cart to be reshelved. Chloe set hers next to them.

"Half were behind the moral philosophy books; the rest were behind the ag books—specifically the ones on the environmental impact of commercial meat farms. Our book hider has a sense of humor."

Astra chuckled.

"Can you wheel these up front?" Astra asked, and Chloe

scooted off. At last, she could finalize the budget. All the number crunching had been done for days; now she needed to make it accessible to people who only thought about the library's finances once a month. It needed to be ready and approved at tonight's board meeting. Not that she expected any problems, but she liked to anticipate any questions.

The overhead intercom beeped.

"Astra, please come to the front desk," said the voice of her circulation desk manager, Billy.

She prayed Mr. Whitney hadn't decided to make a scene because then she really would need to ban him.

As she came around the stacks and the circulation desk came into view, a deep "woof" greeted her, followed by a sweet whimper and nails clacking on the tile floor.

"Bernie! What are you doing here?" Astra asked, greeting her dog with ear scratches and a nose boop. Bernie, a giant Bernese mountain dog and Lab mix (she guessed), had a long coat, mostly black except for a streak of white starting on her forehead, then trailing down her throat and onto her chest, with another spot under her tail, making her look like a cream-filled chocolate-dipped cannoli. Three of her four paws looked dunked in white paint, like she'd made a mess during a home improvement project. She was named for one of Astra's favorite characters, Bernadette Fox from *Where'd You Go, Bernadette*. Like the titular character, Bernie had a small circle of people she adored; she found the rest to be annoying gnats (small children excluded—they often had snacks to share), not to be bothered with, except the squirrel who lived in the front yard, who was her nemesis. She spent hours making sure the little rodent didn't sneak into the house.

After grabbing the leash and wrapping it around her hand, not that Bernie would ever leave her side, Astra finally addressed the man who had brought her. Trent Bradley. The ex-husband. Once upon a time she had thought him the center of her universe, with his short blond hair, striking gray eyes, and magnetic charm, until he had decided he didn't love her and left—simple as that. One minute they were married; the next they weren't. He got the house, she got giant legal bills, and they shared custody of Bernie— the true love of her life and only remaining tie to her former lover.

Which was of course the reason Trent had fought for joint custody. He might not want to share her bed, but he loved when she solved all his problems. As Trent's personal Google, she found the best local plumber, how to set up a router, even where to hire a dog walker. Top that off with the convenience of knowing she'd happily watch Bernie whenever he needed her to, often with little or no warning, like today—Trent had every motivation to keep her in his life.

Until Bernie crossed the Rainbow Bridge, something Astra refused to spend time pondering, or she convinced Trent to give her full custody, she had to put up with his continued existence in her life, like the weed in a flower bed that never went away no matter how many times she yanked it out.

"Seriously, what are you doing here?" Astra asked again. He held a plastic bag in one hand.

"I know, I know," Trent said. "But I had a last-minute work trip come up."

"Then call the dog sitter." She didn't really mean it, but she couldn't make it too easy on him.

He cleared his throat.

"She's not responding to my texts." Trent actually looked guilty. He'd certainly been making the most of his singleness.

"What am I supposed to do? You know this is my girls' weekend."

He absolutely knew. His supposed work trip was most likely a bro trip to Vegas that he'd known about for weeks. He wanted to know if she'd still drop everything for him.

"I'm sorry, but I have to go," Trent said. His gaze wandered to a group of young moms checking out stacks of children's books.

He held his hands wide as if he had no control over his schedule. As if he couldn't have done anything to make her life easier. He was the worst. Once she had thought him worth all her attention, cutting out time with friends and family to be with him. The classic mistake. She hated herself for giving up so much for him and would never make the same mistake again.

"You can leave," Astra said.

Her staff did a good job pretending this wasn't at-work entertainment.

"I'll pick her up on Tuesday," Trent said.

"Don't bother. If you can't take care of her this weekend, she may as well come with me to Florida. I'm leaving on Monday."

Astra entertained the idea of flying with Bernie in a crate but couldn't stomach the idea of her under the airplane. What if it was too cold? What if she thought Astra had abandoned her? No, she'd have to rent a car and drive, finding pet-friendly hotel rooms along the way. She should cancel her trip to Florida to see her parents, but she knew Bernie would love the ocean and her parents would love spoiling their grandpup.

"If that's what you want." He paused and held out the bag in his hand. "Can you hem these for me?"

Astra breathed deeply and glared but still took the bag. Trent grinned and leaned in to kiss her cheek. Astra stepped away.

"Merry Christmas," he said, then left.

Thank goddess. Astra looked down at Bernie.

"Now, what am I going to do with you, sweetface? Can you be a good girl and stay in my office?" She noticed Bernie's boring black collar. "We'll have to do something about your festiveness, too."

Bernie sat and gave her a serious look, letting her know that she could handle the important responsibility that Astra proposed.

"Puppeeeee!" The preschool reading group had just let out and a small crowd of under-fours headed in their direction, with moms struggling to get arms in sleeves and hats on heads. Before Astra could get Bernie away, children surrounded them and Bernie's tail reflected her excitement. Little hands and faces coated in Goldfish crumbs and applesauce drips were in easy reach of her soft, warm tongue. She snuck in kisses as the children giggled and touched her fur.

Astra's librarian mode kicked in.

"Be gentle and don't push. Two lines, please. Give her a chance to sniff you. That's how she gets to know you. Then you can all pet her. This is Bernie; she's a Bernese mountain dog and Labrador retriever mix, so she loves to play catch, go swimming, and give kisses."

One little boy looked up at her. "Does she make big poop? My mom says we can't get a big dog because they make big poop."

Astra could tell immediately which mom belonged to this fellow. The mom covered her face to keep from laughing, then mouthed "sorry" to Astra. Astra winked at her, then gave the boy her full attention.

"She makes really big poops. Your mom is right."

His eyes got wide and his mom reached into the crowd and eased him out.

"Time to go; we need to get your sister," the mom said as she scooped him up. Astra gave them both a wave and turned her attention back to the kids, who peppered her with questions about the dog's white paws and if she snored, until the parents slowly collected them and she and Bernie were left alone.

"Well, Bern, we should probably call the parents and tell them they'll have another guest. Then see if a neighbor wants a giant furball for the weekend." Barely holding the lead, Astra led Bernie to her office, Bernie staying snug against her sensible black pants, leaving a smattering of hair. Before she could give the command, Bernie crawled under Astra's desk and lay down. This wasn't the first time Bernie had come to work with her, but she tried not to take advantage of it since she wasn't an officially trained service animal. Still, Bernie knew the routine.

Astra slipped in her earbuds but paused before calling her mom to take a few breaths. She hadn't slept well last night, but she'd had the most vivid dream about a man in a bakery. While he looked familiar, she couldn't remember where she had seen him. In the dream, he'd given her some kind of baked good. Why couldn't she find someone like that in real life? What could be sexier than a man who baked?

After another deep breath, she pressed Call on her phone.

"Hey, Bun," her mom answered. "Bun"—the nickname that had evolved from "Snow Bunny," a play on their last name, to "Bunny," to just "Bun." It stuck. "Is your flight all set?"

"Did you read my mind?"

"Oh no, what happened?"

"Good news and bad news. Bad news, I'll be a few days late getting there. Good news, you get to spoil Bernie."

"That jackass." Her mom knew without her even having to say anything.

"Yep. He just dropped her off at the library with no notice and I have to scramble to work her into the weekend."

"I'm sure you'll find the perfect solution. What should I have for Bernie when you get here? She'll be our first canine guest."

"I'll bring everything, so you don't need to do anything. Though I'm sure she would love some special treats."

They chatted for a few minutes and she got ready to hang up.

"Wait, your father wants to talk to you."

"Hi, Snowflake." Another nickname. Honestly, why did they bother giving her a name when they never used it?

"Hi, Dad."

"Your mom will update me on the particulars, but I wanted to remind you to let a tap drip while you're gone so your pipes don't freeze. And set some lights on a timer so people think someone is home. Did you tell the post office to hold your mail?"

He did this every year, as if she'd never left home before, but she loved it. He couldn't help but watch out for her.

"I've got it on my list to do before I leave. And I even have a neighbor checking on the house every few days. I've got to finish some work and search for best places to stay with a dog . . . and maybe some long-car-ride tips." She added that to her running to-do list.

"That's my girl."

"See you soon, love you."

She set the phone down, kicked off her shoes, and tucked her feet under Bernie's already snoring body. She had a few hours left to prep for the board meeting. Once that was done, she was gone through the New Year, kicking off her vacation with her favorite people. It was the one thing she counted on, the one predictable high point in her year—a weekend of laughter, friendship, and memories she would never forget, followed by getting spoiled by her parents until Christmas. All of it was even more wonderful this year because she didn't have to deal with Trent. That's what she wanted every Christmas—no, every day—to be like. No weed-like ex-husband and Bernie all to herself. Astra needed to find a way to pull Trent out by the roots.

Chapter Three

ALONE IN THE LARGE WHITE-TILED KITCHEN THAT ENCOMpassed most of the footprint of Kringle All the Way, the only bakery in the Julemarked, Jack fed pastry dough through a rolling machine, much like making fresh pasta. In the center of the room stood an enormous ancient butcher-block counter, scarred and battered from centuries of use. Every night he and his brothers scrubbed the counter with lemon juice and salt, wiping away the day's dusting of flour and sugar until the old wood grain came into focus and the kitchen smelled like a summer afternoon—or at least what he assumed a summer afternoon smelled like, having never experienced one. Above the large sink along the side wall, a single light glowed, allowing Jack to prolong the dreamy quality of early morning.

Normally, his brothers would be with him and they'd be doing this assembly-line style, but he couldn't sleep, drawn from his bed as if pulled by strings. When you lived in the Julemarked, you learned to go with those types of urges. Something was different about today and lying in bed wouldn't help.

With the effortless flair garnered from decades of repetition, he lightly floured a parchment paper square in front of him and gently laid the freshly pressed dough rectangle onto it, the long edge closest to him. He trimmed the dough to a precise thirty-inch-by-six-inch rectangle by sight.

Next to the dough sat a bowl of softened almond paste mixed with their cherry filling—Door County cherries cooked in sugar. Simple and delicious, like all the best things. Using an offset spatula, he spread the filling over half of the dough, folded over the uncovered pastry dough, and pinched it closed, encasing the cherry-almond filling inside. Confidently taking both the ends, he formed the filled tube of dough into an oval. Maneuvering it onto a baking sheet, he slid it into a preheated oven. While it cooked, he prepared a second one, this time with separate layers of almond paste and cherry filling.

As he waited for the first kringle to finish baking, he poured a cup of coffee into his favorite large mug, with a white-and-gray exterior textured like stone and a dent opposite the handle providing a natural resting spot for his thumb when he held it with his fingers looped through the handle. Glazed a bright Christmas red on the inside and made at the pottery shop in the Julemarked, the mug fit his hand perfectly. He sipped the black coffee, the bitter liquid hitting the back of his tongue, warming him from the inside. That first sip was always the best, except maybe the satisfying sip after a bite of a sweet pastry, or the sip after a long dinner with his family. Actually, every sip of coffee was the best. The brew alone made life worth living most days.

He sniffed the air in the bakery; the smell of warm bread and almonds had become more pronounced. The first kringle was done. After so many years, he could tell by the smell alone. A minute or two longer and it would start to burn. He gulped down his coffee and pulled out the golden-brown ring, set it on the counter, and replaced it with the second kringle.

With his personal baking project mostly done, it was time to start the day in earnest. From the large refrigerator, he pulled out a huge tub of dough, dumped it onto the counter, and separated it into chunks, each one a future kringle, lining them up next to the dough roller like soldiers ready for battle. That finished, he made a small batch of glaze, a simple mix of powdered sugar, cream, and vanilla, the default combination they used for most of their kringle, not measuring any of the ingredients, but aware he had the right balance from the resistance on the spoon as he stirred. A quick taste using a separate clean spoon let him know to add a splash more vanilla. He added a small dash, stirred, then spread the glaze onto the first kringle while still a little warm to his touch, letting the excess artistically drip down the sides. He'd add a second layer once it had cooled completely. When the air smelled right, he pulled the second kringle from the oven and set it next to the first.

"You're up early." Mads had arrived. Jack's younger brother by only eleven Yules, he was the one Jack was closest to, an adventurous spirit who would try anything once. While Jack chose to rarely leave the Julemarked, Mads left frequently and returned with tales of new flavors, people, and most importantly, experiences. Mads ran a finger around the mostly empty bowl of cherry and almond paste filling and stuck his finger in his mouth. "Nice. Why don't we do that all the time?"

"Restraint?" Jack said. "Most cherry fillings have almond flavoring, so the sugar and sweetened almond paste seem like over-kill."

"Restraint is for the timid. Be bold, my dear brother. Mix cherries with almond paste." Mads smacked a hand on Jack's shoulder as he passed behind him on the way to the coffee.

"I know you're screwing with me, but I like my restrained life."

Mads leaned against the butcher-block counter behind him, pouring in a healthy dose of cream and sugar—the only one of them who added anything to his coffee.

"I'm merely saying it wouldn't kill you to leave the Julemarked once in a while. There's a great big world out there, and all you ever see are these brick walls." Mads waved his hand toward the front of their store and the alley beyond.

"Everything I need is here."

"It's not about need, brother, it's about living. What's the point of all the extra years we get that those on the Outside don't, if you're not going to use them?"

Mads raised his eyebrow at Jack and Jack rolled his eyes back at him.

"I'm surprised you don't have literal horns coming off your head. Do you try to get vegans to eat bacon and eggs, too?"

"Does that mean you're coming out with me tonight?" Jack could also see the hope in Mads's eyes that he might say yes.

"Not a chance. You know I get nauseous." Jack said.

Jack spread the glaze onto half of each kringle and they were ready to test. He sliced two wedges of off each for Mads and him to taste. Already he liked the contrast in the cherry and almond-paste layers, bright red next to the creamy white rather than the uniform pink of the mix.

Mads sighed.

"You wouldn't get nauseous if you came out more often. It's all about tolerance. I barely feel sick when I leave the Julemarked now. And I don't notice it after a few drinks." Mads took a huge bite of one kringle and then the next. They both chewed in silence. "The layers are better. And the glaze needs a little something to offset all the sweetness."

Jack hadn't needed to ask for Mads's opinion. They'd been doing this so long, if a baked good was handed to you, an opinion was wanted. He agreed with Mads; the layers were the better option. As for the glaze, he took another bite to think as the intense sugar slapped his taste buds. Cream cheese. That would add a tanginess to counter the sweet. He mixed a new glaze, adding a pinch of cinnamon, and spread it on the unglazed halves so they could sample right away.

"Should I keep the cherries whole or chop them up so you don't get a giant glob in your mouth?" Jack loved the flavor but didn't always like it when he took a bite and an entire cherry came out. For his taste, it was too much cherry in one chunk.

"Chopped. Always chopped. Why would you even ask that when you know you're going to do it anyway?"

"Sometimes you manage to change my mind."

"Really, of all the things I could convince you to do, you think I'm going to make my stand on whether or not cherries should be chopped for filling? That is not the hill I'm going to die on."

"Why would you die on a hill?" Jack knew it was an idiom, but it drove Mads nuts when he pretended to not understand colloqui-alisms.

"Are you deliberately obtuse?"

Jack smiled that he had gotten a reaction.

"You're a dick." Mads grabbed a handful of flour and tossed it at Jack, coating his dark blond hair in white. Jack reached to grab his shirt but missed.

"Quit making a mess and get in here and help me before Carl and Orn show up and yell at us." Jack scowled, but it melted into a smile. He couldn't pretend to be grumpy. Not today. Not in a Mil-waukee Yule.

Mads pulled an apron on and started clearing the counter, getting everything ready for their assembly-line approach to kringle making. Jack had started rolling out one more special kringle when the kitchen blazed into full light; his eldest brother, Orn, stood by the switch. He didn't even say anything, just shook his head to convey that he thought Jack was an idiot—for what, he was sure Orn would let him know soon enough.

"Is there a reason you're making kringle in the most ineffi-cient way possible?" Orn asked, not making Jack wait to learn why he was a fool. He poured a cup of coffee from the freshly brewed coffee carafe.

Jack kept his eyes on the dough, focusing on rolling it to the ideal evenness, something he'd done so often it was almost a sixth sense, knowing by the feel of the rolling pin, the give in the dough as it rolled over the top. Mads noticed he had ignored Orn's ques-tion and stopped pulling fillings from the shelves and came to stand next to Jack at the island.

"Why. Are. You. Hand. Rolling?" Mads said.

Why did brothers know exactly how to irritate and make a person uncomfortable at the same time?

"I want it to be special." Jack shrugged.

"So we're going to hand roll them all? Shouldn't they all be special?" Orn asked.

Jack met Mads's eyes behind Orn's back.

"No," Jack said. "Just this one."

Understanding bloomed in Mads's eyes and a smirk took life.

"And why just this one?" Mads asked. When Jack didn't answer, Mads continued. "Come on, Jackie-boy, tell your brothers why all our kringle don't deserve this special treatment."

The dick was going to make him say it. Brothers could be the absolute worst.

"She's going to come in today. I can feel it."

Jack shot Mads a look implying he wanted to be done with the conversation and hoped Mads understood.

Orn ignored their conversation, instead sipping his coffee as he looked for flaws in the finished kringle laid out on the counter, taking a small bite from each one. At last he gave a little nod, drained his coffee mug, and set it next to the pot to use in precisely forty-five minutes, when he would drink his second cup. He looped a clean white apron around his neck, wrapped the ties around his lower back, then tied them in front. He joined Jack at the island.

"You roll, I fill," he said.

"And I'll shape," Mads said and took the spot next to Orn.

"I guess that leaves me on tray duty," Carl said. He pulled a stack of baking sheets off a shelf, then stacked parchment paper sheets next to Jack. Jack would lay the finished dough on the parchment paper and trim it, then slide it to Orn, who would spread the filling and seal the dough tube. He would then slide the filled dough to Mads to form them into circles. Then Carl would lift them onto a baking sheet and slide it onto an open slot on the rolling cart—then put them in the giant oven once there were enough. Working this way, they could assemble thirty kringle an hour—their record was forty-five, but they had pre-rolled a bunch of dough. A few hours of this and they'd have enough kringle to sell for the day. Jack should be sick of the routine, but he loved it.

"Nora is pregnant," Carl said, dropping the news with no preamble and few words. They all stopped for back slaps and hugs, then got back to work. This was kid number five, after all. It had stopped being news after Nora had announced she was pregnant with their third.

"When is she due?" Orn said. As the only other father among them, he knew the questions to ask. Jack really only cared that the babe was healthy.

"In six Yules. Nora is hoping for somewhere warm."

"Will you finally name this one after the best uncle? Johan for a boy, Johanna for a girl?" Jack said. He'd always gone by "Jack" to differentiate himself from the two other Johans at the Julemarked. It was a common name in their small community.

"Dream on. Nora wants Thor." Carl rolled his eyes and frowned. "She saw one of the movies when we were in Melbourne and decided it was a crime that we didn't have any boys named Thor."

"I can't believe you let her out to see a movie," Mads said, grinning because he knew how Carl would react.

"Nora is her own woman and can leave the Julemarked anytime she wants. She and Freja like movies." Carl finished with a shrug as if to say he couldn't understand why. Jack liked movies too, but leaving the Julemarked was too much of a bother. Going to the Outside made him achy and nauseous, followed by a few days of recovery, having to do with the way time worked between the Outside and the Julemarked. For Jack, it was easier to stay put. After all, why leave the best place on earth? Everything he wanted was here.

The brothers had finished their work and readied the bakery to open, sliding whole kringle and trays of buy-by-the-slice pieces into the pastry case in the shop. It took up the entire length of the store, allowing customers to gaze at all the delicious goodies as they made their way to the cash register. Orn studied the case from the customer side, polishing off any lingering nose- and fingerprints revealed in the morning sunlight finding its way through the front window. When everything met his standards, he flipped the sign and the customers soon followed. Through the day, the brothers would hear on repeat some version of "I didn't know this was here and I've lived in Milwaukee my entire life. Is it new?" The brothers would smile to themselves, knowing that the customers would forget about it again until next year, when they would have the pleasurable experience of discovering it all over again.

It had been only two years since Jack had last seen the woman who'd captivated him, but because time worked differently in the Julemarked, it had been much longer to him, especially because he could never fully put her out of his mind.

He would look the same, but she might be different. Would her hair be a different color? Would there be an extra laugh line from the corner of her hazel-green eyes? Would she be smiling and laughing with her friends or coupled with someone, hanging on his arm?

Would she remember him?

When she (over all these years, and all the times they'd found each other, he still didn't know her name) finally walked into Kringle All the Way, he couldn't stop from staring. Like looking at the night sky on a cloudless evening—the more he stared, the more he discovered. She wore new glasses with green frames that brought out the color in her cheeks and lips. Her auburn hair almost blended in with the knit Santa hat she wore—the same as her friends. The same one she had given him, which now topped the bedpost in his cottage.

Her appearance was like when the last star in a constellation comes into focus, completing the picture. The waiting was over and he could finally take action.

While helping the customers in front of him, he watched her progress, inching closer to the pastry case. Her pale cheeks glowed from the cold air he felt every time the bakery's door opened. It felt good to him in the warm building. At the end of the bakery case, Mads slid kringle into boxes or bags and pushed them toward Jack to ring up. He caught his eye.

"Switch," Jack said.

Mads looked at the next group in line, nodded, and took the spot behind the register, unable to completely hide his grin.

"At least find out her name this time," Mads whispered in his ear as they passed.

Jack looked up and there she was, half-turned to speak to one of her friends.

"What did Cassie want? Almond? Chocolate?" she asked. Her voice registered lower than he remembered, with a gentle rasp like she'd shouted into the eye of a storm a few nights ago.

"Chocolate," one of her friends answered. "I want the almond. What about you, Ronnie?"

"Cherry." Ronnie nudged her toward the case. "You order." A grin split Ronnie's face like there was a joke, but Jack didn't get it. That happened often enough.

At last, she turned to him, her lips curving in a smile and her cheeks even pinker than when she first walked in, the dimple jumping to life.

"Hi," she said, blinking a few extra times when she saw his face. Was that a glimmer of recognition? The moment passed and he wasn't sure if he'd imagined it.

"Hi," he said back. "What can I get you?"

"I'll take a chocolate, two almonds, and a cherry. All slices." She paused to bite her lip as she studied the case. "And a whole . . ."

Now was his chance.

"I have a special flavor that's not in the case. A cherry-almond with a cream cheese–cinnamon glaze. There's one left in the back if you'd like it."

There, he'd kept it casual. It shouldn't be obvious that he'd made it special for exactly this moment.

Her eyes widened.

"That's perfect. All my favorites in one. It's like you could read my mind."

"I'm not that good. Let me get it, or if you'd like, give me your name and you can pick it up when you're done at the market."

He held his breath, hoping she chose option number two.

"Really? You'd let me do that? We might be late. How long are you open?" She looked around for the hours.

"I promise, we'll be open."

Mads looked over at him and raised an eyebrow. What was one little lie? It's not like they had any special plans besides cleaning up the bakery and getting things started for tomorrow to do it all again. As they spoke, he slid the requested slices of kringle into waxed paper sleeves, quickly folding the ends in a practiced, precise motion. He slipped them into a white paper bag, added napkins, and slid it down the wood counter to his brother.

"Astra," she said.

"What?" He wasn't sure he'd heard her correctly.

"Astra Snow. It's my name. So I can pick it up later." Her wide smile sparkled at him.

Her name. He had her name at last. He pulled out a pad of paper and wrote it out in neat square letters. "ASTRA." It fit her perfectly.

"Do you need my number, too? Something to prove it's mine."

"I'll remember." He paused. "I'm Jack, in case one of my brothers is here when you get back. But I guess it couldn't hurt to have your number."

She rattled off her number and he wrote it down. Not like he could call her, but it seemed important to have it. Significant to have those digits, like a secret password to learning more about her. He had her name and her phone number. He stared at the ten digits as if they would unlock her secrets right then. What was her favorite color, food, book? How did she take her coffee? He wished he had a number to give her in return.

"Do you need any more information?" Astra said, peering at the pad of paper atop the glass case between them.

"That's it. Mads can ring you up." He set the paper on the side counter.

"Don't sell my kringle to anyone else." Astra pointed at the paper. "We'll be back later. I promise."

"Your pastry is safe with me."

She laughed and paid for the treats and walked out the door with her friends, already digging into the bag. He wanted to follow her out the door. Out of the alley. He wanted to follow her everywhere.

"Smooth," Mads said.

"Shut up," Jack said, but the smile stayed on his lips.

"She's pretty," Carl said, having come in behind him. "I wondered what was up with the new flavor."

"Wow, you've impressed Carl—I didn't think that was possible," Mads said.

Carl shoved Mads in the shoulder, all while they continued to smile and help customers. After as many Yules as they'd worked through, it was second nature, the natural rhythm of taking orders, filling them, and getting the customers out the door. In a few hours or days (depending on the person), those same customers' memories would slowly fade, leaving them with only the taste of sugar on their lips as a clue to the wonderful bakery they'd patronized. But she'd be back later. Twice in one day. That was new. That was different.

This time would be different.

Chapter Four

Astra cradled the white bag, glancing back in the window at the man who'd helped them. Jack. He looked so much like the man from her dream, down to the warm smile that crinkled the corners of his eyes. How strange that she'd dreamed about him.

Her friends gathered around one of the picnic tables distributed along the walls of the Julemarked. They'd been visiting the Milwaukee Christmas market every year since they had graduated from a tiny college outside of Green Bay. Right after graduation, they had scattered across the Midwest, agreeing to one sacred weekend a year, usually the first one in December, to meet up. Over the years, they slowly moved closer and closer together, until now, when they could all be at any of their houses in thirty minutes, depending on traffic and construction on I-94, of course.

The first year after graduation, they chose the Christmas market in Milwaukee as their destination for its central location and the convenience of Astra's apartment—cheap was the important part. They had so much fun, they decided to return every year. Now they stayed in a posh room at Saint Kate's Hotel, but the Christmas market remained the same. Gooey raclette on crusty French bread, spiked hot beverages, and Christmas shopping.

Astra used her phone to take a few pictures of her friends, liking to snap candid shots, like one of Cassie carrying a tray of hot cocoa, steam rising from the top vents, with the wrought-iron arch of the Julemarked entrance behind her. She set the tray in the middle of the table.

"Everyone take a big gulp," Ronnie said as she pulled a small bottle of coffee liqueur from her blue puffy-coat pocket. Astra removed the lid to blow on the cocoa, taking a test sip before drinking enough to make room, then set the cup on the table. Ronnie filled each cup to the brim. Astra put the lid back on, then held up her cup toward her friends, each wearing the red-and-white knit Santa hats she'd bought the first year.

Ronnie with her loud laugh and long legs was always the first person anyone noticed when she entered a room. She was blunt, brash, a literal blond bombshell, but she'd walk through fire and beat down anyone who threatened one of her girls. She would tell you exactly what she thought about your mistakes, did not suffer fools, but also never held a grudge or judged you. She'd tell you how stupid you were, then help you clean up the mess with a hug and a smile.

Cassie was tiny and quiet, with light brown hair she always wore in a ponytail. She was easy to overlook next to Ronnie but had a quick wit that would catch you off guard when you first met her. She had moved here from Florida with her parents in high school and still wasn't used to the cold, even though it had been more than twenty years. In college, she would break out her ankle-length coat by the end of October and wore long underwear past Easter. She currently led a team in the cancer center of the local hospital—the team you went to with a rare illness, who usually found a way to treat it. Of the four of them, she would save the world.

Steph held them together. She organized their annual trip, made reservations, and checked in with everyone on their fifteen-year-old text thread. Without Steph, they would have drifted apart years ago as life's currents pushed and pulled them in separate directions. She was the rope tying them all together. Always sensible and mature, she rarely lost her patience and always gave precise and practical life advice. Plus, she had great taste in clothes and wore the same size as Astra—which came in handy anytime Astra needed something fancier than her librarian wardrobe contained. Steph's dark brown hair was always smooth and shiny, her hands warm, and she had a near magical ability to sense big changes in the air—be it a storm or a job.

"To the beautiful, strong women in my life. Where would I be without you?" Astra said.

"Still crying over the jackass," Ronnie said.

"I love you too much to answer that," Cassie said.

"You'd be exactly where you needed to be. You're stronger than you think," Steph said.

Astra smiled and tapped her paper cup against each of her friends'. The coffee liqueur added extra heat as she swallowed the chocolatey drink, remembering the time they'd made their first toast together.

It had been their freshman year in college and they had lived on the same floor in the all-girls dorm. At times, it was so smoke filled that a perpetual haze hovered in the hallways, occasionally dispersed by opening the windows at the end of the hall. On a rare occurrence, class had been canceled due to a huge blizzard dropping thirty inches of snow over two days, making it impossible for professors to safely get to campus—though somehow the cafeteria staff had managed—proving who the true heroes were.

The second semester had just begun. Steph, Cassie, and Astra, with a few other stragglers from their floor, stomped through the snow for the impromptu Blizzard Brunch being served in the cafeteria, including the ever-popular waffle bar. Astra imagined it was easy for the kitchen staff since they only had to put out the batter and toppings, then clean up the inevitable mess left by the college kids. The students didn't care that they were doing the majority of the work, piling their waffles with strawberries, whipped cream, and sprinkles.

The girls pocketed bagels and small packs of peanut butter to bring back to their rooms. Cassie, ever the planner, had brought a Ziploc bag to fill with cereal and a bottle to fill with milk. They could feast on carbs later that night.

As they trudged through the snow back to their dorm, a car struggled to get into the student parking lot, stuck on the ridge of snow left by a city snowplow. Behind the wheel was Ronnie, cursing loudly enough for them to hear her through her window, or maybe it was just that her emphatic enunciation made it clear which words she shouted. The car's wheels spun in the slippery snow. It was the damp kind, heavy and perfect for making snowmen, but the worst for driving.

Steph tugged Cassie's sleeve, instructing her to "go grab a few cafeteria trays." Cassie dashed off in the snow like she skittered on top of it, rather than sinking deep like the rest of them. Astra got what she had in mind. You didn't grow up in Wisconsin without knowing a thing or two about getting a car out of a snow pile. Astra knocked on Ronnie's window and she rolled it down.

"You're making it worse."

"What am I supposed to do? Leave it here?" Ronnie's sharp words stabbed through the blizzard. They all knew Ronnie, but she tended to run with a group of sophomores, going to parties more than the rest of them. She knew the entire hockey team, and more importantly, they knew her. Loud, brash, and stunning, she dominated every room she entered, and Astra was more than a little intimidated by her bold confidence.

"That's what we're here for." Cassie returned and handed out trays, and Steph directed them to scoop snow away from the tires, shoveling a path through the icy ridge. "Give us a few minutes."

Once the snow was cleared, Steph told her to drive forward, but she got stuck once the car hit the twelve inches of snow in front of it.

"Stop," Steph shouted, and Ronnie listened. "You need to create momentum. Once you get enough, you'll break free and can get to your parking spot. Back up ten feet, then drive forward with a medium amount of gas. Not too much or you'll spin your tires again. We'll push from the rear."

Ronnie nodded and everyone fell into place. With one well-timed shove, Ronnie broke through the barrier and coasted into her spot. Cheers rose from the nearby dorm windows where an audience of boys had been watching.

"You could have helped," Cassie shouted at them. She made a lot of noise for someone so tiny.

"More fun to watch," a disembodied voice shouted back.

Ronnie emerged from her car carrying some plastic bags heavy with bottles.

"Ladies, I was going to take these to the hockey house, but I think you deserve them more." She reached into one of the bags and pulled out a bottle of margarita mix—the kind with the alcohol already included. Just add ice and enjoy.

Collectively, everyone woo-hooed—a unified fierce group of women. When they returned to the dorms, bowls of fresh snow were brought in, and everyone on the floor lined up to fill cups and water bottles with snow, then poured the margarita mix over it to create the perfect slushy frozen margarita. Steph, Cassie, and Astra helped Ronnie dole out the rainbow-colored concoctions of strawberry, lime, orange, and blue raspberry. Buzzed and warm, Astra looked around at the three other women.

She raised her margarita-filled plastic coffee mug; the three others did the same.

"To girl power," she shouted.

"To girl power," the other three echoed.

All of them finished their drinks and refilled them, spilling more as the night went on, making their cheap Target floor rug look like a toddler's art project.

At some point, they'd ordered pizza and tipped the delivery guy extravagantly for making it through the snow on a snowmobile. Music blared from the speakers tucked among the books above Ronnie's desk and they all shouted along to Kelly Clarkson, screaming the lyrics to "Since U Been Gone" at the top of their lungs, pizza crusts being repurposed as improvised microphones as they danced in the small dorm room, bodies bumping against one another, laughter leaving them breathless. When they flopped onto the tiny bed, a pile of alcohol-numbed limbs and sloppy smiles, something had changed. Looking at each of their faces, Astra knew these were her people, who would have her back through anything. After all, there was nothing quite like the friendships forged in close living quarters, then tempered with copious amounts of bad pizza and cheap booze.

From that day on, they were a foursome. Whenever they weren't in class, they studied together, partied together, watched movies together, consumed vast quantities of waffles together. They rallied when hearts were broken and celebrated when tests were aced. After college, they stood up at one another's weddings, were the first at the hospital when babies were born, and picked up the pieces when things fell apart. Astra's greatest regret was drifting away from them while she was with Trent. She had missed the birth of Steph's last two children as a result.

She'd never let that happen again. These were her people.

Astra sipped her spiked hot chocolate, though the warm liquid could never warm her as much as her love for these formidable women.

"Astra's got a date later," Ronnie said.

Cassie's eyes widened and Steph chuckled.

"It's not a date. I have to come back later to pick up the kringle I bought."

"He has a special flavor for her," Ronnie said.

"It's not a big deal. He didn't make anything for me. We've never met and he doesn't even know me from the next person. I ordered cherry and almond slices, so he probably assumed I'd like one with both those flavors." She opened the bag and handed out the slices. "Speaking of, here you go."

She slid her slice out of the parchment paper sleeve, a few sliced almonds falling out along with it. The sweet almond scent rose from the golden pastry, and she could see the pale almond filling peeking out the ends where it was sliced. Biting into the kringle, Astra closed her eyes to savor the sugary almond, following it up with a chocolatey swig of her spiked cocoa. This kringle was by far the best she'd ever had.

It had been a rough few years, but getting to this point, surrounded by her friends at their annual vacation, her shoulders sagged with relief. She had made it out the other side. Recovered from the sudden loss of Trent to realize she'd almost lost so much more. But friends like hers were hard to lose, and they helped her pick up the pieces. If only she could wrestle full custody of Bernie away from Trent. Living on her own, with a public employee's salary, wasn't easy after her divorce. But all of it would be so much harder without the women beside her.

"I'm so grateful for you all," she said, her voice thickening.

"Nope. None of that behavior," Ronnie said. "Christmas is not about crying."

"Have you seen *It's a Wonderful Life*?" Steph jumped in.

"That is the worst Christmas movie," Ronnie said. "I don't want to be depressed and watch some dude who's too blind to realize he's got a great life. And it's the wife who gets screwed. She had a great job as a librarian in the alternate reality and didn't have those snotty kids to watch or a whiny husband to deal with," Ronnie said.

She wasn't wrong. Astra could testify that librarian work beat out a needy husband every time.

She finished her kringle, wishing she'd bought another slice, even though she knew there was a long day of snacking ahead of her—and that she'd be picking up an entire kringle at the end of the day.

Astra studied the alley of the Julemarked where it zigzagged off the Milwaukee Christmas market proper, wondering when they had built it. It was a great addition. The muted redbrick walls were broken up by the bakery, a glassblowing shop that sold mostly ornaments, a toy shop, and a few other stores they had yet to explore. Small fires burned every twenty feet in outdoor fire pits. A young man would come along every so often and add more wood into each of the black steel cages, the fires giving off enough heat to make the cozy alley a huge draw for those wanting to take a break from the more open market outside. Lights and pine garland draped overhead, alternating between green and glowing. It was her new favorite part of the market, and not just because of the flirty, too-attractive baker.

She slugged back the rest of her hot cocoa, tossing the cup into the empty bakery bag. She looked at her phone out of habit but couldn't get her mail to refresh. There must be too much brick around to get a decent signal.

"None of that," Cassie said as she grabbed the phone and slipped it into the deep pocket in Astra's coat. "No work allowed." She pointed at Steph and Ronnie. "That goes for both of you, too." Everyone tucked their phones away. You didn't mess with Cassie.

"Ready for round two?" Steph said, pointing at the mulled-wine stand. It was barely eleven, but the citrus and cinnamon were wafting toward them. They lined up and handed over their money and received a tiny ceramic cup of steaming spiced goodness. The little mug would be refilled many times over the rest of the day as they wandered from stand to stand, Christmas music pumping over the loudspeakers when live carolers weren't roaming the crowds or a local choir wasn't on the stage.

With a mug in one hand, Astra looped arms with Steph.

"How are the littles?" Astra asked.

"Adorable nightmares. But what kids aren't." The glowing smile on her face revealed exactly how much she loved her little monsters. The eldest had upended her life more than seven years ago, almost eight years if you counted her pregnancy. She had been sick from the beginning, but that hadn't stopped her from making their annual Christmas outing, even though she had to wrap a blanket around herself because she refused to buy a winter coat large enough to fit over her giant belly. She walked the whole day without a complaint, but her ankles disappeared. "They love the books you sent. I have to read them every night, exactly two times."

"That was the plan. Start them out young," Astra said, failing to ignore the small pang in her heart.

Would she ever have children of her own? Even if thirty-seven wasn't that old to start a family, her window of time was cranking shut rapidly. She wanted to hold a child close to calm them. She wanted to have pancake Saturdays and Sunday movie nights.

She wanted to decorate Christmas cookies and paint ornaments each year. She wanted to read to them so much that she kept a stockpile of picture books in a closet just in case, like a literary hope chest. More than anything, she wanted more time to make a family a reality.

Holding on to Steph's arm, she passed the window of Kringle All the Way, and Astra couldn't help looking in the window again at Jack, the lines of his face familiar to her, like watching the movie *Marie Antoinette*, then visiting Versailles in real life. She'd seen it before and now wanted to explore. He looked up and waved and her heart skipped a beat.

She'd had enough disappointments. Tonight, she'd live a little.

Chapter Five

Jack had slept late, and it was almost five in the morning when he shuffled into the bakery to find Carl and Orn already rolling out dough. Mads came into the kitchen holding a local newspaper.

"Milwaukee. Same year as last Yule," he said, conveying that the Julemarked hadn't moved on to the next year yet. Snow melted in his hair from the heat in the kitchen as he stepped out of his boots and into the comfortable leather clogs they all wore indoors.

"At least it's snowing," Carl said. "I'll never be a fan of Yules where it's ninety degrees. It's not right."

Orn pulled extra dough out of the fridge. They always sold more kringle in Milwaukee. Jack downed a mug of coffee before their local contact arrived to get their supply list. They had people all over the world who would show up on December 1 to help get the supplies they needed.

"I'm meeting John," Jack said, checking the order and adding a

few things they could only get in Wisconsin that they liked to stock up on, like Door County cherries and Spotted Cow beer. Under his arm he tucked a bankers bag with enough cash to pay for everything.

Jack pulled a green cable-knit sweater over his head, added the soft red knit hat he'd been wearing since their last Yule in Milwaukee, and changed into his own boots to meet their contact. When he arrived at the Julemarked entrance, discernable by a black wrought-iron arch with the word "Julemarked" spelled out in elegantly curved letters, Anika Pedersen was already waiting.

"Hi, Jack," Anika said. She was as tall as him, and broad in her shoulders, like she'd spent a lifetime lifting hay bales instead of yarn skeins. Her long blond hair was piled on top of her head. He'd grown up with her, made snowmen with her, and even had his first kiss with her. Despite their long shared history, he had no interest in it ever becoming more, and she felt the same, despite their mothers shoving them together at every chance. It was probably why he was put on order duty this morning, because his mom knew Anika would be doing the same for A Stitch in Time.

"Morning, Ani," Jack said, looking around the empty beer garden that connected the Julemarked to the Christmas market for any sign of their contact. Sadly, it was empty, with only the tables and chairs to keep them company. The bar was closed at this early hour, as was everything else. He could see a few people moving around the Christmas market, pushing carts loaded with boxes, making sure the trash cans were empty from the night before. Without leaving the Julemarked—he didn't want to deal with the rush of nausea that always hit him, he slid onto one of the Julemarked's nearby picnic table benches to wait. Ani moved to join him, then paused to touch his hat.

"This isn't one of ours."

"No. A customer gave it to me the last time we were in Milwaukee. I like the fit."

"Can I see?"

Jack handed over the hat, not bothering to tidy his messy morning hair. Ani studied it, even bringing it to her nose for a sniff, then handed it back.

"The stitching is a little uneven in spots, but that wool is dreamy. Baby alpaca, I think. I wonder where they got it." She pulled out her own list and made a note.

"You're here," a man's voice interrupted.

Jack and Ani looked up to a see a handsome man wearing sweatpants, winter boots, and a fitted navy wool coat and scarf. Jack stood and held out his hand to shake.

"Hi, John, nice to see you again," Jack said.

Ani one-upped him and pulled John into a tight hug; John's eyes widened in surprise and Jack held back a laugh. Ani had a firm hug. She released him.

"Sorry I'm late, I almost forgot it was December first and I needed to see if it showed up." He nodded toward the arch.

"I'm happy to say the Julemarked decided not to skip Milwaukee this year," Jack said, then pulled his list from a pocket. "I've got the bakery's orders. As well as the toy store. I think Ani has the rest."

They handed over the paperwork and a couple of bankers bags and John gave them a once-over.

"Assuming there isn't anything unusual or hard to find, I should have most of it tomorrow." John looked over his shoulder to the Julemarked's entrance. Then he looked at Jack, then Ani, and took a deep breath as if trying to decide if he wanted to ask something. "How's Mads?"

"Good. You can come say hi if you want."

John looked at the alley entrance again.

"Maybe tomorrow."

He gave them both a nod and went back the way he'd come.

Ani looked at Jack with a raised eyebrow.

"Mads and John?"

"They had one wild night and now they've been tiptoeing around each other. Maybe we'll have to find a new contact if they ever get together."

"You're assuming John will move to the Julemarked. Mads could just as easily stay here."

Jack snorted.

"Why would he do that? What could be better than living where it's Christmas all the time?"

Jack gave her nonsensical comment a dismissive wave and returned to the bakery.

Later that morning, during a lull in customers, he stepped outside and joined the line at the Yus' hot chocolate and mulled-wine cart next to one of the always-burning fires. Some hot chocolate sounded good. With his paper cup in hand, he stepped away from the cart to make room for the next customer, and his foot met some resistance.

"Ouch," a woman said.

Jack looked down to see his black-booted foot covering a woman's. He stepped off of it.

"I'm so very sorry," he said, finally noticing the woman with her red hair trailing out of the same red hat that he wore.

"No worries." She smiled up at him, a dimple sparking to life, sending a jolt of recognition to his core. He'd seen this woman before.

"Hat twins," she said, pointing to her own hat. She was the woman who had given him the hat that he currently wore. What were the odds he'd see her again?

"Looks better on you," Jack said. "For crushing your foot, please let me buy your drink."

"That's not necessary, I'm buying for me and my friends." She pointed to a nearby table where three women laughed.

"All the more reason for me to insist. Then you and your friends can talk about what a gentleman I am."

"How can I refuse? Four hot chocolates, please."

"Put it on my tab, Mr. Yu."

Mr. Yu smiled at him. "Sure, Jack." The Julemarked residents didn't keep track of such things, but Jack was happy to take the credit.

"Your tab?" the woman asked. "You work here?"

"In the bakery, with my brothers." Jack pointed to Kringle All the Way. "You should stop in when you're ready for something sweet."

"Brothers in a bakery? That's a romance series waiting to happen. I wouldn't be able to keep those books on the shelf."

"Do you work in a bookstore?"

"Better. I'm a librarian."

She beamed as she spoke about her job. Jack felt the same when talking about kringle. It was all he ever wanted to do.

Down the alley, Mads stepped out of the bakery and waved to him.

"I have to get back before they come and drag me. Make sure to stop in."

"We will." The woman held up her drinks. "Thank you."

In the middle of a morning rush, Jack slid another tray of precut kringle slices into the pastry case, not paying much attention to the din of a baby wailing above the noise of customers talking. Breaking through the cries, a warm, slightly familiar voice spoke.

"You weren't kidding about the four brothers," a woman's voice said. By the way his heart added an extra beat, he knew who it was before he looked up. The red-hatted, dimple-cheeked woman.

"I'm the best-looking, though," Jack said.

"Indubitably." Her dimple danced.

Her attention returned to the pastry case between them and Jack studied her as she studied the kringle.

He couldn't help but pay more attention to her. Every time she smiled, that dimple lit up the space around her like a star in the night sky. They saw so many customers in so many different places that they all blended into a general humanity, so it was rare when someone stuck out as memorable. But now she had his attention.

"One cherry, one almond, and . . ." She chewed on her lip as she thought, looking over the options in the case. Watching her lips stirred parts of him that had been dormant for far too long. Lost in thought, he started when she pointed at the case. ". . . one cranberry. That sounds interesting."

He cleared his throat.

"Right away," Jack said.

He quickly wrapped the slices and slid them into a bag. On a whim, he grabbed a nisse and shoved it in the bag along with the pastries. It was one he had carved and painted during the last Yule. The green hat sat on the small gnome's head while he held a tiny rolling pin in front of a bright white apron. He set the bag next to Carl at the cash register. "You can pay down there."

He pointed to Carl. She gave him a little smile and handed Carl her money.

Before leaving, she smiled at him one last time. "I'll see you next year." Then she walked out the door.

Would he see her next year? Would the Julemarked come back to Milwaukee? If it did, she was unlikely to remember their flirtation. Could it even be called that? It had been so long since a woman had piqued his interest that a flirtation felt like climbing onto a rusty bike—he could do it, but it wasn't pretty and made a lot of awkward noises.

Carl frowned at him. "What's up with you?"

"I met her last Milwaukee Yule, though she doesn't remember. Today I stepped on her foot and bought her hot chocolate."

"They never remember," Carl said.

"Not true and you know it," Mads joined in. Carl scowled. He had even less interest than Jack did in the Outside. "You've heard Old Johan's stories, and I've had a fair few romantic encounters that have come back the next year remembering me."

"Speaking of, John says hi," Jack said.

Mads blushed and chose to ignore Jack's comment. He continued. "You need to make a connection, do something memorable."

"I caused her bodily harm and bought her a hot beverage," Jack said.

"You can do better than that. Most of mine involved nudity and the creative use of candles."

"There are people in the store," Orn said from behind Mads, adding a gentle smack to the back of his head. "At least pick a different language if you're going to talk like that."

Mads rolled his eyes and they both got back to work, settling into the familiar rhythm. Why was Jack so wound up? It was a fluke encounter, a tiny flirtation. It wasn't like he'd ever see her again. This was just a coincidence. He was sure of it. If she ever returned, then maybe it would mean something.

Chapter Six

THE FOUR WOMEN TITTERED AS THEY PEERED IN THE LARGE glass window of the bakery, Ronnie knocking loudly on the door.

"Ronnie," Astra said. "The door is open. He's right there."

Astra could see Jack through the empty and clean pastry cases, staring at the ruckus they were causing, the bells jingling merrily as they bustled into the quiet business. He set a book on top of the case and smiled.

"I wondered if you'd forgotten," Jack said.

"I could never forget about this kringle, it's the most amazing thing I've ever put in my mouth," Astra said, blushing at her word choice.

Maybe she shouldn't have had that third shot before they left the bar. It had had more kick than the previous ones, and she didn't want to make a fool of herself in front of this handsome man. And he was extremely handsome. She couldn't shake her dream about him. How could she have envisioned what he looked like when they had never met?

Earlier today, she had focused on what was inside the case instead of what stood behind it. Now she couldn't stop staring. Tall, with blond hair that darkened near the roots, longish all around his head, like he'd forgotten the last few haircuts; his bangs almost dangled in his eyes—more like rugged outdoorsman than a surfer dude. His sharp jaw was dusted in the barest of stubble, which stopped at his high cheekbones, and his green-blue eyes that had brightened as they walked in. He looked strong, but not overly muscled. He still wore an apron over a white T-shirt and cargo pants, though it wasn't smeared with fillings or dusted with flour, as if he'd put on a fresh one while he waited. He was a lot of wonderful to look at, and Astra didn't want to stop looking.

"You're reading *Outlander*?" Steph said, pointing to the book cover.

Astra loved that book, about a woman who had escaped into the past to live another life and find true love. She had reread the entire series three times and here he was reading it. Such a surprising choice. She would have expected him to read something by Tom Wolfe or Stephen King, maybe even some presidential memoirs, but certainly not a time-traveling historical romance. She should know better than to try to predict a person's reading preferences—they were never what you anticipated.

Jack shrugged and set her kringle on the countertop.

"I like how even time can't keep two people who belong together apart."

Astra appreciated that he didn't act ashamed about reading it. It told her everything she needed to know about him. Maybe she had already had too much to drink, or maybe she was thinking more clearly than ever before, but the next words she spoke surprised her more than anyone else.

"Come out dancing with us. We're going to drop this at our hotel, then hit a club until they kick us out, dancing like we're too young to be there," Astra said.

Now that the words were out, Astra had never wanted anything more than to be dancing next to this man, sweat dripping off them as the lights flashed, letting themselves feel the music until it set them free. She really wanted to be free and feel young with this man.

Her three friends' heads turned in unison toward her, but their mouths stayed shut, waiting to see what would happen next.

Jack's head tilted as if he were thinking over the offer. Was he thinking of a reason to say no? She checked for a wedding ring—his finger was bare, but she still prepared herself for the coming rejection, the thumping club music in her head morphing into a sad trombone.

"Sounds fun. I'll grab my coat."

With practiced ease, he untied his apron and slipped it off his neck as he went into the kitchen.

"Holy shit. What did I just do?" Astra said, the words a whisper so only her friends could hear.

"Let your cooter steer the ship." Ronnie grinned.

"Never say that word again," Cassie said. "She has a vagina, not a cooter."

"Fine, she's letting her vagina steer the ship, and it's about time."

"Shut up, he'll be back any second. What do I do?" Astra said.

Steph gently grabbed her face so they were mere inches apart.

"You do what you said. We drop off the kringle. We dance like we're twenty. Whatever else happens can be attributed to the magical quality of the holiday season." The perfect wise words. "And Lord knows that man would look fantastic wearing a bow and nothing else."

"Yeah, he would," Ronnie said.

"Ready?" Jack had returned with a light wool coat. All four ladies' heads snapped toward him.

With wide eyes and her lips curled in between her teeth to stop from laughing because he'd surely heard what they had been talking about, Astra nodded yes. It was all she could manage.

"I should probably get all your names." Jack pointed at Astra. "I know you're Astra."

Ronnie elbowed her as she flushed. Jack had a way of looking at her that made her think they knew each other, that he knew her secrets and she knew his, that this was one of many looks they had shared, and it made her knees a little wobbly. Ronnie finished the introductions as they walked into the night.

"Don't you need to lock the door?" Steph asked as the door shut behind them without Jack making a motion to do anything. "It's getting late, and who knows who might meander by."

Jack smiled.

"The door doesn't even have a lock. We've never needed them," Jack said.

Steph looked around the quiet alley, and they noticed a solitary man sitting near a fire, his clothing gray and worn, his shoulders bunched against the cold. Her brows scrunching together conveyed that she was unsure about his logic.

"But this is downtown; surely you have homeless people that wander in. They could just walk into any of these stores and take things." She pointed at the man with his hands outstretched to the warmth.

"Why would they do that when we give it to them? See?"

A tall, strapping woman came out of the knitwear store carrying a pile of warm-looking clothing. The man happily swapped his hat for a new green one that covered his ears with flaps and dangling tassels. He stood and removed his coat to put on the multicolored sweater with prancing reindeer over his worn black sweatshirt. After he'd donned his coat, she wrapped a warm scarf around his neck and set a blanket on the table for him to take. A frizzy-haired man appeared carrying a tray of steaming soup, bread, and some wrapped items that the homeless man quickly slipped into his pockets. The man and woman left the man alone to enjoy his warm food.

"If that's what you do for every homeless person who strays in, why aren't you inundated? Word has to spread," Steph said.

"Maybe they don't want to lose out on the best-kept secret." Jack shrugged and seemed unfazed by the question as they left the Julemarked.

With a quick stop at their nearby room to drop off their breakfast—or more likely late-night snack—they were soon in line at one of the clubs. When Jack leaned close to Astra, his breath smelled like ginger.

"Do you do this often?" he asked.

"Not since college, but it feels right, doesn't it?" Astra said. The night seemed full of opportunity as they stepped into the club, flashing lights matching the beat of the bass. Bodies tight on the dance floor, and snug around the bar.

"Grab a spot, I'll get drinks," Ronnie said.

They found a high table with one stool still under it. They piled their coats on top of it, already too warm to wear them. At least bars weren't smoky anymore, so she wouldn't need to Febreze it like she had to back in college, when she would wake up the next morning, her mouth like cotton, her hair reeking like an ashtray, the pile of clothes she'd worn the night before needing to be washed immediately before she got sick from the smell.

Ronnie arrived quickly with a tray of red and green layered shots, two for each of them.

"Aren't they fun?" Ronnie shouted over the music. "It's crème de menthe, peppermint schnapps, and grenadine. It's called a Santa's Night Out." She set two shots in front of each of them. Jack looked skeptical but held his first one in front of him, waiting for the cue to drink it. Astra leaned toward him.

"You don't have to if you don't want to."

"I'm good. I'm just not sure about the combo."

Ronnie held her shot high. "To annual traditions and old friends who know all your secrets."

"And new friends who still think you're perfect," Cassie added with a wink toward Jack. "That ends real soon."

With a quick toss back and a hastier swallow, the first round was gone.

"That was worse than I thought," Jack said.

"More like Santa's Undercarriage," Ronnie said. "Might as well get it over with. Maybe it won't be so bad now that we know." Shot number two went down the hatch.

"Nope," Astra said, covering her mouth. "Definitely worse. Why do you hate us?" she asked Ronnie.

"Nothing but love, babe." Ronnie kissed her forehead. "Now,

let's get to it." She grabbed Astra's hand, and Astra grabbed Jack's arm—a spontaneous need to touch this man as much as possible. Steph and Cassie stayed at their table—the lessons learned in college held fast: always leave two to guard the table. They'd swap places later, though Cassie never liked dancing, often getting stepped on because of her height—or because of that one time a drunk football player lifted her over his head and passed her around the dance floor.

Somewhere in the middle of the floor, they gave up trying to proceed, but stopped and moved to the music, no semblance of a circle, only a mass of moving bodies. Astra could see Ronnie to her right and Jack to her left. The floor was so full of people, she could have leaned in any direction and not fallen down. She closed her eyes and let the music pound out her stress and inform her body how to move. Sweat already coated her skin.

The last few years had been a nightmare. Trent leaving their marriage, but then not leaving her. She resented how she'd let him separate her from her friends, to the point of not making it to the hospital when Steph had her last two children. He had claimed he needed her to go with him to some work event that turned out to be after-hours drinks. It still stung that he'd managed to get the house and partial custody of Bernie, her beautiful galloping black-and-white mutt so full of love, it had turned her paws white. She'd caved because the lawyer's fees were going to bankrupt her and she had naively hoped that she'd convince Trent to eventually give her full custody. But nope, he used it as a way to inconvenience her at every possible turn, taking advantage of her like he always had. Asking her to watch Bernie, then take in his mail or water his lawn or hem his pants.

He hadn't always been an ass. They had met during the Friends of the Library book sale, where she was hauling in boxes of donated books and sorting them onto tables while he browsed for books for his high school classroom. They had coffee, then dinner. A few months later she cheered him on as he coached the basketball team for the high school where he taught, watching him with the players, the way he encouraged them to be the best. She knew he would have been a great father. It never occurred to her until after they were married that he might not want his very own children. It was her own fault for not asking, for not having the discussion. She was young and stupid and in love.

Astra danced to forget how much she had missed her friends while married to Trent. The distancing had happened so gradually. First it was a missed brunch, then a missed birthday party, then a missed birth. She didn't realize how she'd allowed Trent to become the center of her universe until he left it, leaving her without something to orbit around.

Astra danced to forget all the nights she'd spent crying. The struggles at the library when she had to let go of three part-time employees due to budget cuts, even though they were like family. The constant stream of small fires she had to put out that distracted her from programs she felt passionate about. Patrons complained about not having enough diverse books, then other patrons complained there were too many. The library was for everyone, yet no one seemed to be happy with it.

Astra danced to forget how much she missed her parents during the winter when they escaped to Florida for the sunshine. She'd worried so much that they would get sick and she wouldn't be near to help them.

It had taken her almost a year to feel like her own woman again. Astra danced to celebrate her freedom. Freedom to spend all night out, to eat kringle, to dance like no one was watching in a room packed with people.

The mint cherry concoction jumbled in Astra's stomach, fueling her dancing spree, letting her inhibitions slide away. Sweat dripped down her back and her breath mingled with laughter no one could hear. Her elbows and hips bumped the people dancing around her, her feet hopped to the thumping base of a song she'd never heard, but it moved her all the same. She danced out the pain until only joy was left.

Joy that she was with her friends.

Joy that it was nearly Christmas.

Joy that she would see her parents soon.

Joy that a handsome man was smiling at her, his hair stuck to his forehead, his T-shirt becoming more transparent.

On a whim—and Astra would later blame it on the Santa Claus shots—she wrapped her arms around Jack's neck and pulled his lips to hers. The shock of it caused them both to stop dancing as the minty-cherry taste in her mouth mingled with the ginger on his breath. Tentative at first, her lips waited for him to respond, a sign he was open to sharing her joy. She was about to pull away, hot embarrassment kindling to life in her cheeks, when his hands went to her hips and his lips moved with hers, and her mouth opened for him. Their kiss found its own rhythm on the dance floor, moving them closer together as the people bumped around them, but Astra didn't care. She only cared that this kiss reminded her that she liked kissing, she liked being touched, she liked feeling wanted. It had been so long.

Her hands grabbed at his shirt as he moved his kisses to her neck. She moaned but too softly for anyone to hear over the music. Lights flashed and swirled on the ceiling; the air pulsated with heat. She was dizzy and breathless. Her hands pressed against him, savoring how well they molded to his curves and angles.

Her lips found his again, and she wanted to be closer, wishing she could wrap her legs around him and have her way. Her knees quaked as his hands explored the way her jeans clung to her butt and hips, finding the hem of her shirt and touching her lower back, heated skin on heated skin. He wanted her as much as she wanted him. She broke the kiss long enough to look into his eyes: they flashed from blue to green to black with the disco lights, his hair dark with perspiration, and his breath coming as fast as her own. Now that they'd kissed, she knew what it was about the way he looked at her. He looked at her like this moment had been inevitable, a done deal, foretold years ago. And she believed it. The feeling left her even more light-headed.

Perhaps it was the cheap shots or the excessive heat or the perfect kissing, but Astra's knees wobbled, then gave out, quickly followed by the club going dark.

She came to with a flashlight blinding her.

"What the hell?" Astra batted at the flashlight and tried to sit up, but was shoved back down. Cassie was much stronger than she looked, especially with irrational patients. Jack and her friends were in some sort of office lined with cases of liquor and a desk buried in papers.

"Stay. You passed out. It doesn't look like anything serious. Probably a combo of heat, booze, lack of oxygen from sucking face,"—Cassie couldn't help but smirk at her—"and age."

"You had to add that last one? We aren't that old. Where are we?" She chose to ignore the sucking-face comment, for now. While Jack wasn't quite a random stranger, it was still very unlike her to kiss someone she'd just met.

"The club's office. It was this or the bathroom and I figured you'd rather not be lying on the bathroom floor of a club that's approaching closing time."

"Good call," Astra said.

"Jack carried you in here like a superhero. It was damn impressive. Between that and Cassie taking over like it was an episode of *Grey's Anatomy*, this has been a truly epic night," Ronnie said.

Astra moved to sit up again and brushed away Cassie's hand.

"I'm good," Astra said. Over her shoulder, Jack stood against the wall, his brows furrowed in concern. "Can we leave now?"

"Do you feel up to it?" Cassie asked, watching Astra carefully as she stood and tested her balance. She felt normal, just tired and in need of a shower.

"If not, Super Jack can carry you again," Ronnie said.

Jack blushed.

"Sorry," Astra said, following Steph out of the office door and into the cool night. "And thank you. If you hadn't been there, I could have been trampled."

"If I hadn't been there, would you still have been, how did Cassie put it, sucking face?"

Astra glanced at him and cleared her throat before she spoke. "Unlikely."

Jack nodded and grinned.

"Then you wouldn't have swooned."

"Are you implying that your kisses made me pass out?"

"Perhaps we can do some testing on the matter, to rule it out."

They walked side by side and a light snow started to fall, just enough to dust everything in white and hide all the dirt and grime of the city. Downtown Milwaukee had every street draped in Christmas lights so it was like walking through a Christmas village. When her foot slipped on a patch of ice, Jack put an arm around her waist to steady her, then left it there. Astra leaned into the sweetness of his touch.

"I'd like that. Should I text you? Or you text me—you already have my number."

"I don't have a mobile phone."

"Really? Old-school. Interesting. Then call me."

They stood under the wrought-iron arch that marked the Jule-marked entrance. Her friends had walked a little bit ahead to give them their space. It hadn't taken long to get to the Julemarked from the club. He rubbed his jaw.

"Perhaps we could set the date and time now? The bakery phones aren't always reliable. How about tomorrow? We could have dinner?" Jack asked.

"I'm sorry, that won't work. Tomorrow is my last day with the girls, and then I leave for Florida to spend Christmas with my parents."

"Come on, Snow, it's not getting any warmer out here," Ronnie shouted, interrupting them.

"I get back on New Year's Eve. Let's ring in the New Year together. You could come over and celebrate with Bernie and me. She gives great sloppy kisses. I'll come get you at eight."

It was so unlike Astra to set the plans. It felt good to be making decisions and doing what she wanted.

Jack opened his mouth to speak but was interrupted.

"My boobs are becoming titscicles." Ronnie shivered. "We're leaving."

"Sorry about my friends. See you soon." With that, she kissed Jack on the cheek and ran off without giving him a chance to say no or tell her he had other plans.

Chapter Seven

ASTRA WOKE WITH A FACE FULL OF RONNIE'S HAIR IN HER already too-dry mouth with all the covers piled on top of her, explaining why sweat drenched her clothes as if she had slept in a sauna. She gently spread the sheets over Ronnie and slipped out of the bed, grabbing her phone and sneaking into the bathroom so she didn't wake any of her friends. Their hotel room overlooked the performing arts center and was a short walk to the Christmas market, while also being close to Old World Third Street, Water Street, and Cathedral Square—a convenient location for their annual get-togethers.

The previous night, she and Ronnie had flopped onto one of the double beds, leaving the other for Steph and Cassie. Cassie had handed out bottles of water she had stashed in the fridge, while Steph used a flimsy plastic knife to cut off hunks of the cherry almond kringle.

"No one falls asleep till they've eaten some food and chugged their water," Cassie said, pointing her finger at Ronnie, who was already dozing on her pillow.

"Why is it now that I am at an age where a few glasses of wine seem essential and deserved after a long week, the hangovers become brutal," Steph said before drinking half her bottle.

"Do you actually want an answer for that or do you just want to complain?" Cassie said.

"Complain. I don't want to hear that I'm old."

Cassie took Steph's head between her hands and kissed her on the forehead.

"You will always be the twenty-year-old I'd bring extra rubber bands for when we went out because I knew I'd be tying your hair back by the end of the night."

Steph held her bottle up as if to toast.

"To eventually learning to carry my own rubber bands."

Astra bit into the kringle slice that Steph handed her. It tasted even better with a buzz. Like cherry pie she could eat with her hands. Ronnie roused herself enough to discover a red ukulele in the corner and strummed a few very out-of-tune notes until Steph sternly took it from her hands and set it back on the stand.

"No. Under no circumstances."

Ronnie distracted herself with the colored pencils and roll of paper on the desk, seemingly having gotten a second wind from the sugar and hydration, sketching the four of them walking through the snow. Astra chewed her pastry and watched as the scene came to life, snowflakes dotting their red-and-white knit hats, their arms linked, colored lights glowing in the night around them. It was a quick sketch, a doodle by the most generous of standards, but a wonderful representation of their fun night.

"You forgot Jack," Astra said.

"Jack?" Ronnie paused and looked at the drawing.

"You aren't drinking," Cassie interrupted and poked at Astra's bottle. She took a few sips to wash down her last bite of kringle. Steph had a found a record player and some records—another feature of the eclectic hotel room—and in a few moments, Elvis crooned "Blue Christmas."

"My mom used to play this every year," Ronnie said. She set down the colored pencils and picked up the album cover. "It's like I'm five again."

"If only that was how it worked," Steph said. "I'd be listening to Kelly Clarkson on repeat until I was twenty-two again."

"You couldn't pay me enough to be twenty-two again," Cassie said.

"I'll agree with you tomorrow, but tonight, I want to have perky boobs." She cupped her chest and looked down.

Ronnie grabbed her own.

"They have a wonderful procedure that can help you with that." Ronnie had had her boobs done five years ago. Tasteful and firm. They looked great.

"Rob already can't keep his hands off them. I'd never get anything done if I had yours," Steph said.

"They can be distracting, but there are plenty of benefits." Ronnie waggled her eyebrows.

The conversation devolved into hysterics and horrible innuendos after that, until they drifted off to sleep as Elvis sung "O Come, All Ye Faithful."

Astra was glad Cassie had made them all drink the water and eat some food last night, or her head would be hammering.

On her way to the bathroom, Astra grabbed the last slice of kringle they hadn't devoured the previous night, wishing she had bought more to take home. Maybe she should swing by the bakery before driving to her parents' in Florida.

Thinking about the bakery brought to the surface the dream she'd had last night. Jack had been in the bakery, slipping a tiny gnome like the ones decorating the store and her house into the bag with the kringle. It was exactly like one she had—her only one that wore a green hat and held a rolling pin. In her dream, she had fixated on his hands, large and strong from rolling dough, yet careful and precise in the way he handled the gnome and the delicate pastries. It made her mouth dry, but not from her hangover.

She chugged another glass of water, then took a bite of the kringle, her stomach silent in appreciation. Sitting on the side of the tub, her phone in one hand and the kringle in the other, she saw she had a voice mail from an unknown number. Her phone showed her the text, and it didn't make any sense. She clicked Play in case it was something to do with her parents. At their age, she was always a little worried their neighbor or doctor would call to tell her they were in the hospital for something awful.

The message started with a squeak.

"Hi . . . Jack . . . see you on New Year's Eve . . . explain . . . come to the . . . there . . . will I. Please come . . . I am . . . you get . . ."

It ended with a shriek.

She listened again, and didn't pick up any new words. No wonder the voice mail to text was nonsense. Jack had mentioned their spotty phone service and he wasn't wrong. If this went anywhere, she'd have to get him a usable cell phone. She would research which phone models and plans were best for poor service areas. There had to be a solution.

She took another bite of the kringle, appreciating how she

tasted just the right combination of flaky, tender pastry and scrumptious filling in each bite. She could see the layers in the dough, but they didn't flake off like a turnover or croissant. The almond cherry filling and cream cheese glaze were the perfect balance of sweet and tangy. With a man who could bake like this, she could almost see herself in another relationship.

Before closing her phone, she checked the time.

Crap.

It was almost eleven. They'd all crashed like back in their college days. They'd planned a brunch so she would have time to be on the road by four with Bernie. As she shoved the last of the kringle in her mouth, she roused her friends, realizing that picking up another kringle would have to wait for another time.

Chapter Eight

WITH ONLY A WEEK UNTIL CHRISTMAS, JACK WAS RESTLESS. BE-
fore coming to the bakery, he'd tried on the red knit hat and taken it
off three times. It was soft and warm and didn't make his head overly
hot, yet he felt wearing it meant something he couldn't quite grasp. Before leaving the house, he took it off his head and tossed it onto an armchair near the door.

The woman who had given it to him had come through the bakery
one more time since he'd last seen her, but it had been so busy he could
only flash her a smile as he slid another nisse into her pastry bag—
something she could enjoy after she forgot about the Julemarked. It
meant something that she was back, didn't it? Seeing her three times
wasn't a coincidence anymore. It meant something and he wanted to
find out what. He had wanted to chase after her then, find out her
name, but he hadn't found her when he took his break fifteen minutes
later.

This Yule, he looked up whenever the door opened, checking the clock, as if waiting for the start of a much-anticipated event. Normally the shiny tiled walls of the bakery were inviting and homey, but today they crept closer and closer with each customer, pressing in on him, his skin tingling with unreleased energy. He imagined people who drank too much coffee felt like this—he was so immune to the stuff, he'd never experienced it himself. To try to work out the excess jitters, Jack wiped down the pastry case between customers, chasing away every fingerprint to the point that customers were noticing and not touching the glass.

"That's enough," Orn said, his words curt, but he had sympathy in his eyes. "Go clean in the kitchen, where you won't bother the customers."

Jack nodded. In the kitchen, he spread handfuls of kosher salt over the butcher-block counter and squeezed fresh lemon juice over the surface. Using the emptied lemon husks, he scrubbed the counter until his arms ached and the salty lemon juice found its way into every tiny nick on his hands—the stinging provided a welcome distraction. Next, he filled a bowl with warm water and wiped away the lemony salt until the island was clean and smooth, only to be dirtied again when they made the dough later that night.

From there, he swept and mopped the floor, and even removed everything off the shelves to wipe them down. It hadn't released any of the tension.

He needed to get out of the bakery. He needed fresh air. The sun was already setting, the light in the alley more fire than sun. He grabbed a cream cable-knit sweater from the back of a chair, not sure if it was his or not, and pulled it over his head, pausing long enough to add a dark green knit hat and matching scarf. He left out the bakery's entrance, patting Orn on the shoulder as he passed. They would know why he'd left. They all had moments when the elysian brick walls of the Julemarked became too tight. It never lasted long, and happened less often to him, but when it did, he knew not to ignore it. Only fresh air and freedom could cure it.

Tucking his hands in his pockets, he walked into the cold night air. He could feel puffs of warmth as he walked by the fires dotting the alley and paused as he approached the iron arch marking the line between the Outside and the Julemarked. It was strange that a simple arch could mark such an important line—between his small world and another much larger one. Taking one step at the right (or wrong) time could radically change a person's life.

He rarely crossed the line, but today it was as if an unseen force shoved him. With a deep breath, he lifted his foot and crossed the border into the Outside, and a wave of dizziness rolled through him as if he'd stood up too quickly. His mouth began to water, sweat beaded on his forehead despite the cold, and Jack regretted ever eating anything. He heaved the contents of his stomach into a nearby garbage bin and hoped any witnesses dismissed it as too much mulled wine.

When he finished, he wiped his mouth with a handkerchief and popped a slice of sugared ginger into his mouth. That seemed to take the edge off the spinning and settled his stomach enough that he could continue.

Right outside the Julemarked was a biergarten where people sat at tables sipping steaming mulled wine and cold beer. He walked past the tables to the market. Among the market's stalls, white lights crisscrossed above him, their glow reflecting on the small snowbanks lining the walkways and white roofs on the stalls, a vision out of a Christmas card. He braced his hand on the wooden pole of a tent selling Christmas ornaments that could be personalized with family names, children's faces, or dogs, as his head still spun like he was whirling on a carnival ride. After a few deep breaths, it settled to a steady undulation, like a boat riding choppy waves. Unpleasant, but he could manage.

Shoppers crowded around the stalls buying everything from knitted sweaters to hand-carved nutcrackers to Christmas cookies for their dogs. People laughed and smiled and a few even sang along to the Christmas music playing over the speakers that dotted the area. A line for raclette, the Swiss cheese that was melted and scraped onto French bread, already ten deep, lengthened as he watched. At this time of day, almost everyone carried hot mulled wine in the Christmas market souvenir mugs. This year's was shaped like a boot.

The festiveness in the air was contagious and was why he loved living in the Julemarked. The cheer hung in the air like garland, connecting people together through the Christmas spirit. At the Julemarked, this was his everyday life. Everyone living in anticipation of family and feasting and gift giving. Generosity and kindness, laughter and song. Something about those magical days leading up to Christmas brought out the best in humanity. More than any piece of ginger, that calmed his queasy stomach.

Cinnamon, warm bread, and citrus joined with the smell of firewood and pine, blanketing the market. On the far end of the grounds, a row of picnic tables allowed visitors to sit with friends and family to enjoy the festivities and rest their feet. His breath puffed into the night air, and when the white plume disappeared, he saw a familiar face sitting alone at one of the tables in front of him.

She wore the red knit hat that she always did, a puffy black coat with a blinking Christmas tree pin, and large red wool mittens. She *had a few packages sitting next to her. On a whim, he bought two boot mugs of mulled wine and walked to her table.*

"Excuse me," Jack said. "Is it okay if I sit?"

Her hazel-green eyes looked up at him and narrowed that tiniest bit, as if trying to remember something or deciding whether or not it was worth letting a strange man sit with her. He didn't blame her for the caution, but he hoped the decision would fall in his favor. He knew he was in before she said anything; her lips curved into a welcoming smile before she responded.

"Sure," she said. "My friends will be back shortly, but I'm sure they won't mind the additional company. As long as you don't mind raucous women."

"My favorite kind." *He slid onto the picnic table bench not quite across from her, setting the mugs on the table in front of him.*

Astra nodded toward the two mugs.

"Do you have a friend joining you?"

"They gave me two," *he fibbed,* "and told me to keep the extra one. Can I offer it to you? It will be cold by the time I finish the first one."

She narrowed her eyes at him. He understood. A woman couldn't be too careful when by herself.

"I promise it isn't poisoned," *Jack said.*

"That's exactly what someone who had poisoned it would say."

He set both mugs in front of her.

"You pick."

Using both of her mittened hands, she pulled one closer to her. He pulled off his own mittens and pulled the tiny remaining boot mug to him, enjoying the warmth as it transferred from the ceramic to his skin. She took her right mitten off and did the same, taking a sip.

"See, no poison," Jack said, drinking from his own mug. "So, your friends left you here?"

"I finished my shopping and decided to claim a table so we'd have a place to sit." She pointed to the bags next to her.

"You're a glorified 'reserved' sign." Jack nodded knowingly. He liked understanding these little pieces of Outside life.

"Precisely." She looked around them. "But this is the best place to people watch, so I'm happy to. And now I have some company."

He warmed a bit at having qualified as "some company" as opposed to some random stranger, or some creepy guy.

"Are you here with someone?" she continued.

"No, I work in the Julemarked." He pointed back toward the alley, wondering if she'd remember it. "At the kringle bakery."

"We walked by there earlier. I love kringle."

Jack smiled. She still remembered it.

"You should have come in."

"We had just eaten our weight in raclette and strudel. Maybe next year." She took a drink from her mug. "I love all the little nisser decorating the alley."

Jack blinked at her comment. It took him a moment to register that not only had she said "nisser," but she had pronounced the word correctly—the way he had taught her the first time they met. She might not remember him, but she remembered something about their exchange. There was something different about this woman. They always found each other when the Julemarked appeared in Milwaukee. Especially today. He never left the Julemarked, but he had today and almost walked straight to her. He needed to learn more about her.

"I carve them." Jack reached into his jeans pocket and pulled out a small wooden nisse no bigger than his thumb. He had carved it from *a pine branch off a tree behind his cottage and painted it. He set the small figure on the table in front of her. "Here. One to remember me by. My initials are on the bottom."*

She picked up the small figure with a snowy white beard and pointy red hat. This one held a bunch of green mistletoe. Her finger traced all the little details, like the curls in the beard, and his pinkish nose sticking out from under the hat. She flipped it over to see the JC on the bottom.

"You made this? It's amazing. I couldn't possibly keep it." She set the small gnome back on the table.

"Why not?"

"I don't know you. I can't take something like this that's clearly worth something."

He nudged it closer to her.

"I don't sell them. We use them for decoration. Please, take it."

She picked up the nisse again, then set it down.

"I have a growing collection of them that I set out every year for Christmas. I think my friends sneak some in every year, because they seem to multiply when I'm not looking. He would be a wonderful addition."

A collection. She still had the other nisser that he had given her. He picked it up and moved it closer to her on the table.

"Now you have to take him. It's meant to be."

She curved her uncovered hand around the figurine.

"Thank you," Astra said. "He's my new favorite."

They sat in silence for a moment or two. It was peaceful.

"Are you always at the Milwaukee Christmas market, or do you go to other markets?"

How could he answer this without sounding delusional?

"A little of both. I've been to Christmas markets all over the world."

Astra leaned in.

"Really? That would be so fun. Do you have a favorite one?"

"Milwaukee."

She rolled her eyes.

"It is not," she said.

"It is. Milwaukee is my favorite. The market is the perfect size but still draws a nice crowd, the weather is winter appropriate, and . . ." Jack swallowed. "I like the people."

"Okay, I'll give you that, but I have to believe there are more interesting places."

"Interesting isn't really what you want at Christmas, is it? You want comforting, familiar, cozy."

She nodded.

"True, I'd be sad if I didn't get my mom's Christmas cookies or my dad's roast pork and potatoes."

"Exactly. Christmas is about tradition, and is there anything more traditional than a snowy holiday, with good food and family?" he said.

"And friends, of course," she said, looking up as her three friends found her. His time was up, it would seem.

"Who is this delicious Christmas treat?" the tall blonde said.

The tiniest one smacked her arm. "He's human, not some object for you to devour."

"He might be. We've only just met."

"I warned you," she said. "Raucous."

"I'll take that as my cue to leave. I'm not one to get between friends. Happy holidays, ladies," Jack said with a nod. He rose from *the table, and when he looked over his shoulder, the four women had their heads close, but their laughter was loud. He was happy she had such people in her life who brought her so much joy. He tucked his hands in his now empty pockets, the nisse having found a new home, and whistled as he walked back to the Julemarked. He expected he'd see her again—it was only a question of when.*

Chapter Nine

IT HAD BEEN A VERY LONG TWO DAYS OF DRIVING FOR ASTRA. With a butt sore from hours of sitting and her teeth grimy from so much junk food that she worried she'd never get the taste out of her mouth, Astra wanted to shower and sleep, but Bernie was ready to party. She ran down the sandy beach, chasing waves, then dashed back to shore as they pursued her. Astra lay on the lounge chair, where her mom joined her, setting down a piña colada in a red glass with Santa on the side, the air condensing on the outside into beads of water that grew until they streamed down the side in winding streaks. Astra came by her love of Christmas honestly. She sucked a quarter of the drink down, letting the chilly concoction cool her, then finished putting a fresh layer of reef-safe sunscreen on her face.

"I needed that," Astra said.

"I can't believe you made it in two days. That's too much driving for one person," her mom said. Though anyone walking by wouldn't think she was her mom, maybe an older sister. She had thinning dark hair pulled into a low ponytail below her large floppy hat. A filmy pale green cover-up went to her mid-thighs, but Astra knew she still had a bikini on underneath. A tasteful and appropriate-for-her-age bikini, but a bikini nevertheless.

"Bernie doesn't love the highway, so I thought it best to get the journey done as quickly as possible. Plus, finding hotels that allow big dogs isn't as easy as it should be. They're either so gross we were both likely to get fleas, or so expensive I might as well have chartered a private plane to get here."

Her mom smiled and raised an eyebrow.

"I doubt they were quite that much. Your dad and I can help if you need it."

Astra knew that, but she hated needing help. She'd already used up her allotment of parent bailouts during the divorce, needing them to cosign to get the mortgage. It embarrassed her to be in her late thirties and need her parents to help her buy things. She had the money (mostly), but the bank wouldn't take the risk on her as the sole payee. With both her parents retired, she didn't want to eat away at any of their savings, so she made sure her mortgage payment was always early, though she some-times resorted to meals of cheap ramen at the end of the month. She was too old to eat like a college student. Her mom had taken to ordering groceries delivered to her house once a month when Astra made the mistake of mentioning it.

"I can see you worrying about us," her mom said. "Trust me, we're good. I married a smart man with foresight. If we don't give it to you now, you'll just get it later."

"Maybe let's not talk about your inevitable demise," Astra said.

Bernie had lost the race with the most recent wave and

emerged from the water soaked. She trotted toward where they sat in the shade, paused to shake off the excess water, then proceeded to noisily drink from the ice cream bucket filled with water they had sitting out for her.

Her parents lived in a town house on the gulf side of the Florida Keys. They resided there just long enough to have residency every winter and avoid the Wisconsin taxes, then rented it out the rest of the year to help cover the costs. The entire complex was made up of couples who did the same thing. They had bought it five years ago, and that's when the family started celebrating Christmas on the beach.

Astra missed the snow. Christmas didn't seem quite right when the lights were wrapped around palm trees instead of pine trees and she wore a swimsuit instead of a sweater. But it made her parents happy and she didn't really have anywhere else to go. She made sure to get her fill of the snow and cold before heading south.

At least Bernie seemed to love the change of pace, and Astra couldn't argue with the on-demand cocktails.

"You ready?" Her dad joined them, carrying two sets of snorkel gear. This was the one very big upside to Christmas with her parents—there was moderately decent snorkeling off their beach. If she ever gave up on the four distinct seasons of Wisconsin, it would be for year-round snorkeling out her front door. She didn't love the heat, didn't really love the sun since she was more of a night owl, but snorkeling would get her up and out the door every time.

"Ready? I've been waiting all year for this. What took you so long?" Astra said.

Astra took a huge gulp of her piña colada and grabbed the gear her dad set on the end of her lounge chair.

"Did you do the masks?" she asked.

"Not yet." Her dad handed her a tube of toothpaste. She squirted out a dab and rubbed it around the inside of the mask, then used some of her bottled water to rinse it off. Then she spit into the goggles and repeated the process.

"Don't they make spray for defogging?" her mom asked.

"That's not nearly as much fun," her dad said with a wink. Astra agreed. It was a weird process, but a fun ritual she enjoyed. Who knew if it was all necessary? But she did know that if she did those two steps, her mask never fogged up.

"Keep an eye that Bernie doesn't follow us," Astra said. While Bernie could swim, she didn't want her swimming too far out and getting tired.

Her mom held up a bag of bacon.

"Way ahead of you."

Bernie sat down in front of Astra's mom without even acknowledging Astra's departure. Now she knew where she ranked compared with bacon.

She waded into the gulf with her dad, dipping her mask in the water, then slipping it over her eyes, pressing to check the seal. The familiar sucking feeling on her eyes let her know it was tight enough. She put the snorkel in her mouth, then started the process of getting her feet into the flippers while waves tried to knock her down, making her feel like she'd never done this before. She'd yet to discover a graceful way to get into flippers without falling over. At last she pushed off into the water, cool against her sun-warmed skin even though she wore a long-sleeved swim shirt. It had been two years since she'd last done this, and the first few breaths were always tricky. Her body resisted the urge to breathe with her face in the water even though her mind knew the snorkel would get her the oxygen she needed. She focused on taking long, slow breaths, letting herself float on the gentle waves until her body and mind agreed they weren't about to drown. Her dad had already kicked his way toward the small reef off the shore.

Instead of racing toward him, she took time to acclimate herself. Sea grass dotted the sand, with a few small fish hiding among the leaves. Picking out the hidden sea life was what she loved most about snorkeling, and that she couldn't bring her phone. It was just her and the ocean.

Small tan fish darted around under the sea-grass blades, the antennae of a spiny lobster poked above the grass, and a tiny crab scuttled across a sandy patch. The sounds of the world muffled around her, leaving only crackling in her ears, like a staticky radio station. Astra took a deep breath through her snorkel, letting the stress of driving almost sixteen hundred miles wash away with the waves. Her arms drifted at her sides as her flippered feet gently kicked her toward the jumbled line of craggy rocks that her dad had zoomed off to see, where most of the sea life dodged in between boulders and around growing corals, but it was in the sea grass where she might spot a manatee hoovering the vegetation. While a bit cold during December for manatees this far south, she always hoped for an unexpected encounter.

Astra reached the rocks—they had been placed there intentionally to attract sea life several years ago, and had now grown into a mini reef with dark green and purple sea fans waving in the current, corals poking out from the crevices, and yellow and blue fish darting around. Snorkeling made her feel free and weightless, and she let her mind wander while her eyes sucked up all the beauty. It was here three years ago that Trent had blindsided her, revealing he had never wanted kids. Ever. Astra could still taste the regret of not sorting that detail out before the "I do's." He had picked up on her disappointment, because when they returned home, he presented her with Bernie—a wonderful but ineffective attempt to fix things. A few months later, he presented her with divorce papers. Now she only wanted him out of her life for good.

Nearby, a sea turtle munched algae growing on a rock and Astra floated to watch, staying as still as the rolling waves would allow so she didn't startle it. Her life was so much better now. She just needed to get Trent to agree to give her full custody of Bernie, and she would never have to see him again. Get him out of her life forever. That's what she wanted now. And maybe there was even romance on the horizon for her, now that she and a certain baker had a date on New Year's Eve.

Astra's toes dug into the cool sand on the Bahia Honda beach for her father's favorite activity—stargazing. She sat at the corner of a large blanket with her mom next to her, her arms wrapped around her bent legs. Her mom lay on her back like a starfish, limbs stretching toward the four blanket corners. Astra picked up the wine bottle they had stuck in the chilly sand and poured herself and her mother a glass of the crisp white. Her dad crouched over the new telescope he had unwrapped earlier in the day, pushing buttons on a keypad, causing the telescope to slowly move to a new position.

"Did you make a wish, Astra?" her mom asked. That was their thing. Dad looked at the stars, and she and her mom wished on them.

"Incredible," he said. "It finds the object I select on this." He held up a small black controller.

Astra's mom turned her head toward Astra and winked.

"I know, dear," her mom said. "That's why I bought it for you. Now you don't have to waste all your time fiddling with the dials and swearing when you can't find what you're looking for."

"You know me so well," he said, turning back to the view-finder. Her mom had gotten him a new, computerized telescope that did all the tedious work for him. He had gotten her cozy clothes and the soft, sand-resistant blanket on which they sat so she could be more comfortable while he stargazed. And a wine-club subscription.

This. This was what Astra had thought she had found with Trent, what she still wanted for herself. Knowing someone so well you could buy them the perfect Christmas gift. She sighed and set her chin upon her knees.

"Why such a big sigh, Bun-Bun?" her mom asked.

Astra sipped the wine.

"Every time I think I'm moving in the direction I want to go, roadblocks pop up everywhere."

"Work still?" her mom asked.

"Who knew local politics could be so time-consuming? Another new board member who doesn't even have a library card. I mean, shouldn't that be a basic requirement to be on the board? Must have library card."

Her mom sat up and rubbed her back, something she'd always

done when Astra complained, and the effect was instantaneous. Her muscles eased and she took a deep breath, freeing all the frustration.

"You'll figure it out, you always do. But something tells me that isn't all that's bothering you." Her mom looked at her the way only a mother can, as if seeing into the nooks and crannies of her heart to find the truths that Astra chose to ignore. "You're lonely."

Damn it.

"Of course I'm lonely. I thought I'd be surrounded by kids and barreling toward my middle age with a husband by my side. Not fighting over custody of my dog so I'm not completely alone." Astra bit her lip. She was leaving in two days, just in time to get home for New Year's.

As if on cue, her mom asked, "What are you doing for New Year's? Are you and the girls going out?"

Astra bit the inside of her cheek to keep from smiling as she admitted her plans.

"I have a date. With a very cute baker."

"Which bakery?" Her mom of course knew to focus on the important facts.

"It's near the Milwaukee Christmas market in this little alley. I'll take you there when you're home next time—assuming it goes well."

The smile refused to stay hidden.

"Astra, you've been holding out on me. This isn't just any date—you really like this man."

"I've only met him once, but . . . I don't know. It's like I've known him for longer. It doesn't make any sense. If only I could align the pieces right, the puzzle would be complete and it would make sense." Astra looked up at the night sky. Her parents had moved here specifically so her dad could be close to this beach, the best stargazing in the Florida Keys. It was so dark she could make out the Milky Way as a cloudy streak across the sky and see more stars than in Milwaukee. After years of tagging along with her dad, she could pick out the major constellations, like Orion and the Big Dipper, and Jupiter, which sat right on the horizon—looking like the largest star in the sky. After all these years, they were always the same, just like her. "Mom, how did you know Dad was the right one?"

Mid-drink, her mom held up a finger to let her know she'd answer as soon as she was done. But her dad took over.

"That's an easy one," he said. "As soon as we met, it was like we had always known each other. Like we had found the home we knew was waiting for us."

Astra's mom swallowed her gulp of wine. "What he said."

"Just like that. It was that simple," her dad said.

"Well, it wasn't love at first sight. But there wasn't that awkward phase where you have to say what you think the other person wants to hear. We just spoke the truth from the start," her mom said.

"She made her thoughts on sitting in the dark and cold very clear."

Her mom tapped the blanket.

"But he found all the ways to make it better."

Her dad turned his attention back to the telescope and waved Astra to join him. Her mom squeezed her elbow before shooing her to join her dad. All her life, her dad had been obsessed with staring into the night sky, but he had admitted long ago that his wife and daughter weren't as delighted by it as he was; still, Astra always loved the time they spent together.

"Found it. Look."

Astra set her eye against the eyepiece to see a velvety black background covered in speckles, some with orange or pink or white hues.

"Stars," she said.

"Ha ha. Not just any stars. That's the Christmas Tree Cluster. It looks like an upside-down Christmas tree from our location. The bright one at the bottom is S Monocerotis. The bright star at the other end is the top of the Christmas tree, then you can fill in the rest around the edges."

Astra couldn't tell one star from the other.

"Dad, you're making this up. You can look in the stars to connect the dots any way you want. It all looks the same."

"I am not making it up. Find Orion."

That was an easy one she could find without the telescope.

"Got it."

"Go to Betelgeuse, go down and to the left and look for S Monocerotis."

Dad always liked to pretend she remembered the names.

"You say that like I remember what S Monocerotis is."

"The unicorn horn on Monoceros." He hid any impatience he might be feeling and Astra loved him all the more for it.

"Got it."

"That's the tree trunk, and go down and you'll see the tree. Let your eyes unfocus and let the bright stars form the picture."

Astra listened to his advice, releasing the tightly held control. Once she no longer tried to force the stars into a shape, it emerged—

a distinct triangle topped with a bright star, and speckled with even more. She pulled her head back from the telescope and looked up at the night sky, finding the two brightest stars that marked the top and bottom, the rest obscured by light-years, but that didn't stop her from filling it in now that she'd seen it, like a beacon of Christmas joy in the sky—a Santa Signal.

She hadn't made her wish yet. Staring at the Christmas Tree Cluster, she thought about what she wanted most at this moment. Someone to share her life with, start a family. She wished for it all, even if it seemed greedy. You never knew when a Christmas wish might come true.

Chapter Ten

SIX YEARS AGO

IT WAS THE FIRST WEEKEND OF YULE MILWAUKEE. IT HAD BEEN three years since they were last here, but so much longer to him. Since time worked differently for them, it made any kind of relationship with someone on the Outside impossible. There was no way to tell how soon the Julemarked would return to a specific location as they criss-crossed the globe.

Jack had been thinking about it a lot.

Saturday had been wall-to-wall people, and his feet ached like they hadn't in a while. Tonight, they would need to make extra kringle dough to keep up with demand if these crowds continued. Jack slipped through the door at the end of the alley, the one next to the bookshop. He had checked the backup storeroom for stock to see what they should consider ordering from their contact, John. Butter and flour were running lower than he liked. After he pushed the large oak door shut, making sure it was closed tightly so no unexpected guests wandered through it, he bumped into someone when he turned, causing the person to drop several bags on the ground.

"So sorry," Jack said, then his heart leapt. It was her. Earlier than normal and stunning in the warm glow of the alley's multiple fires and twinkling fairy lights. She was beautiful. He smiled wide, because he couldn't help it when he saw her. She had that effect on him. His smile got even larger when she returned one of her own.

"It's my fault. I didn't realize I was standing in front of a door," she said, pointing to the door behind him before she bent to pick up the dropped items and collect the bags.

Jack quickly joined her, reaching for the items, grateful it hadn't snowed so they weren't icy and wet. As he reached for the last item, a book, his hand closed over hers rather than the book cover, shooting heat up his arm. He looked down to where his bare hand clasped her mittened one over the cover of the book—Outlander. He'd have to check it out another time. She picked up the book and they both stood with the items they'd collected.

"Sorry again," he said. Jack pointed to a picnic table, where they set all the items, and she worked to organize them, checking to make sure nothing had broken in the collision. "Everything survive? If not, I'll be happy to buy you another one since it's my fault."

"They all made it."

Jack looked at the several packages nearly covering the round bistro table.

"Getting your Christmas shopping done?"

He scanned the area, looking for her friends, but didn't spot any. Perhaps this was a chance to get to know her better, for her to get to know him.

"I hit the jackpot here. I never knew this little alley existed, but I managed to get items for my entire staff."

"Staff?"

Jack waved to the hot chocolate vendor, Henry Yu, who brought them two mugsful, generously topped with whipped cream.

"Oh, you didn't have to."

"It's the least I can do for endangering your packages. For your staff of?" He wanted to know what she was in charge of.

She sat up straighter, clearly proud of her accomplishment.

"You're looking at the newest library director for the Northeast Milwaukee library branch. I wanted to kick off my tenure by bribing the staff into liking me. And there's a few for other people, too." She pointed to a box from A Stitch in Time. "That's for my mail woman, Denise—a scarf to wear in the winter. That one is an ornament for my hair stylist. She has the funkiest Christmas tree in her salon and this ornament will be perfect. That one is a warm hat for my neighbor— poor man lost all his hair to chemo and needs to stay warm."

"Is there anyone you didn't buy presents for?"

"Well, Christmas is literally my middle name." She smiled to herself, and he was only more intrigued. "Besides, who doesn't like an unexpected Christmas gift?"

She shrugged and sipped her hot chocolate. He did the same, using the time to let this new information settle. She was generous and thoughtful of the people in her life.

"And the book?" He pointed to where Outlander sat.

"That's to keep me company while I wait for someone. It's one of my favorite books. I try to reread it every few years."

"I have books like that. Like visiting old friends."

"What are some of your favorites?"

"Most of them are not in English." Jack let his accent get a little thicker as understanding bloomed on her face. "But I've always had a soft spot for Dickens and his sweeping storytelling. The Russians are good on long winter nights, but their novels always veer a bit tragic for my tastes. Without hope for love, what's the point of it all?"

"I couldn't agree more. You might like this one, then." She tapped the cover. "Epic drama, with a lot of love that withstands it all." She leaned in closer and whispered, "And great steamy scenes, if that's your thing."

Jack laughed. Now he knew he'd be reading it. Who didn't love a little steam?

He took another sip of the hot chocolate, using the sweet, creamy drink as a distraction while he decided what else he could ask her about. He set the paper cup on the table.

"Oh," she said, reaching toward his face, a smile on her lips. She'd been smiling nonstop since they started talking, and Jack could feel an answering grin on his own face. Time stretched as her hand came closer to him. He didn't want to miss a moment of what happened when he was with her. His mind frantically scrambled to record every aspect. For the first time ever, he wished he had one of those phones people were always recording their lives with.

"You have whipped cream in your whiskers."

He wiped with his hand. She shook her head no when he took his hand away, and he continued wiping.

"Did I get it?" Jack asked.

She nodded.

"It's my burden to bear as an infrequent shaver."

"The downside of being razor-lazy?"

"Facially negligent."

She snorted and it made him want to kiss her. What an odd reaction to a snort, but there it was. Her head bent toward the ground and she looked up at him, errant snowflakes falling between them, catching the light, making the air sparkle. His brain scrambled to etch every scrap into his memory. He didn't want to forget how the nearby fires reflected off her red hair, making it dance like the flames, or the rosy glow to her cheeks from the cold, or the warm undertone in her laugh that spoke of kindness and light. She was meant to be here.

"That doesn't even make sense." But her grin told him she enjoyed their conversation just as much as he did. Had time slowed for her, too?

A Christmas polka began playing from nearby speakers and a few shoppers started dancing. This was the kind of thing that happened in Milwaukee—the locals knew what to do when they heard a festive oompah-pah. She chuckled at the music. "I thought this was more of a Scandinavian vibe here."

"We embrace all Christmas traditions."

"Since when is polka a Christmas tradition?"

"Polka has no season." Jack stood and held out his hand. "Care to join me?"

She looked behind him at the other dancing couples and set her mittened hand in his. His fingers closed around the soft yarn—the only barrier between their fingers—and his heart jolted. This spark was new and unexpected. He always thought he'd eventually settle down with someone already in the Julemarked, but perhaps his fate was to bring in a new resident. With her love of Christmas, reading, and easy laughter, she would be a perfect fit for their lifestyle here. And him. He'd never wanted something like this before. He willed it through *his hand, closing his eyes briefly, hoping that when he opened them, something would click into place for them both. Would he see a flicker of recognition in her eyes? Would heat flush her cheeks?*

He opened his eyes and felt disappointment when the flood of affection didn't wash over them both. But this time, something was different. He took her in his arms, one hand pressing into her lower back as he led them off in a small circle. He could tell this wasn't her first polka. They both grinned into the cool night air, scented with cinnamon and wood-burning fires, a few scattered snowflakes just starting to fall.

As the music ended, they slowed to a stop, but he didn't drop his hands and she didn't move away. Something subtle had changed during the dance. He longed to feel the satisfaction of when he knew he had perfectly balanced the flavors for a new kringle, but instead, their connection was still missing an ingredient that he hadn't found yet. He needed more time getting to know her.

"What's your name?" The words came out softly. He knew the answer would change everything, and the anticipation in him grew as she opened her mouth, as her lips started to shape the word. He needed to know, but he didn't want the moment to end.

Before she could reply, her eyes glanced over his shoulder and she stepped out of his arms, cold air filling the space between them, and a different smile slid onto her face.

"Hey, sweetie, you found me," she said as a man with short blond hair and a puffy olive-green winter coat stood next to her. He studied Jack, trying to determine if there was anything he needed to be concerned about. The man pulled her to his side and pressed a kiss onto her forehead, all while maintaining the staring contest with Jack.

"Yeah, I did, my beautiful bride." The words hit Jack with all the

weight that was intended. Bride. She was married. He took a half step back, worried he might tip over if he didn't. He needed to test that the ground was still beneath his feet. Everything sped up as the man pulled off the mitten on her left hand and kissed it, making sure Jack could see the sparkling rock. She was taken. Firmly off the market. "Ready to go?" the man said.

The alley walls wavered as Jack grew light-headed.

She looked back to Jack, seemingly unbothered by the connection that had tightened, then snapped between them. He knew she had felt it, too.

"Thanks for the dance, and hot chocolate." She gave him one more of her wide smiles, maybe the last she ever would, gathered her packages from the table, and disappeared down the alley with her husband.

He still didn't know her name.

Chapter Eleven

ASTRA TOOK STOCK OF WHETHER SHE WAS READY FOR THE night. Date-night outfit on, no food stains, legs shaved, bikini waxed. She was just missing the guest of honor. Bernie sat by the door as Astra triple-checked the state of the house. Bathroom cleaned, kitchen cleaned, and snacks prepped. Champagne chilled, bedroom cleaned. Condoms in nightstand. Floor vacuumed, though Bernie did her best to make it seem like it hadn't been. Christmas lights sparkled.

She slipped on her boots, and Bernie scooted closer to her. Though she had just dropped Bernie off at Trent's yesterday after their Florida trip, Trent had returned her while Astra showered. Her jaw still clenched when she thought about it.

Her hair had been sudsy with shampoo when Bernie's nose nudged the curtain enough that a draft found her in the steamy water.

"Bernie, what are you doing here?" But she already knew. Well, Trent would have to wait until she finished. Astra kept scrubbing.

"Hey, babe," a male voice said. Astra's blood started to boil in the already hot shower.

That jerk.

"Get out."

"What? You left the door unlocked. It's not like I haven't seen it all before."

She could hear the smarm in his voice. So annoyed, she didn't trust her response, so she kept quiet.

"Fine," Trent continued. "I'll wait on the couch."

Astra peeked around the curtain to make sure he'd left, then quickly stepped out of the shower to shut the door and lock it, leaving a puddle on the tile floor she was sure to slip on later.

Now that he couldn't get in, she took her sweet time washing her hair, shaving her legs, and letting the hot water ease out some of her anger. Twenty minutes later, she had emerged from the bathroom with her hair wrapped in a towel and her bathrobe tightly tied around her. She could feel her nostrils flare the second she saw him sitting in the middle of her green velvet couch with one ankle crossed over the opposite knee as if he were a king in his own castle. Before she could let loose the long list of reasons why what he had done was out of order, he spoke. Bernie lay curled up on her bed by the fireplace as if she knew she was in for a cozy stay.

"Why's the house so neat? You never clean for the girls." Of course she didn't clean for the girls; they were family. But she knew getting into her having a date would sidetrack the conversation. Best to stick to her list.

"How dare you come into my house, then into my bathroom without notice."

"I rang the doorbell and knew you were home. I could see the light on in the bathroom."

"That doesn't mean you can walk in. You should have waited until I was done, then rung the doorbell again. This is not your house, so what is convenient for you doesn't matter here."

He rolled his eyes and studied her more closely.

"You have a date." His words were flat.

"I imagine you do, too. That's why you're dropping off Bernie." The smarm returned.

"My date's allergic to dogs and we're spending the night at the Pfister for their New Year's Eve party."

Of course those were his plans. He had to have had it booked for months.

"And why didn't you ask me earlier to watch Bernie? I could have just kept her."

"I didn't think about it. And I thought I'd see if you have those pants hemmed."

He shrugged. There was always an ulterior motive with him. He never thought about what would be convenient for other people. She should talk to him about getting custody of Bernie, but she just wanted him out. Out of her house and out of her life.

"No, your pants aren't done. You'll get them when I finish them. Yes, I'll watch her even though you've only had her for a whole day and a half." She stared at him but he didn't move. "You can leave now."

Trent stood, clearly pleased with himself. Astra went to the front door and held it open. He paused in the doorway, just a few inches from her.

"How about a pre–New Year's kiss?"

She could smell his cologne. He still wore Polo in the green bottle, and now she'd have to burn a candle to get the smell out of her house before she picked up Jack. She had an hour before she had to leave. Cassie had lent her one of her cars so she could drive back and forth to pick Jack up without spending a fortune on cabs.

Astra could only stare at him.

At last he took the hint and gave up. Halfway out the door he turned to her.

"I'll call you in a few days to get Bernie."

"When?"

"Not sure." She knew he did this as some sort of weird power play, but it was more annoying than anything else, though that didn't mean she didn't want to occasionally return his petty behavior. Why did divorce make people so crazy?

"Fine." At last, when he was far enough out, she shut the door and locked it before he stepped off the porch. Bernie tippy-tapped next to her, assuming they were going for a walk.

"Not now, girl, but I won't be gone long. I'm just getting my date. You're going to love him. He's funny and handsome and a really good kisser. And he actually smells fantastic, even when he's sweaty. That's a great sign."

Astra finished getting ready and, an hour later, put on her navy blue pea coat, tied a navy-and-pink scarf around her neck, and perched an adorable knit hat carefully on her hair so it wouldn't get so flat that a quick upside-down hair plumping wouldn't fix the problem.

She tried to remember the street the Julemarked was on, but

couldn't. She knew it was near the Fiserv Forum, where the Christmas market was. When she arrived, she couldn't find available parking for several blocks. Astra had forgotten that the Fiserv Forum was having a blowout New Year's Eve party complete with a giant cheese wedge dropping down a pole at midnight. After paying twenty dollars for parking ten blocks away, she hiked back. At least she'd had the sense to not wear her heeled boots. She would have broken an ankle on the wobbly salt chunks dotting the sidewalks. She was grateful to be walking with the flow of pedestrian traffic. Walking back would be a challenge, but at least she'd have great company.

Crossing the street to the Deer District, the name for the plaza near the Fiserv Forum where there were several restaurants, she searched for the iron arch that marked the Julemarked. Around the open plaza, people were scattered in clumps, staking an early claim to watch the cheese drop, making it difficult for her to find the entrance. She walked the perimeter of the space, then up and down the alley between the restaurants where she had been certain it was located, but the Julemarked was nowhere to be found. She did the circuit again, then again, finally stopping in front of a plain brick wall near a beer garden that stayed open all year long, where she knew the entrance to the Julemarked had been.

To the left and right were two large sports bars. Tables sat next to tall heaters where patrons could sip their drinks while enjoying some protection from the elements. Above, the alley was partially covered. She remembered discovering the Julemarked was like finding a hidden treasure and wondered why there weren't more signs directing people toward it. There were two police officers nearby wearing bright yellow vests over their winter gear, puffs of breath coming out of their mouths as they spoke to each other.

"Excuse me," Astra said. "Do you know where the Julemarked is? I could have sworn it was here." Their blank expressions told her it didn't sound familiar, so she continued, hoping something would cause their memory to return. She put her hands on the brick wall, as if that would make it clearer to them. "It has a big arch of wrought iron that says 'Julemarked.' There's a bakery, bookstore, glassblower . . . Does that ring a bell?"

"Ma'am, I work here almost every day and all through the Christmas market. I've never seen what you're talking about. It sounds more like the Third Ward near the Public Market. Did you try there?"

Astra shook her head. "No, that's not possible. We weren't anywhere near there. It was here. I know it was here. I need to pick someone up and I'm late. He'll be waiting and I won't be there." Her voice rose, and her chest tightened. The possibility that she might not see him pulled at her. For a week she'd been looking forward to this night, bragging to her parents about it. Trent even knew about it. He'd love it that she was stood up.

"Ma'am, I think it's best if you move along. What you're looking for isn't here. He's not waiting for you here."

She stepped back as if buffeted by a strong wind. Astra pulled out her phone to check the time. Eight forty-five. Would Jack even still be waiting? Why didn't that fool have a cell phone like a normal person? If she could call him, this wouldn't be an issue.

She tried to google Kringle All the Way but wasn't surprised when it didn't come up. If he didn't have a cell, he surely wouldn't have a website.

What did people do before the internet?

And why couldn't she remember where it was?

Steph would remember. She never forgot anything, including the anniversary of when they all first met. She had the phone to her ear; it was easier than trying to text in her mittens.

"Hey," Steph answered.

"I'm picking up Jack and can't find the Julemarked. I thought it was in the Deer District, but it's not here."

"What are you talking about? Who are you picking up?" Steph asked.

Astra checked the phone to make sure she hadn't muted herself. It was unmuted.

"Jack. Remember, the guy I kissed at the club who's from the kringle bakery."

Steph paused.

"I kind of remember the guy. Real cute, dark blond hair, sweaty T-shirt. It's coming back to me. You have a date with him? That's fantastic. We need details at brunch." The girls met at least one Saturday a month for brunch at Blue's Egg in Wauwatosa. It was a nice middle distance between them all and had the most incredible hash browns.

"Obviously. But where was the bakery? It's not where I thought and now I'll be over an hour late."

"Huh, I don't remember. I remember the kringle we ate at three in the morning, but I don't remember where we got it. I didn't think I'd drunk that much."

"You didn't. We were there earlier in the day, right before Ronnie boozed all our hot cocoas."

"Did she roofie us, too, because I don't remember any of that. That's weird, right?"

"Very. I'll check with Ronnie and Cassie. Maybe they'll remember. I know Cassie dumped half her drinks because she didn't want to get wasted."

Astra hung up and called Ronnie and Cassie but got the same response. They vaguely remembered Jack, they remembered drunk kringle devouring, but they couldn't remember where they had bought it. Defeated, Astra walked the ten blocks back to her car, bumping against people as she plowed through the crowd, peeking down every alley as she trudged by in case she could spot the Julemarked. Disappointment fueled her search.

How could an entire alley disappear?

She hadn't imagined the connection they shared, no matter how many foul shots Ronnie had bought them. Something was off and she was going to figure it out. As a librarian, if there was one thing she was great at, it was finding answers. She just had to ask the right questions.

Chapter Twelve

Jack was strolling the Julemarked, to escape the bakery for a *few minutes for some fresh air, when he saw her. He had thought a lot about the woman in the red knit hat and her husband since he was last in Milwaukee. While she couldn't remember him, he found himself thinking about her often. Did she like her job? What did she read? Was she happy? It wasn't that he had fallen in love, but he couldn't ignore the spark they shared, like the thrill of reading a book's description that seemed custom written for him. The anticipation of unraveling all the twists and turns, the ups and downs of emotion, and enjoying the journey as much as the ending. They had the potential to be great together, and that didn't go away even though he knew she was married.*

As if he had summoned her with his thoughts, she appeared, wearing the same warm red coat he'd seen before, but a different knit hat, green this time, and it looked lovely next to her red hair. She walked next to a shorter woman with light brown hair, both cradling steaming mugs of mulled wine. They stepped into JulBooks at the end of the Julemarked, the one next to the large wooden door that patrons never went through and rarely noticed. The one near where they had danced. The sharp bells jingled through the muffled din of the Julemarked. He followed her into the store's warmth, Old Johan nodding to him from where he sat behind the counter, as Jack entered.

Old Johan was the oldest resident of the Julemarked, the keeper of the stories and their history, the bookstore being a natural extension. He remembered when women wore long, bell-shaped sleeves and men wore short pants and heeled shoes. He remembered the original residents of the Julemarked.

Jack walked the winding aisles, the dry, musty scent of used books a marked change from the yeast and sugar he normally smelled. An aisle over, Jack heard her and her friend speaking in hushed tones.

"How's Trent?" her friend asked. Trent. What a bland name. He hated that he knew the husband's name but not hers.

"He's Trent. We just had our annual fight about whether I needed to come on this weekend or not."

Her friend let out a low growl. "He can't keep you from us."

"I'm here." An edge sharpened her voice.

"It's okay if he's not the center of the world," the friend said. She sighed.

"I know, but it's different when you're married. You know. You've been married for a few years."

"My husband would never ask me to give up these weekends. It's just as important for our marriage that I get my girl time as it is for me to spend time with him."

"Trent is different. He needs me around."

"You mean he needs you to do things for him and validate his existence."

"He's not like that."

The friend huffed, then drew another deep breath before replying.

"You deserve better. And that's all I'll say about it. Nothing has happened that can't be undone."

Their voices went silent. He wished he could see her. Jack tried moving some books around to peer through the shelves, but they were too clogged, with books stacked in front of books. He'd have to empty both shelves on each side to see through, and there was no way to do that without being obvious.

Jack waited to hear her response, but a phone binged.

"It's him," she said. "The reception is crap in here. I'll have to call him later."

"He doesn't need to check on you."

"He likes to know I haven't forgotten about him."

Another long pause.

"You know I say this only with love. You haven't seemed happy lately. Think about why that is. You're the only one who can figure that out. Nothing is permanent and you deserve happiness. You know I love and support you no matter what you choose to do. Now I'm going to look for some books for my mother-in-law. Maybe they'll have something with curse words and steamy sex scenes that will shock her enough to never speak to me again."

One set of footsteps shuffled away and her friend walked past the end of his aisle. Jack pulled a book from the shelf to make it look like he wasn't eavesdropping. He was in the travel section and held a book *on the best places to snorkel—as if that was on his bucket list. He opened it to a random page and strained his ears to hear.*

He heard a sniff, then footsteps that followed the same path her friend had taken. Jack looked down at the book in his hands. A sprawling photo of blue water stretching as far as the eye could see took up both pages, the water shifting from clear aqua to dark blue until it blended into an even more vibrantly blue sky. Could there really be that much blue in the world?

He looked up to see her enter the aisle, her cheeks pale, lacking their normal bloom from the cold, the skin around her eyes pink. She scanned the books quickly, then stopped, drawing one carefully from the stacks, holding it almost reverently, her diamond ring flashing like a warning as she turned the book over in her hands—screaming that she was already in a relationship. Jack raised his book so he could see the pages and her at the same time. She opened the book carefully, its spine creaking as she scanned the first few pages, careful not to damage or stress the old book with its tattered cover. Jack couldn't tell which book she held, but Old Johan had hundreds of ancient tomes collected over the years from all around the world.

"Holy shit," she whispered, checking the title on the spine again, then cradling the book to her chest as she walked toward the front of the store. Jack slid his book back onto the shelf, not caring where it belonged, and followed her, glancing at where she'd grabbed the book from—fairy tales. Specifically, Hans Christian Andersen. It should be no surprise they had an entire bookcase dedicated to his titles.

When he caught sight of her approaching Old Johan, he found cover behind a nearby display. What about the book in her hand had caught her attention?

"Is this really a signed first edition?" She set it reverently on the counter. "And how much?"

Old Johan looked at the book and looked at her, his eyes squinting.

"I wondered where that had gotten to. Yes, it's a first edition, signed by the man himself." Jack was certain Old Johan had gotten it in person. "But I'm sorry, it's not for sale. It's been in the family for decades and I couldn't part with it."

She nodded.

"I understand. It was a treat just to see it. Thank you."

Her friend joined her as she left empty-handed. Jack wanted to grab the book and deliver it to her, certain she should have everything she wanted. He could see her through the large window at the front of the bookstore, where she waved her friend on and stopped, checking to confirm she wasn't blocking the door. She took a deep breath and turned her face to the sky, where large white flakes drifted down, landing in her auburn hair, winter blooms on a field of red. She closed her eyes and let the flakes kiss her cheeks, eyelids, lips.

Never before in his life had he been jealous of snowflakes. Opening her eyes, she stared at the strings of twinkle lights stretching back and forth along the alley. A smile twitched on her lips. She liked what she saw and Jack couldn't blame her. The alley was almost as beautiful as she was, especially on an evening like tonight. He almost stepped toward the door to join her when she brushed a snowflake from her cheek and followed after her friend.

"You can come out now," Old Johan said.

Alone in the bookstore, Jack joined him at the counter. He didn't get much traffic being at the end, and that was the way Old Johan liked it.

"She's an interesting one," Old Johan said.

"I know."

"But married," Old Johan said.

"I know." Jack's voice lowered to match his spirits as he was forced to admit the truth yet again.

"Don't be so down. Nothing is forever." Jack snorted at the sentiment coming from someone who seemed like he had been around forever. "Not everyone can find this book." Old Johan tapped the cover. "Only people who have a connection to this place. Her story isn't done yet."

Hopefulness surged. His life had been all but perfect. Surrounded by his loved ones, never wanting for anything—why would he have needed to hope? But he could only describe the soaring feeling in his chest as hope. Hope that he wasn't wrong about their connection. Hope that she would someday return here unattached. Hope that their story wasn't done. A wide grin spread across his face.

"Thank you, Old Johan. That's what I needed to hear."

Jack moved to leave and Old Johan held out the book.

"Put this back where she found it."

Jack grasped the book, its linen cover rough in his hands, his fingers warming where her fingers had so recently touched, tracing the invisible paths that hers had traced. His imagination swirled as he envisioned the time they could spend together, getting to know each other. He couldn't wait to show her all the secrets of the Julemarked.

Chapter Thirteen

Two days after New Year's Eve and Astra's head still felt like the inside of a cement truck, each revolution causing a nauseating head thump. She could feel the pulse in her ears and eyes. She'd moved from Tylenol to Advil to the I'm-not-fucking-around dose of three Aleves she reserved for her worst period headaches, and still the pounding continued like her head was a timpani drum, spiked mallets banging on her brain. Drinking two bottles of champagne alone had really taken its toll on her thirty-seven-year-old body.

She pulled out another three blue pills and double-checked her math. It had been three hours since the last dose. Not the best idea, but desperate times and all that. She tossed the pills into her mouth and chugged half of the water bottle she'd filled at the library's bubbler. She'd been gulping water for thirty-six hours trying to rehydrate, and her body still dragged as if full of sand. Was this what being forty would be like? Was this more than a brutal hangover?

After returning home without Jack, Astra had put on her pajamas, grabbed the first bottle of champagne, and flopped on the couch next to Bernie, flipping between the various televised New Year's Eve parties. After taking her first swig straight from the bottle, Astra poured the entire thing into the giant stainless-steel cup she used to drink water at work, the same one she had just used to take the Aleve. A bottle of champagne—no, it was sparkling white wine from California—had fit perfectly. After the second bottle, an hour before midnight, she'd fallen asleep curled around Bernie until her furry companion woke her with a sharp bark at nine in the morning, letting her know it was time to go outside.

Two days of water, very little food except buttered toast, and Astra wondered if this was beyond a hangover. Of course she was upset that her date with Jack had failed, but there was more to it than that. While she didn't know Jack well, they had a spark. It could go out as fast as it came to light, or it could be the beginning of a long, slow, delicious burn. He'd been charming and funny, and that tiny lilt in his speech like he had grown up speaking a different language set her skin tingling. When they had danced and he'd set his hands on her hips, she could still feel their strength, like he was consciously being firm and gentle, having complete control over the pressure they exerted after years of manipulating dough into delicate shapes. The thought warmed her cheeks and set her stomach aflutter.

The memory was viscerally real; she could still feel where his hands had been, the brush of his lips, the lingering scent of sugar and ginger when they kissed. She didn't imagine it, but being unable to find the bakery combined with her friends' missing memories had questions multiplying faster than Tribbles. Why did she remember more than her friends? Where was the Julemarked? Where was Jack?

Taking a fresh yellow pad of legal paper from a stack she kept on a shelf above her desk, she wrote down her questions, leaving space between them for notes.

She opened her browser and typed in "Kringle All the Way." She knew this wouldn't get her far, since she'd already searched there, but it established a baseline. If she started her process at the beginning, she knew she wouldn't miss any steps, and the internet always changed, so it was possible something might hit this time. She pressed Return.

Nope, nothing new.

Now it was time to get serious. If you knew how to search, you could dive past the surface results based on ads and SEO manipulation and truly mine the international well of knowledge.

This first basic search came up with nothing but a very strange short movie about a talking Christmas cookie and a craft beer, which was definitely not what she wanted. Next, she tried "jule-marked," but that brought up millions of results about all the different Christmas markets around the world, not the specific one she wanted. Or if it was there, she'd have to wade through thousands of websites. She put an asterisk next to it as something to circle back to if she didn't have any success. With each search, she noted the parameters so she didn't repeat herself. She stretched her arms, took a long drink of water, noting that her headache had finally disappeared, and had settled in for some deep-dive work when Chloe appeared at her door.

"Mr. Whitney is back."

"What's he watching?" Astra asked.

Chloe snorted.

"He's not watching anything. You have to see it."

Astra sighed, noted where she left off, and slipped back into her shoes under her desk, then followed Chloe to a corner of the library where there were huge windows looking out over a small snow-covered patio and picnic table. In the summer, they would host nature programs and story times out there. On the interior side of those huge windows were tables, each with a lamp and outlet on the surface so patrons could easily plug in their electronics. It was a popular spot for students to study, as it was generally quiet and bathed in natural light during the winter.

Even before she picked out Mr. Whitney at the full tables, Astra could smell his new antic—the unmistakable odor of bacon and toast.

The thing about Mr. Whitney was you never quite knew what you would get. There was the time he kicked off his shoes, propped his feet up on a table, and proceeded to snore so loudly he cleared an entire section of the library, or the time he tried to hand out suckers to the children to keep them from chattering. While his antics were technically against library policy, he was never belligerent when asked to stop. He was a lonely old man who either didn't see the line between appropriate and inappropriate behavior or, more likely, enjoyed the excitement of tiptoeing over it to see what would happen. She knew he lived alone on a nearby street and often walked to the library. Recently, his face seemed more drawn and his clothing more baggy, which made today's antics particularly hard to shut down.

Spread out on the table in front of him, he had an open package of bacon, a loaf of whole wheat bread, a carton of eggs, and American cheese slices. And a waffle maker, the older type that would make four small waffle squares rather than a giant Belgian waffle. Using a bent fork and gloved hands, Mr. Whitney lifted a piece of bacon from one square and set it on a piece of bread in another square, then moved a cooked egg from the third quarter and topped it with a piece of cheese and another piece of bread. He closed the lid like it was a panini press, steam leaking from the sides as the sandwich cooked. At last, Mr. Whitney looked up to see Astra standing across the table from him.

"Astra, would you like a sandwich?" A wide grin brightened his face. He'd forgotten his teeth today, but it didn't make the greeting any less warm. "I'm making some treats for these hard-working students." He waved a trembling fork at the students sitting at the tables around him. Most had the good sense to hide their sandwiches under book covers or in their laps under the table.

"Mr. Whitney, as well-meaning as this is, you can't cook and feed people in the library."

Mr. Whitney peeked into the waffle maker and closed the lid. The sandwich must not be done to his standards.

"There isn't a policy about preparing or sharing food. Only that you can't do it around reference materials. As you can see, I don't have any library items. And the kids are all using their own books."

"This is meant to be a quiet study space and your impromptu kitchen is very distracting."

"Just trying to help out the kids. Eggs are brain food."

He nodded to a nearby table where a brother and sister were studying. Astra guessed they were between the ages of ten and twelve, and she didn't know their names, but they came here every day after school until their mom collected them around six. Their clothes looked faded but neat and most likely secondhand. The younger girl's boots looked too big for her as she slipped her feet in and out of them under the table. Their mom probably felt better with them here than alone at home, and Astra didn't mind. They were always well-behaved and did their schoolwork or read. They weren't the only kids who came in after school. Sometimes she would even bring out the leftover snacks from the staff room to share with the kids. These two always accepted whatever was offered with quiet thank-yous. Right now, they had split a sandwich and were taking huge bites before she suggested they throw them away—which she had no intention of doing.

Mr. Whitney was full of surprises. While this wasn't something she should allow, it was hard to tell him to stop. There were days at the library when she felt more like a judge than a library director, weighing transgressions against the broad policies and what precedent it would set if she allowed a behavior to continue. Like any good parent or teacher, she shouldn't pick favorite patrons and let their bad behavior slide.

While she thought, Mr. Whitney's sandwich finished cooking and he slid it toward a nearby table, where the teen looked at Astra. She nodded to the teen to give her approval, and the teen picked it up and nibbled on the edge, returning to the book in front of her. Ingredients for only a few sandwiches remained.

"Since you're almost done, you might as well finish up what you have. Chloe will bring you some cleaning materials so you can completely wipe down this table." Mr. Whitney's gummy grin shone up at her. "Next time you want to feed the young minds, run it by me first. I'm not sure their parents would appreciate them taking food from a stranger."

"Mr. W's not a stranger," the teen at the table said, her sandwich now gone. "He's always checking up on us. Helped me with my math last week, too." A few of the other kids nodded. Just when she thought she had a patron pegged into their neat little square hole, they changed into a star shape. Mr. Whitney was laying the last two pieces of bacon on the waffle iron and closed the lid. It hissed and crackled, followed by spitting oil that echoed through the quiet area. A few of the kids covered their mouths to hide their giggles. Mr. Whitney had won this round.

"The point remains, we can't have a short-order kitchen in the library, no matter how nice."

As Astra walked away, ideas started forming, questions that needed answering. While they couldn't turn into a soup kitchen, they could have an after-school program that taught kids how to make healthy study snacks. It would be a way to get them some food and teach them about nutrition. That's what libraries were for, teaching and helping the community. Steps she needed to take, money she'd need to budget, space she'd need to reserve . . . all the crucial points started filling in the canvas in her mind like a Georges Seurat painting. That familiar tingling of a plan coming together zinged through her body. Moments like this, when the Venn diagram of learning, helping people, and building community formed a perfect circle, were why she had become a librarian. She sat at her desk, her mind filled with the promising new idea, and started jotting notes, questions she would need to ask, and whom she could contact.

All other thoughts were banished for the day.

Chapter Fourteen

ASTRA KNEW IT WAS A DREAM THE WAY SHE KNEW WHEN SHE read a great book—she just did. If pushed, she could come up with defensible arguments based on specific facts: like an unexpected plot twist, imagery that echoed through the story, or a vividly described setting. The primary reason she knew this was a dream was because it never happened. It had to be a dream.

She sat across from Jack at a picnic table at the Christmas market, and her heart thumped at how handsome he looked in a cream wool sweater with a matching dark green hat and scarf. The hat and scarf brought out the green in his eyes, making them appear darker than she remembered. His strong hands cupped a cooling mug of mulled wine as he smiled at her. She knew it was cooling because she had one just like in front of her, too distracted by his smile to drink it.

The dream filled in vivid details she must be pulling from other, real memories of her trips with the girls, like the classic Christmas carols playing over loudspeakers, the smell of cinnamon and orange rising from her mulled wine, and the cold, hard bench under her. She wished she'd worn a longer coat and was envious of how Jack seemed unaffected by the chill.

Would he mind warming her up?

She said something to him and then he pulled out a tiny Christmas gnome—a nisse; the name popped into her head—made of wood and no more than three inches tall. With intricate details like a white beard so fluffy she was surprised it didn't yield when she touched it. The tiny nose had a pink tinge as if the gnome had been standing in the cold. She could make out each leaf and berry of the mistletoe the figure held, tied together with a bright red ribbon that matched the nisse's hat.

Handling the carving with care, she flipped it over to see two initials carved on the base. JC. Jack Clausen.

Astra awoke to the sound of Bernie barking and jumping off her bed. Her heart beat faster as all the possibilities scrolled in her brain but kept circling back to the worst: someone was breaking into her house.

The barking ended quickly and she could hear Bernie's nails on the hardwood floors. If it were a break-in, Bernie wouldn't have stopped barking. Astra slid out of bed and peeked around her partially open bedroom door. It was worse than a burglary.

Trent stood in her kitchen.

The jolt of the inviting dream ending so abruptly and the reality of Trent in her house made her head spin. It had only been two weeks since she'd last seen him, making it much too soon to see him again. Still in her pajamas and undercaffeinated, she wasn't ready to deal with her ex-husband showing up uninvited. With a deep breath, she pushed her bedroom door fully open and walked out. He looked up and grinned when he saw her.

"You can't walk in here whenever you want, especially when it's earlier than I expected." Astra wasn't going to bother with niceties. As she walked past a mirror on the wall in the living room, she admired the state of her hair, like a cow had licked it, leaving it in swooping, irregular waves. She refused to do anything to make it neater. "How did you get in?"

Her arms crossed tightly over her braless chest while she started the coffeepot and it began gurgling and hissing.

"Your door was unlocked." Shit—she must have left it unlocked when she let Bernie out to pee in the middle of the night—not smart or safe. Trent continued. "But I'm only an hour early. And I wanted to pick up those pants." He looked around her kitchen as if they'd be hanging there neatly pressed. They were still on the bed in her spare room, where she planned on leaving them. She was done fixing things for Trent.

"We were supposed to meet at the dog park," Astra said. "I planned to leave in thirty minutes so Bernie would have time to play before she went home with you."

Bernie lay under the kitchen table, watching their conversation and seemingly trying to melt into the floor. She knew what would happen next and it broke Astra's heart to allow him to take her. An idea started to form about how she might keep Bernie, but she'd attempt plan A first.

"Trent, I was thinking." She dropped her arms to the sides of her body so she seemed less guarded. "Bernie spends so much time here and you're always busy with school and coaching . . . maybe it's time I took over. Full-time."

Trent opened one of her cupboards, pulled out a coffee mug, and helped himself to a cup of the still-brewing coffee.

"No. We agreed. We share custody."

"True, we do share custody." She'd spent so much time thinking about how to broach this subject—she had to make him think it would be in his best interest. "You did get Bernie for me. She was my dog. Think of all the time you'd save not having to drop her off and pick her up."

"If we start tinkering with the agreement, then we'll have to get the lawyers involved again." He took a drink of the coffee and set the mug on the counter.

Astra let out a slow exhale, consciously not clenching her jaw—it took a lot of effort. He knew she didn't have the money. If she didn't love Bernie so much, she would block Trent's number and be done with it. Trent took a step toward her and Astra walked around him into the living room, where her Christmas gnomes still decorated the mantel.

Trent followed her. "So, do you have those pants?"

Astra tried not to snort and failed. Bernie was his free pass to getting her to do things for him. She resisted answering him right away, her attention drawn to one of the nisser, the one carrying mistletoe. The one she'd just dreamed about.

Trent forgotten, she picked up the gnome and held her breath as she turned it over. There on the bottom, exactly like in the dream, was a JC. She knew she'd never noticed it before. She picked up another wooden one, this one with a star. Another JC. She checked the bottoms of six different wooden gnomes, and all had the same JC. How was that possible when they hadn't met until this past year?

"Astra?" Trent said.

She set down the nisse in her hand and faced Trent.

"They aren't done. You should take them to a tailor because I don't know when I'll get to them."

"But you do such a better job."

Once his flattery might have worked, but now she just wanted him out of her life so she could focus on what mattered—like discovering how Jack's initials had gotten onto the bottom of those nisser. "Just go. I'm sure I'll see you in a few days when you have another dog-sitting emergency."

She picked up the leash and called Bernie to her. Bernie slowly stood and walked to Astra but kept an eye on Trent. Astra hooked the leash and handed it to Trent, then bent over to give Bernie a kiss.

"Be a good girl and I'll see you in a few days."

She was determined to stop putting Bernie and herself through this. It was time to take action.

Project Save Bernie Commences

Astra texted Steph, Cassie, and Ronnie as she lay alone in her bed. Well, not entirely alone. In her free hand she clasped one of the gnomes. Holding it gave her strength, and she needed it. She had come up with a plan and it was time to rally the girls.

Ronnie responded first.

I have no idea what this is, but I'm in.

Astra grinned in the dim room. Ronnie was always in with her say-yes-get-details-later approach to life. Astra appreciated that more as the years passed, because Ronnie pushed her outside her comfort zone.

FINALLY!

Cassie texted. Steph gave a thumbs-up, followed by,

When do we begin?

Astra reviewed the email from her attorney back when she and Trent were going through the custody case. She had only given up because the lawyer fees were rising faster than she could earn money and she didn't have the energy to take on a second job.

According to her attorney, she needed to provide evidence of his neglect. Trent might be a selfish, self-centered turd, but he would never hurt Bernie, so that wasn't an option. They had to get Trent to voluntarily give up his custody.

Astra thought for a moment, then continued.

Wine and brainstorming.

A stream of hearts and suggested dates followed until they found one that worked with all their varied schedules. She hadn't felt this optimistic since the day she'd left Trent. This time things would be different.

With their help, she could accomplish anything.

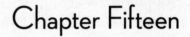

Chapter Fifteen

TWO YEARS AGO

JACK HAD SPENT THE LAST 442 YULES THINKING ABOUT WHAT *he would do when he saw her again. Everything from walking around the counter and kissing her (which would probably earn him a well-deserved slap) to absolutely nothing—the most likely of the options. In his favorite fantasy, she would walk in and recognize him, asking to know where the bakery had been, then looping her arm through his so he could tell her all about the Julemarked. After which, she would agree to become the newest member of their magical secret world and they would live happily ever after. It was possible Jack had been reading too many fairy tales lately.*

Despite not having any real plan, Jack insisted on working the counter from open to close, not wanting to risk missing her, needing to at least see that she was still out in the world.

"She'll be here," Mads said.

"And if she brings her husband?"

"I won't stop you if you want to punch his face. They won't remember in a few hours anyway."

"They don't get mind-wiped," Jack said.

"It's the same effect. If you can't remember where something was, it's still lost, even if you know what it was. At best, they remember hazy feelings of a good time."

Jack studied his brother. "When did you get so smart?"

"Always been. The smoldering visage throws people off."

Jack shoved him in the shoulder.

"Sure, that's what it is."

The morning carried on in the usual fashion. Customers lined up, they sold them sugary goodness, repeat. The crowd had thinned and only apple and raspberry cream cheese kringle remained in the case. They were still delicious, but they were always the last to go. His brothers had retreated to the kitchen, where they had started the dough for tomorrow's kringle. The door jingled and Jack's instinct to greet his new customers kicked in before he could think about the possibility that it was her.

And it was.

She filed in with her three friends, all holding the Christmas market mugs of mulled wine and wearing their slightly worn red hats—no husband in sight. He was grateful she wore mittens so he didn't have to see the ring. Without a line, the four women came directly to the counter, though she paused to study one of the nisser sitting on the counter, taking off the mitten on her right hand to trace the edge of the bright red hat.

"Afternoon," Jack said, his eyes taking in as many details as he could without being too obvious. Her hair brushed the top of her scarf—shorter than last time, her cheeks a little thinner, a new tiny *wrinkle at the corner of her mouth that could only be caused by abundant smiling. He wanted to kiss it.*

She searched the case and her face fell.

"Awww, you're out of almond and cherry. I was going to get one of each," she said.

He felt compelled to give her anything she wanted, but even he couldn't speed up kringle dough.

"I wish I had a secret stash, but this late in the day, this is it. I promise it's all still good."

"It could be filled with dog doodoo and it would still taste good," the blond and heavily eyelinered one said.

"We're good, but I think that would be a stretch even for us," Jack said.

"Do you get to close up shop once they are gone?" she asked. Her voice was raspier than he remembered. Each time she spoke it was like she traced a finger down his spine.

"We do." Jack swallowed.

She studied the case—there was almost enough to make two whole kringle if reassembled.

"Are you thinking what I think you're thinking?" the tiny one said. "Cause I'm in."

A smile took over her face.

"We'll take what's left. If we don't eat it all, I'll smash a piece on Trent's pillow—maybe shove it in his face."

Jack's surprise at this unusual conversational direction must have shown on his face.

"No need to be alarmed," the quiet one said. "She's going through a divorce and they still live together."

"Steph," she said, "he doesn't need to know all that."

But he did. He did need to know all that. The husband was on his way out and a part of him cheered despite knowing it was a painful experience for her. But in this instance, he couldn't help but be selfish. She would be single again.

"Assuming this is something to celebrate . . ." Jack said, pausing to give her time to respond. He wanted to make sure he understood the divorce to be a positive turn of events for her.

"Definitely a celebration," the tall blonde said.

She nodded in agreement.

"Then I'll wrap this all up for you. On the house. My gift to you and your friends."

"We can't accept that," she said.

"Truly, you'll be doing me a favor, because then I can clean out the case and get back to the book I'm reading."

"Oh, a man who reads. We should take him with us," the blonde said.

"Let's avoid kidnapping charges today. I swear, we haven't had anything besides the mulled wine," she said.

Jack pulled out the trays so he could access the pastries, leaving the women to talk.

"Have you figured out who gets the house?" the small one asked. Jack assumed they were talking about her divorce.

"He is. I don't want anything," she said.

"Not even Bernie?" the quiet one asked. Who was Bernie?

"It's not looking good. Even though he gave Bernie to me as a gift, because he bought her, his lawyers are being difficult. I can't imagine losing my beautiful puppy."

"If he gets the house, it seems only fair you get the dog," the tall one said.

Bernie was a dog; that made sense.

"Fairness in a divorce depends on your lawyers, and he can afford a much better one."

Jack wrapped up the rest of the kringle, sliding it into a bag, adding a tiny nisse that he'd kept on hand for just this occasion, something for her to find later. The tiny gnome held a bouquet of delicate gardenias. Even though she never seemed to remember that he gave them to her, he couldn't help hoping that one year, she would.

"Leave one out, doesn't matter what flavor," she said. "I don't want to wait."

He set a raspberry cheese slice wrapped in parchment paper on the counter and she slid it off, biting the corner with an "mmm." Her eyes closed as she chewed and swallowed, taking another large bite with an even more audible sigh.

"That is indecent," Steph said. He wished he could figure out the rest of their names, but at least time was on his side again.

"It is indecent in the very best way," she said. "Everything tastes ten times better than it ever did before." She held out the pastry to each of her friends so they could taste, all nodding in agreement. Most patrons didn't eat their treats while still in the building, and it was wildly satisfying to witness her enjoyment, titillating even. Parts of him tightened that hadn't tightened in response to another person in much too long. One of the friends pointed out the fleck of glaze perched on her lip and she licked it into her mouth. Talk about indecent. He placed both of his hands on top of the pastry case to steady himself, his knees suddenly unstable like he'd spent a morning moving bags of flour from the kitchen to the cellar. He was grateful the apron covered the front of him.

The tiniest friend grabbed the full bag and headed to the door.

The woman he couldn't stop thinking about, the beautiful soon-to-be-divorced woman, reached over the pastry case and set her left hand on top of his. It was warm, soft, and wonderfully bare of any jewelry.

"Thank you. That was very generous of you and I promise we won't waste a crumb of it." She squeezed his hand, her fingers lingering a moment longer than necessary, then walked to the door, raising that same bare hand in farewell.

"See you next year," she said.

Jack stood in the empty bakery as the bell echoed off the tiled walls, echoing like the feeling of her touch on his hand.

"At least you didn't embarrass yourself," Mads said. "Oh wait, there's drool all over your shirt." He used the corner of his white apron to dab at Jack's face. Jack shoved him away but couldn't stop grinning. What had been a bland Yule was now one of the best.

"Did you hear?"

"We all heard. Congrats."

"That seems premature," Jack said. "I still have to ask her out. I don't even know her name yet." He lifted off his apron and tossed it on the counter, already planning to chase the group down. He didn't want to waste another Yule. The spark he'd recognized years ago had taken light again and he planned to help it burn brighter.

"Here's some ginger," Mads said.

"And why would my son need ginger?" His mother stood in the archway to the kitchen. For someone with as many years as she had lived, she stood tall and strong, her spine straight and proud like a queen rather than the wife of a retired bakery owner who spent her days teaching her grandchildren and enjoying the peace and comfort of the Julemarked. Her white hair was in a neat line even with her chin, with just a little bit of bounce, her cheekbones high and strong despite

a lifetime of eating sweets. She wore a thick, brightly colored wool sweater from A Stitch in Time across the alley, dark pants, and black slip-on wool shoes that she wore in every weather. She'd raised four strong, uniquely different boys with extravagant amounts of love and generous hugs, believing you can never love a child too much. All of them grew up only wanting to keep her bright smile on her face. Since that was what their father wanted, everyone was happy.

Jack stopped his escape and his mother joined him in front of the pastry case, where she wrapped her arm around his lower back and leaned her head on his shoulder, nearly as tall as him.

"Tell me," she said.

"The one I told you about years ago . . ."

"The married one?" His mother's mouth pursed.

"She won't be married soon," Jack explained. He didn't want his mom thinking poorly of her. "Now's my chance. I'm just not sure how to find her. I don't even know her name."

"If it's meant to be she'll come back."

"She's come back almost every time the Julemarked has been in Milwaukee."

"But she doesn't remember you yet. How can you be so sure it's right when she can't remember you?"

A thousand "buts" began to stack up, reasons he should be chasing after her. But his mother was right and his back slouched when he accepted the truth. If she didn't remember him, then did they even have a real connection? Maybe it was all him.

"In the meantime," his mother continued, "I know the Pedersen girl sneaks peeks at you every time you go in the knitting store."

Jack knew she did, because they were rolling their eyes at each other because they knew what their mothers were doing.

"Ani and I are just friends. How many times do I need to tell you that?"

Mads stood behind their mom and stuck out his tongue like a child.

"If the Pedersen girl isn't for you, perhaps someone else. Your brothers found wives from the Julemarked and they're both very happy."

"Why aren't you bugging Mads about this?"

"Because she knows I'm just as likely to marry a guy as a girl, and a guy isn't going to get her grandchildren," Mads said.

The Julemarked was a better place to live than anywhere else, unless you wanted to adopt. There weren't any adoptable children here.

"You know that doesn't matter. Orn and Carl are doing fabulous work in the grandchildren department. I just want you both to be happy and I know how much you love the Julemarked, Jack. My heart believes you need to find someone who loves it as much as you, and that seems most likely to happen here. Have you asked the Pedersen girl out? Spent time with her lately? She might surprise you."

"We grew up together, how can we not know everything about each other? I'm not going to settle until I know for sure this woman and I don't have a chance. I can't stop thinking about her. The way you knew with Dad."

"Well, with Dad, it was a bit more complicated. I knew when I got pregnant."

"Wait," Mads said. "Orn was a premarital accident? This is the best news I've ever heard."

"Mads, you will not tease him. I'm surprised you didn't do the math years ago. Orn has known since before he could see over the pastry case. But the point I was making is your father and I were having a bit of fun, but the Julemarked has a way of nudging events in the right direction. Look at us, four beautiful grown boys later. Don't overthink it."

"I'm not, Mom." But he was. He was already running plans on how he could connect with her again.

"You should probably find out her name first," Mads said.

Jack punched Mads's arm, but only half-heartedly. He was already envisioning how he'd ask her out—maybe make her a special kringle to show he had been paying attention. He had a hunch that the next Milwaukee Yule would change his life.

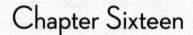

Chapter Sixteen

WITH JOBS, KIDS, HUSBANDS, AND HOUSEHOLDS, IT TOOK UNTIL late February for Astra to assemble her girls and brainstorm how to get Trent out of her life permanently.

"I know people," Ronnie said. "Well, my brothers know people who know people, who probably know people."

She was curled onto the couch, a giant fishbowl-size glass of red wine in one hand while her other absentmindedly played with Bernie's soft ears—another last-minute ask. Astra had to take a cab and tip the driver extra to let her bring Bernie into his car, money she really couldn't afford to be wasting. Cassie sat on the other side of Bernie and ran her fingers through the long fur on Bernie's back. Bernie, being the lady that she was, snored softly, her top lip wobbling with each exhale, lulled to sleep by the adoring ministrations.

Steph entered the room carrying a charcuterie board with sliced summer sausage, prosciutto, cheddar cheese from a local dairy, a local Parmesan, hummus, carrot sticks, crackers, and pita chips.

"We're not trying to kill him," Steph said, always the voice of reason. "Just get him to give up his claim to Bernie so Astra can forget he ever existed."

"Maybe you're not trying to kill him. I happen to think a well-timed car accident could solve a lot of problems." Ronnie shrugged.

"We aren't killing him. Or maiming. Or threatening," Astra said from her spot on the floor in front of the gas fireplace, flickering with its anemic flame. For too long, that's how she'd felt after Trent left her. A weak, flickering version of herself. She'd lost herself bit by bit during their marriage and it was taking her too long to rediscover those pieces, like scrounging through a bin of nuts and bolts looking for the right pair that would hold her together.

Steph set the snacks on the coffee table and went to the large pieces of paper she had taped to the wall like they were about to start a corporate strategic planning session. She scrawled "Bernie Custody Plan" on the top of one sheet. And wrote:

1. Plant evidence that B is a bad dog (even though she is the bestest dog ever).

2. Let T think B did the naughty things and is more trouble than worth.

3. Offer to take B and pay for any damages.

4. Never see T again.

"Pay for damages?" Astra said. "You know I'm on a public employee's salary, right?"

"We'll work it out," Steph said. Cassie and Ronnie nodded in agreement.

"What kind of evidence do we need?" Cassie asked.

"Anything that will frustrate him and make him think Bernie isn't worth it," Steph said. "What would make you want to get rid of a dog?"

Steph wrote the best ideas on the next sheet of paper as they shouted out ideas.

Bad Dog:

1. Pee on bed.

2. Bark at night.

3. Run away.

4. Chew T's dining room table.

5. Diarrhea everywhere.

6. Whining.

"What's up with the dining room table?" Cassie asked.

Astra tried not to roll her eyes, but failed. "He used our wedding money to buy it."

"That's kind of sweet, isn't it?"

"All of our wedding money. Without asking my opinion. It's a four-thousand-dollar table." Cassie's jaw dropped. "Don't get me wrong, it's a beautiful wood masterpiece, but we rarely ate on it because he was afraid we'd scratch it. He'd freak if Bernie chewed on it."

"It has potential." Steph nodded, looking over the list. "But we do have to be careful about not getting caught," Steph said. Astra could see her sorting out the logistics before moving to the next sheet.

Steph led them through the plans with military precision, and soon they had contingencies on contingencies, and three empty wine bottles. For the first time in years, Astra knew something would work to turn things in her favor—it had to with these incredible women by her side. After all they'd been through, they had never let her down. She wished she could say the same. She'd never forgive herself for not being there when Cassie's dad passed away or when Ronnie had to have her gall bladder removed. She wouldn't make that mistake again.

"Are you sure you know what you're doing?" Astra said to Cassie, who crouched in front of her at Trent's back door in the dark. Both women wore black, as did Steph and Ronnie, who were posted at the front corners of the house, keeping a watch for any sign of an unexpected return. He'd left twenty minutes ago, presumably to go on a Friday night date, because they could still smell his cologne lingering in the air like a fart in the shower.

"You'd be surprised what you pick up in med school," Cassie said.

"Don't you need a light?"

Astra heard metal scraping against metal in the dark; she had her phone out, ready to flick on the flashlight.

"It's all about the feel." A soft click sounded. "And we're in." Cassie gave a soft hoot and Ronnie and Steph came into sight as shadows silhouetted by the streetlamp two houses down. Steph crouched into the shadow of the bush next to the door, disappearing even though she was a few feet away. Seeing how easy it was to break in with minimal planning, Astra realized she really needed to up her own home security.

"Get in," Cassie said, leading Ronnie and Astra into the dark house. "Ronnie and I will keep watch and you and Steph do the deed."

Astra dug into her pockets and pulled out a water bottle full of yellow liquid. For the last day, she'd been peeing into a cup and filling up the water bottle, not the most ladylike maneuver, but easier than chasing Bernie around the yard trying to get her to pee into a cup.

"Good God, could this be more of a bachelor pad?" Ronnie held the fridge door open to reveal leftover Chinese food containers and beer.

"You're not supposed to be snooping," Astra whispered as she headed toward the bedroom.

Ronnie moved on to the overpriced dining room table, giving it a shake to test its sturdiness.

Astra opened the bedroom door to find Bernie sitting and waiting for her to open it, her tongue lolling out of her mouth in a sloppy grin.

"Hey, my beautiful Bernie." She kissed her nose and rubbed

her ears in greeting. Bernie gave her a quick kiss back and went to say hello to the other guests in the house. Astra looked around the bedroom. It was spare, just the bed, Bernie's bed, and a dresser. Trent was always careful about his things, so there weren't any dirty clothes on the floor, no loose change on the dresser. Neat and tidy. Even the bed was made, more neatly than when they had lived together. She never understood the point of making a bed. Getting into bed at the end of the day should not require work.

Astra unscrewed the cap on the bottle, and holding it over the center of the pristine white comforter, she slowly poured it out, careful to stay out of the splash zone. Behind her, Steph winced. It was hard to watch the liquid soak into the bedding, going against human decency everywhere. But this was what Trent had pushed her to. Breaking and entering with urine. As the last bit soaked through, Bernie returned and immediately hopped on the bed to investigate. In the dark room, they could hear her sniffing.

"We gotta go," Steph said, keeping them on track.

Astra reached out to Bernie, who was still sniffing, and gave her a pat on her back.

"See you, girl. I hope you don't get into too much trouble," Astra said, leaving the bedroom and closing the door behind her. She knew Trent wouldn't do much besides a few choice curse words under his breath.

The ladies filed out of the house, locking the door behind them.

Mission One complete.

Chapter Seventeen

Jack sat alone in his small cottage, which was not much more than a bedroom, kitchen, and bathroom. He had turned the tiny living room into a woodworking room. A potbelly stove took up a corner. In addition to heating the room, it was a convenient place to get rid of all the wood scraps. A heavy oak table sat in front of a wall covered in pegboard, where knives, chisels, and gouges of various sizes hung in easy reach, most meant for delicate carving. Scattered around the room were boxes of branches, planks, and scraps of wood from around the world that he had collected, though most of it came from the trees around his cottage, pine and maple.

Soft music played from a speaker attached to an iPod. They might not have the internet, but some technology was too good; it was worth the inconvenience of asking Mads to help him. Mads would load it up with music on the Outside, which made for some unexpected choices, like an entire musical about Alexander Hamilton. Currently he had on some classical, heavy on the strings, just loud enough for background noise while he carved.

A magnifying glass perched on his nose as he picked up the small piece of maple he was carving. He liked how it allowed him to create minute details in the wood without cracking, and this particular piece was special. It was for her, something to reflect everything he'd learned about her over the years.

The nisse held a stack of books and he was carving the titles on the tiny spines. He would paint the delicate letters in gold. The books were Outlander; Fairy Tales by Hans Christian Andersen; A Christmas Carol; Circle of Friends, by Maeve Binchy; and Lily and the Octopus. With a tiny V-tool, he etched the letters, the thinnest shavings of wood falling to the table. When he finished a word, he blew on it to clear away any remaining bits.

Behind him, the door opened, letting in a rush of cold air that felt good in contrast to the heat radiating off the stove.

"Want to join us?" Mads said, not bothering with a greeting.

Jack turned to see who the "us" was. Ani stood next to Mads.

"Where?" Jack asked.

"Pub crawl," Ani said. "You can see at least eight from the Julemarked entrance. I love Ireland."

This Yule they were in Galway, where the Julemarked arch nestled between a pub and a shopping center on Eyre Square, where the Galway Christmas market was in full swing, complete with a Santa train, carousel, and Ferris wheel.

Jack looked down at the figure in his hand. He had a few final details in the beard and the books to finish before it would be ready to paint.

"I want to finish this."

Mads rolled his eyes.

"You can finish tomorrow. Come out with us."

The door opened again, and this time it was his mom and dad. With four extra people in his tiny workroom, the cottage had become claustrophobic. His dad moved a box of wood out of the way to make room for them to stand near the fire.

"I thought I saw Anika come in here," his mom said, giving her a pat on the shoulder as she shuffled by Ani.

Ani covered her mouth with one mittened hand to hide her giggle.

"She and Mads are trying to recruit me for a night of debauchery," Jack said.

"You should go. It would be good for you to get out and take a break from"—she looked at the small figure in his hand and sniffed—"your hobby."

"I thought you liked my carvings," Jack said. His dad studied the tools, probably searching for one to borrow for his own "hobby." His dad was the one who'd taught him, and now that he wasn't working in the bakery, a lot of Jack's carvings were sold at Wooden It Be Jul.

"I just don't like to see them go to waste."

Jack pointed to the dozens of small figures scattered around the room.

"There are plenty, Mom."

"You shouldn't lock yourself up in here. You'll go stir-crazy during the next Nulstil and break out."

"Not possible," his dad said. "Remember Gunter?"

Jack's mom shivered.

"Who the hell is Gunter?" Mads said. Ani and Jack nodded.

"It happened before you three were born," Jack's mom said.

His dad rubbed his chin, a sure sign he was about to tell a story. He didn't speak much, so when he did, people listened. Like Old Johan, he knew a lot of the Julemarked history.

"Let me see, Gunter. It was during the Great War on the Outside."

"They call that World War I now, Dad," Mads said.

Their dad waved his hand at Mads to be quiet and continued.

"The weather ... I'd never seen anything like it. Ten straight Yules of blizzards, huge snowdrifts that would almost reach the Julemarked sign, like it knew something bad was happening and wanted to keep us safe. Back then, we didn't stop in as many places, probably because there weren't as many Christmas markets around the world. The ones that we regularly connected to were smack-dab in the middle of war zones. We couldn't open properly because just when we'd clear a path, another snowstorm came. We finally gave in and did nothing. But Gunter ... he liked to leave and see the sights wherever we unbricked. Stretch out his legs. Mads reminds me a bit of him."

Their mom looked up in alarm, but Mads only grinned.

"He had the wanderlust, and being cooped up in the Julemarked got to him. It was right when Nulstil began; after the clock struck midnight and the bell finished echoing, something snapped in his head. Gunter ran at the brick wall with a blazing stick of dynamite—no one knew where he got the thing, but he barely jumped out of the way before it exploded. It knocked the clock clean off the wall."

His dad paused to stare off into the distance. He always loved to draw out a story. Ani cracked first, not used to how he would toy with a captive audience.

"And?? Did he break through?" Ani asked. His dad couldn't hide his small grin of satisfaction.

"Finish the story, dear," his mom said.

"*For the briefest of moments, the bricks scattered around the entrance, but in the snap of a finger . . .*" His dad actually paused to snap his finger, and Jack gave a knowing look at Mads, who did his best to hide his grin. "*It was back as if nothing had happened. Not a chink was missing from that brick wall; even the clock was back in its place. Only smoke remained. It wasn't until the end of Nulstil that we understood the real damage. When the wall unbricked, five years had passed.*"

"*That was the one and only time someone tried to leave during a Nulstil,*" his mom continued. "*We don't understand why it happened. Old Johan has a theory that the Julemarked would let someone out for the right reasons, whatever they might be. Clearly Gunter's were not the right reasons.*"

"*What happened to Gunter?*" Mads asked.

Their dad rubbed his face again as he recalled the particulars.

"*As soon as Nulstil ended, he was gone. Last we heard, he died from influenza a year after leaving.*"

"*And that is why you never leave the Julemarked,*" his mom said.

"*I thought you wanted me to go out with Mads and Ani,*" Jack said.

"*You know that's not what I mean.*" She wagged her finger at him. "*It's the not being here during the Nulstil where it becomes a problem. That's when you lose the benefits. Gunter wasn't protected anymore and he got sick and died.*"

Plenty of people left the Julemarked and lived long and happy lives. His mom worried they would all leave her, though Carl and Orn weren't going anywhere.

"*On that happy note,*" Mads said, directing himself to Jack, "*you coming?*"

Jack looked down at the figurine he was so close to finishing. Hearing the story about Gunter didn't change his mind about anything; he never planned to leave the Julemarked permanently, but that didn't mean he couldn't get out a little more. He'd take Mads and Ani up on the offer of some fun.

Chapter Eighteen

A WEEK AFTER THE RUINED MATTRESS, TRENT CALLED ASTRA. She'd been waiting for this.

When she saw his name on her phone, she almost looked forward to the conversation, curious if he would even mention the pee. She answered the phone.

"Hey, babe," Trent said before she could say anything.

Ugh. Trent always made her regret speaking with him, but this might be the record. She hated this generic term of endearment, somewhere between objectification and infantilization; it made her skin crawl. From different lips, it was innocuous, but from his, it felt like a word he used to address every woman because he couldn't remember their names.

As eager as she was to get Bernie, she didn't want him thinking she had looked forward to this call in any way. He'd use it as an excuse to call her more and more, which was really the heart of why he kept Bernie, to keep her taking his phone calls.

"Hey."

"You're looking good."

He always made this joke, as if he were watching her through the windows. It was never funny.

"That's creepy."

"You always take things so seriously. I'm joking."

Astra rolled her eyes.

"When do you want me to take her?" Astra asked.

"You make it seem like that's the only reason to talk to me. I might be calling for another reason."

"If you are, then I'm hanging up. You know that's the only reason I talk to you."

He sighed. She supposed on some level, he had cared about her, enough that he had wanted all her attention. And he certainly valued her ability to find solutions to most problems that sprang up in his life, but she was done being his personal problem solver.

"Don't hang up. I need you to watch Bernie. I'm going out of town for the weekend."

"You know this wouldn't be a problem if you'd give me full custody. Isn't it a pain to always have to hand her off?" Astra let the words she'd been practicing flow naturally, hoping to lead him into admitting the mess he found on his bed. "Your life would be so much simpler if you didn't need to care for her. Feed her, take her to the vet, clean up after her. I know how much she sheds. Drinking so much water. She's always making messes."

Would he take the bait?

"She does that at your house, too?"

Bingo.

"She does it everywhere. She's a giant dog with long hair; she's going to leave piles of hair wherever she goes. Even when she's here for a few days, I find it on everything."

"Oh, that's not what I meant." He paused and she knew he was thinking about whether or not he wanted to mention anything. "Has she ever peed inside?"

"Not since she was a puppy. Not at my house." Now to pile it on. "Were you gone a long time? Maybe she couldn't hold it. Was it by the door?"

"No . . . on my bed. I had to get a whole new mattress. It soaked through all the bedding."

"Ew. That sounds expensive. Where did you sleep?"

"Three nights on the couch until the new mattress and bedding could get here. My back is killing me. I don't even think she feels bad about it."

"Dogs don't remember that long after they've done something naughty." Astra wasn't entirely sure that was true, but he didn't need to know that. If you said anything with enough authority, it was almost always believed. A little trick she'd learned at the library.

"Relax, I know you think I'm the villain, but I would never punish her." He paused. "But she is a lot of work. You can take some pleasure from knowing that I realize how much work you used to do."

"Pleasure taken." Now was the time to turn the screw. "It's possible Bernie is feeling neglected. Peeing on the bed feels personal. That's your space and she marked it. Pets have been known to do that. You might want to check your shoes before you put them on. I can send you some articles about it."

Homework. Trent hated homework or admitting he didn't know things. It was one thing to ask her to give him the information, but he would never admit it was because he didn't know how to find it—only that he didn't have time.

"I'm fine. I'll figure it out." He paused. "Hey, can you unpink laundry?"

Astra had known there was something else he wanted.

"Did you not separate colors?" As she spoke, she did a quick internet search, something he could have easily done.

"Obviously not. I just need to know if I can fix it or do I need to buy new T-shirts."

Astra found a good site.

"There is a product you add to the laundry that will take the dye out. Or if they are all white, you can bleach them. And yes, I'll watch Bernie. I can pick her up after work. I have to stop at the store, so I'll swing by and get her."

"Since you're going to the store, can you pick the stuff up for me? You could start the load for me when you're here so it's done correctly."

Astra ran the math in her head. If she said no, would he retaliate by being more difficult about Bernie? Picking the product up wasn't too difficult, but she'd be damned if she would do his laundry.

"I'll get the stuff, but I'm not starting your laundry. You can read the bottle just as well as I can."

"Cool." He seemed too happy with that outcome, making her think he'd gotten what he had expected and she was the losing party. Dammit.

She looked at the piles of paperwork, to-do lists, and plans for a new addition to the library; work was going to dominate her life for the foreseeable future. She didn't have time to take the next step with her ex, let alone look into a certain missing bakery that hadn't left her thoughts. She shoved the mystery aside temporarily and dove into her work.

For the first night in months, Astra poured a huge glass of her favorite sparkling white wine, turned Netflix on in the background, and curled up on the couch with her laptop. Now that her after-school snack program was off the ground and the new construction was well underway at the library, Astra could turn her attention to other matters. Like how it was almost the holidays again and she was ready to find the missing Julemarked.

Deep into her second glass of wine, she finally discovered a trail by doing an image search with a photo she had taken of Cassie in front of the Julemarked arch. She ran a reverse image search. It led her to a private group on a discussion board titled "A Holiday Brigadoon."

The profile image was of the Julemarked's iron arch. This had to be what she wanted.

She clicked Join. The next screen had a question.

"Why do you want to join this group?"

While a lot of groups had questions new members needed to answer to weed out the bots, this felt more purposeful. This group didn't want casual visitors. Honesty was the only way in.

"I kissed a man who worked in the bakery. When I went to meet him for our second date, the entire Julemarked was gone, but no one else remembers it."

She submitted it and a confirmation screen let her know the

administrators had gotten her response and would reply when they could. Would it be in a few minutes? A month?

She stared at her laptop, willing the acceptance to come, but nothing happened. After finishing her wine, she put the glass and bottle in the kitchen, switched laundry loads from the washer to the dryer, handwashed the wine glass and set it to dry, then took some frozen ground beef out of the freezer to thaw for tomorrow. Another exciting night.

She checked the computer again. Nothing.

Waiting wasn't going to help. She closed the laptop.

Now what?

It was 8:12 on a Saturday night. Too early for bed, too late to make plans.

Was Steph home? With young kids, she and her husband normally stayed in on Saturdays. Maybe she'd want to talk, or watch a movie together while on the phone.

She called her and Steph picked up quickly.

"Hey," she said. "Everything okay?"

"Yeah, bored and lonely," Astra said.

"What is that like?" Astra heard a scream in the background. "Sorry."

"Looking for an excuse to get away from it all?"

"Want a roommate? I don't take up much space."

"You know I'd love to have you. But seriously, want to watch a movie? Lock yourself in your closet and get snarky with me?" Astra said.

Astra stood up and stretched.

"Ooooh, that sounds like exactly what I need. I have some wine that goes perfectly with snark. What movie are you . . ."

There was a loud commotion in the background.

"Mama!"

Steph sighed.

"In a minute! Have Maria start the tub. Not too hot," Steph shouted. "Daddy should have been home by now. Sorry, A."

"No worries. It's more exciting than watching *Downton Abbey*. Again."

Astra heard Steph run up the steps, her breath getting a little shallower, like a creepy call in a horror movie. Steph gave her kids instructions and helped them into the tub while Astra listened, a voyeur to their domesticity. It was a sad state of affairs that this was the most excitement she could expect all weekend.

A blip interrupted the noise.

"Hang on. Rob is finally calling. Probably stopped for drinks with the boys."

Astra's quiet house pushed in on her; a little, lonely world. On weekends, there were days when she didn't talk to anyone or even leave the house, almost as if she were the only person left in the world, the absence of humans another reminder of her failures in love. Maybe if she hadn't cut herself off from almost everyone she knew while she was married, she might have developed a circle of single friends, joined a book club, or started bowling. She didn't mind being alone; as a lifelong reader, she would happily escape into a book whenever time allowed. But loneliness was different. More pervasive. Loneliness was the absence of someone to love. She wanted the completeness she saw in her parents or with her friends' families. The wholeness of having someone who needed you and for you to need.

Steph clicked back.

"Sorry, Rob was late because there was an accident on the ski hill. The downside of having medically capable people in the family is they feel obligated to help."

"It must be horrible being married to a thoughtful and smart man."

"It's really inconvenient sometimes."

They joked, but Astra could hear the relief in Steph's voice. With a mobile phone in every pocket, not being able to reach someone usually meant something horrible had happened.

"I hope everyone is okay."

"Sounds like some broken bones. I get that it's fun and exciting to do tricks, but those terrain parks are death traps. Rob swears he doesn't go on them, but I'm not an idiot. Telling a middle-aged man he is too old for something guarantees it is on the top of his list."

Astra walked back into the living room, stopping near the fireplace to stretch. The older she got, the harder it was to sit for long periods.

"Would you rather it be something blond and bendy?"

"Depends on the day." Steph laughed and they both knew the truth. Steph and Rob would only ever have eyes for each other. "Now that I'm settled, you okay?"

Astra sighed.

"I'm trying to figure out my bakery-boy mystery."

"I can't believe I don't remember anything about its location. That's so weird."

Astra loved that none of her friends questioned that she remembered it and they didn't.

"Very. Entire places don't disappear."

"Found anything?"

Astra looked at her collection of red-hatted gnomes, which she hadn't taken down. Their oversize hats, white beards, and whimsical nature made her happy.

"Searching is like trying to find a tiny island in the Pacific. There's nothing, nothing, nothing, then you look in the right direction at the right time and you find it. But what are the odds? I have one lead, but it's testing my patience. I don't know why I'm wasting my time. We were drinking and a dude ghosted me. I should let it go."

"There's nothing wrong with hope."

"I cannot hope, for that way lies doom." Astra tried not to snort at herself.

"Melodrama much?"

"Over-the-top, yes. But that doesn't mean it's not true. Hope leads to disappointment. I'd rather assume nothing will go my way and plan accordingly, like a Boy Scout. Be prepared."

She picked up the tiniest gnome, the little wooden one holding mistletoe. The one she'd dreamed about.

"Or Mad-Eye Moody—'Constant vigilance.' That's a depressing way to live."

"I disagree. It's playing the cards I'm dealt rather than hoping for an ace. It doesn't mean if I get an ace I'm not going to make the most of it; I'm just done waiting for one."

And Astra planned to tell herself that until she believed it.

A loud splash came through the phone, followed by a loud, "Mama!"

"Gotta go," Steph said.

Astra set her phone down on the mantel. She flipped the tiny gnome over and traced the letters JC carved into the bottom. Was it possible he gave this to her? If so, then how? Each clue she found led to more mysteries, each one more fantastical than the next. Given how her reality had been going, a little fantastical would be lovely.

Two days later, Astra was sitting at her desk when Chloe arrived with a small stack of books she'd requested from other libraries.

"Looking to make a career change?" Chloe said.

"Some research I was doing. Just set them there." Chloe set them down and left.

She had forgotten she'd requested them. Astra turned the stack to look at the spines: *How Science Works, The Elegant Universe,* and *String Theory for Dummies.* Her descent into that research hole ended as quickly as it began. Learning theoretical physics in her spare time seemed excessive even to her. Astra shoved them to the side. She'd drop them in the return bin later.

Finally! An e-mail had arrived from the discussion board she had requested to join the other night.

She was in.

But did she really want to be? Was she ready for more questions she couldn't answer? Sure, their kiss was amazing. Yes, his strong hands made her mouth water and her knees wobble. More than that, he'd made her feel attractive and safe and interesting. He'd listened when she spoke, like he was absorbing it all to study later. That meant something to her. Never mind that she hated leaving questions unanswered.

Without another thought, she clicked to open the message board. Pages of posts filled her screen dating back years. She clicked the most recent one: **Julemarked Theories**.

whodoes#2workfor: It's a portal into an alien butthole.

AlienzRHere420: I like where your head is at whodoes#2workfor, what if the air is laced with space shrooms and that's why most people forget. Only people who are already stoned remember.

whodoes#2workfor: Yes!! I'll try it out this year. Any recommendations.

SillyString137: Not drugs. Most like a science explanation. Probably a pocket dimension.

AlienzRHere420: Drugs are science. I highly recommend. The drugs, not the science.

OnTheOtherSide42: afterlife? We get to be with the ones we love at Christmas?

SillyString137: Is it hell?

It went on, but that wasn't a useful thread. Entertaining, not useful. There were pages of topics and theories and experiences. Some commenters never found the Julemarked again. Many mentioned that other people who they were with didn't remember it. A few commenters had gone back and found it the next year, and when they asked the residents about where it went, they simply said "magic." Some of the more outlandish theories made it difficult to take any of it seriously—except that she had had the same experience. She scrolled through the list of topics, including "Rate the Julemarked Hotties" (she'd come back to that one), "Rare Book Goldmine," and "Best Shopping Ever," and settled on "Julemarked Didn't Come."

OnTheOtherSide42: Normally it shows up early December (I've been to the Christmas market as early as December 3 and it was there, so it may show up sooner. But this year—nothing. Anyone had this happen? (Chicago)

AlienzRHere420: wasn't here on nov 28. (nyc) came back on dec 1 and it was. not sure y

SillyString137: Based on the data collected from various sources, there seems to be a randomness. If there is a pattern, I don't have enough data to identify yet. I've attached a link to my spreadsheet. As you can see, it doesn't appear in every location every year. If it is going to appear, it will on December 1 and be gone by Christmas morning. Exact times haven't been identified yet.

December 1.

That was this weekend. Her heart beat faster as she planned what to do next. First, what was a pocket dimension? Second, she'd read more threads to see if she could find more useful information. Third—what would she do if she saw Jack?

She wasn't even sure how she felt. Angry? Not quite—he hadn't really done anything wrong. But he also hadn't told her the truth. Or had he? He had left that garbled message the night after they kissed. What if he had tried to tell her then? The possibility made her light-headed and more resolved.

Now that she knew she wasn't crazy, she was ready to follow the trail until she had her answers and, more importantly, found Jack.

Chapter Nineteen

WHEN OLD JOHAN HAD STOPPED BY EARLY THIS MORNING TO let them know the Julemarked had opened in Milwaukee, Jack's heart stuttered, then revved like a car that hadn't been started in a while. Orn had opened the bakery a few minutes ago and already a line snaked out the door. Even though he told himself she wouldn't be there, he still looked up every few minutes from where he cut slices of kringle and slid them into white paper bags. Carl handled the register, Mads shouted out orders, and Orn and Jack filled them. It was a system they could work on autopilot.

Jack didn't expect her to remember him. Not really. He planned to ask her out this year, start the courtship anew, finally make the connection, tell her about the Julemarked, give her the special nisse he'd made her that reflected his favorite things about her. He'd even thought about calling her later from a phone outside the Julemarked to see if she remembered him. He still had the paper with her number, which he'd been using as a bookmark, though he'd mem- orized the digits long ago. He looked forward to a second first kiss.

Even though he kept telling himself she wouldn't come, he

hoped nonetheless. Even though he hoped, he couldn't help but talk himself out of it. It was a depressing circle of self-talk, so when he slid a tray of sliced and packaged kringle into the case and paused long enough to look out the window, as was his habit, he assumed his mind had finally started hallucinating. Yet there she was, standing in the center of the bakery's window like a framed photo hanging on the wall. A black knit hat covering her auburn hair, a thick cream wool sweater, a red and green scarf, and jeans. When their eyes met, she raised an eyebrow and her lips thinned. That told him everything. She didn't look happy, but she was there. He'd never been so thrilled to have someone peeved with him. He could work with that.

It meant she remembered.

"Gotta go," Jack said, clapping a hand on Mads's shoulder. Mads followed Jack's eyes and nodded.

"Be a Viking!"

Jack grinned and didn't bother to remove his apron as he ran into the street with nothing but a T-shirt on, not that he could feel the cold anyway, he was so focused on the woman in front of him.

She waited for him to come to her and Jack couldn't get there fast enough.

"You're here," he said, his breath struggling to keep up with his heart.

"Sorry I'm almost a year late for our New Year's Eve date, but it was hard to get here when I can't walk through brick walls."

Her arms crossed as if she was waiting for him to explain it away with some lame excuse like a superhero trying to keep his identity a secret. He smiled. His only plan was to tell her the truth. All of it.

✶

Astra's heart had been racing ever since she'd arrived at the Christmas market. She'd been coming to the Christmas market in front of the Fiserv Forum every day for the past two days to see if the Julemarked was there. Today was the first day that it had appeared. December 1, just like the discussion board had said.

She'd stood outside the black iron arch for twenty minutes watching people go in and out, commenting on how it hadn't been there before. She'd even asked the nearby officer where it had come from, and he had said it was new this year, as if she were the one missing information or imagining things. With every blink she expected it to disappear again, to be a figment of her imagination. But it was there. And more importantly, people emerged with white bakery bags and bit into beautiful slices of kringle.

When she got to the bakery, she couldn't bring herself to go inside, wrapping her wariness around her like a warm blanket, not letting the heat of it dissipate. She didn't trust him to not try to cover up that the Julemarked was more than it appeared. Never a big fan of confrontation, she braced herself for him to obfuscate what she knew to be true. She had pictures to show him on her phone, had bookmarked the online conversations where other people had similar experiences. She would not let him convince her she was misunderstanding things.

Then he was there in front of her, his hair a little longer, his apron streaked with flour and a red filling, his strong arms striking in the winter sunlight. The same giddy sensation that she had felt the first time they met gurgled up inside her, even though the rational side of her brain told her to shut it down. She was only here for closure, for validation that she wasn't losing her mind. Her friends, while not remembering much from last year, were supportive and waiting for her to text with details. She crossed her arms and waited for him to speak. He didn't look like a man who meant to avoid an awkward conversation. His eyes sparkled and his mouth fought to keep a grin in check. He stood in front of her, a little breathless despite the short distance he'd walked. He looked thrilled to see her.

"That happens when you live in a magical alley that jumps around the globe."

Astra unfolded her arms and leaned forward.

"What did you say?"

Jack looked around them at the crowded Julemarked.

"Maybe we should take this conversation Inside. It might take a while."

She nodded and he led her to the end of the alley past all the shops and tables to a door she hadn't noticed until he set his hand on the handle. A soft click sounded at his touch.

"You're going down the rabbit hole now," Jack said.

Astra didn't even blink, but followed on his heels through the entryway.

And then they were on the other side, and she knew everything he said was true, because there was no way what she was seeing could possibly be at the end of an alley in downtown Milwaukee. Physics didn't work that way—at least not the physics her brain could comprehend.

In front of her were snow-covered hills dotted with pine trees. A frozen pond peeked from behind a sloping rise, and the sun dazzled off the white landscape like it was studded with crystals. Cottages hid beneath towering maples and evergreens, and a few children slipped around the pond like in an idyllic Thomas Kinkade painting. Her head couldn't move fast enough to take in everything. She expected reindeer to wander past, maybe even a talking snowman. Despite the information overload, she couldn't help but feel her entire body relax, like after a long, much-needed massage.

Behind her, the large wood door closed in the brick wall that connected to the back side of the alley's buildings—like walking onto a movie set where behind the scenes was starkly different from where the action was filmed. From this angle, she would never guess she stood in the middle of Milwaukee; no sign of the skyline, no smell of exhaust or greasy food from the nearby restaurants. Only pine and fresh air.

Gently taking her hand, Jack led her to a tiny cottage near four others that were, based on her best guess, behind the bakery. The stone cottage had a steep roof, presumably to keep off the snow. Inside, the whitewashed wood walls added brightness to the small space, only four rooms that she could see. The living room had a potbelly stove, a workbench, and dozens of nisser on every surface. The room smelled of sawdust and paint. She definitely wanted to explore in here, but there were other questions to address first. They stepped into a cozy kitchen with a little table overlooking the hills. The counters were empty except for a coffee maker that Jack turned on and that immediately started brewing. Where did the electricity come from?

"Coffee?"

She nodded. That was all she trusted so far.

"I don't have much else to offer," Jack said. "I only sleep here and spend most of my time in the bakery or at my parents'. They live in the larger house near the bakery. It's small, but it's just me here."

While he set out two mugs, cream, and sugar, then poured them two steaming cups, Astra settled at the table. She doctored hers with cream and sugar, assuming she'd need all the extra calories to handle the shock.

Jack sat kitty-corner to her at the table. Close, but not too close.

"Would you rather ask questions, or should I just start talking?"

Astra sipped her coffee and cleared her throat, hoping her voice would come out strong and confident and not betray her shock.

"Talk and I'll ask questions as they come to me."

Jack nodded, took a deep breath, and started explaining.

"The Julemarked, the alley and this area where we live, is separate from the world. Time and space work differently. I like to think of it as its own little bubble that gets picked up and moved around to different parts of the world. Orn could explain it better. He likes all that science stuff. From December 1 to December 24, the Julemarked appears in a spot. We bake pastries, sell books, knit sweaters, and join in the Christmas cheer wherever we are. Then at midnight on Christmas Eve, the alley bricks up for the Nulstil—our time to reset, rest, and get ready for the next Yule. We have until midnight on New Year's Eve, and then the Julemarked unbricks and it's December first again, but in a new location. Sometimes it's the same year on the Outside, sometimes it's moved on to the next, but we never know when that will happen."

Astra sort of followed what he was saying, but her mind kept trying to align it with the calendar she understood.

"So, you only have Decembers? It's always winter?"

Jack nodded. "It's always Christmas in the Julemarked—the best month of the year."

There were so many things Astra would miss from the other three seasons: the first crocuses bursting through the still-cold soil, robins hopping around in the thawing snow, the sun beating down on her face at a Brewers game, the air sticky but bearable because she knew it would end when the season shifted into fall, the noticeable change in August when the humidity evaporated and the night temperatures dropped, the inevitable morning in October when she woke up to the world iced in frost, like a giant baker had sprinkled everything with powdered sugar.

"How do you know if you've never experienced a different month?"

"While it's always December, I have experienced other seasons when we have Yules in warm places. Sydney and Singapore are regular stops. They can be quite warm, though it's always winter on this side, no matter where we are."

"Is this the North Pole? Does Santa live here?"

Astra couldn't believe she'd actually asked the questions, but if this was real, maybe Santa was, too.

Jack laughed out loud, his wide smile taking over his entire face, so infectious that Astra had to smile with him.

"No, not the North Pole. We're all very normal except for

where we live, and we age slower because of the whole time thing. If Santa exists, he doesn't live here. Though flying reindeer would be very cool."

"No flying reindeer, then?" Astra asked. Jack shook his head. "I'm a little disappointed by that." Astra sipped her coffee as another thought occurred to her. "What do you mean you age differently? Are you like a thousand years old?"

"Not even close. In your years, I'm about 160. We aren't great about keeping track of the specifics, but Old Johan in the bookstore would be able to figure it out."

She couldn't help thinking about all the vampire books she'd read and the judgment she had felt for the characters about the age differences. Perspective was everything when you sat across from someone as handsome as Jack. Astra sipped her coffee before responding.

"You've seen a lot," she said.

Jack's brows crumpled as he thought about her comment.

"Not really. I don't leave the Julemarked often. We get a paper on December first as soon as possible so we know where and when we are—and most other days so we can read the news, but we rarely experience it. We aren't really a part of the world in the same way."

Astra pointed at the coffeepot.

"Where does the electricity come from? Do you plug into the current city?"

"We have some solar panels to generate our own. Same with water. We have wells, though I can't say if we're tapping into local aquifers or if the aquifers travel with us. Not sure how far down we go."

"Wi-Fi?"

"Nope. That's why your phones don't work. The signal gets wonky in the alley."

"So, no TV or movies?"

"We watch discs and tapes, or some people go out to the theaters. Mads, my brother, has set up an account on the Outside so he can download movies onto a computer, then bring them back. He does the same with music for me."

"The Outside."

"Self-explanatory." Jack waved around him. "Inside. Everything else is Outside."

Astra let his words settle as she thought about what they meant.

"Some people? Do you not go to the movies?"

Jack spun his coffee cup in his hands, which were so large they nearly swallowed the pottery.

"Because time works differently, going into the Outside feels like stepping onto a ride that spins really fast. It makes us nauseous—some more than others. It can be jarring. I get so sick, I rarely leave. It's usually not worth it. And if we don't come back at the end of the Yule, we lose the benefits of slow aging."

"But you came dancing with us."

"I said usually. That was more than worth it."

Astra's stomach flipped at Jack's slow smile as they both remembered that night.

"The ginger. Your breath tasted like ginger." She blushed as she remembered why she knew what his breath tasted like. What would his kiss taste like now? Coffee and sugar? She leaned an inch closer to him.

Jack's eyes broke eye contact for a moment, then returned to her face.

"Exactly. And it helped mask those awful shots."

"Horrid things," Astra said. She tapped the side of her coffee mug as she thought of the next question, wishing she had brought a list. "Why do I remember you and the Julemarked but none of my friends do? I thought I was losing my mind and didn't appreciate it."

She frowned.

"Sorry about that," Jack said. And she believed him. "It's part of the magic. While I'm not sure how or exactly why, it makes it easier for us to pop around the world if people don't ask questions. If it was common knowledge that our little world existed, people might try to take advantage of it somehow. We've noticed over the years that a few people remember and take that as a sign that those are people who might adjust well to life on the Inside."

He looked at her as if he were trying to tell her something. And then it clicked.

"You mean me? Living here."

One corner of Jack's mouth lifted in a half smile. Astra had been so obsessed with finding out the facts about the Julemarked, she'd forgotten her feelings. And Jack's feelings. He felt the spark between them, too, maybe even more than her. As she reveled in the warmth of that thought, reality nudged in. Getting involved with someone in the Julemarked would mean leaving her friends, her parents, her job. Everything. She couldn't imagine abandoning them, especially for a man she barely knew, no matter how strong his hands were.

"It's a good life. We have everything we need. Productive and enjoyable work, happy customers, cozy homes, good people, years and years of extra reading time." That comment felt especially catered to her. "Most of the Julemarked's residents are pleasant, but every community has their quirks—but that's what makes it interesting."

Astra looked out the window. It wouldn't be the worst thing, would it? Living in this snowy paradise. Not having to deal with Trent, getting so many extra years with Bernie. The reading. She couldn't believe she was imagining, even for a moment, leaving her life, everything she knew, for whatever this man, almost a stranger to her, was describing.

"What about my family and friends? I have a dog—sort of."

"You can see them whenever we're here, though it won't be as often as you hope, and they'll eventually age and die well before you. Dogs are always welcome."

"I have a job. I couldn't just disappear." She shook her head.

Why was she even considering this? She should leave and be done with it. He had answered her questions. They clearly had no future; time to move on. But something kept her there. Some invisible string that she wasn't ready to cut.

"We have people who help us with the Outside paperwork. Occasionally someone wants to leave the Julemarked and there's no record of any of us, either. They get all the documents we might need, or erase the data that might cause people to ask questions."

"This is a lot to take in."

It was the only answer she could give while her brain sorted the information.

"I know that, but time is limited. If you don't decide by Christmas Eve, then I'm not sure when we'll be back. It could be years to you and much, much longer to me. I'm more than happy to wait, but . . ." He left it hanging, but she knew what he meant. Now that she knew, why waste another year or season?

"Couldn't I just meet you at the next location?" Astra asked.

"And where would you go? On the Outside, we don't exist for 341 days of the year."

"Then you're in several different places at once? That doesn't seem possible. Right now, there are multiple versions of you around the world? Isn't that some sort of paradox?"

"Does any of this seem possible?"

"What if you left one Julemarked and traveled to another? Could you see yourself in another place? We're only two hours from the Christmas market in Chicago. Could I see you there?"

"If the Julemarked is there, you could, but we were already in Chicago this year, so that is a past me. I would be very surprised to see you. Time is still linear inside the Julemarked."

"You could make so much money betting on sporting events and investing in stocks. Buying lottery tickets."

"Why is that always where Outsiders' minds go? What would we do with that money? We already have more than we could ever spend."

Astra and Jack sat in silence. This was a lot to take in, just trying to understand how the time differed from the Outside. She rubbed her forehead.

"I don't expect an answer right now. The fact that you re-member tells me all I need to know, but you need more and I understand that. Let's spend this Yule getting to know one an-other. We won't discuss it, we'll just enjoy each other's company. Let me show you what life could be like here. Give me this Yule and tell me your decision on Christmas Eve. I'm only asking for a chance."

Staring into his blue-green eyes, which reminded her of the beach in Florida, she nodded. She could give it a few weeks. She set her hand on top of his and squeezed.

"Deal. Let's get to know each other."

He sealed the deal by bringing her hand to his mouth and brushing his lips across the sensitive skin, sending goose bumps up her arm and reminding her of how those same lips had felt on hers.

"Want to see my place?" Astra said.

Chapter Twenty

"YOU READY FOR THIS?" ASTRA LOOKED OVER HER SHOULDER at Jack as she turned the key in the lock on her side door. Somehow the day had passed in a blur and the streetlights were coming to life. "You look a little queasy."

He felt more than a little queasy. Jack hadn't left the Jule-marked since they went to the club, and it was as if he were strapped to the mast of a sailboat during a storm. He sucked on the piece of dried ginger but it didn't help much. He knew he needed to power through this. He wouldn't actually get sick, so if he focused on Astra, he could ignore the nausea.

"Ignore that. I'm excited to meet Bernie."

"Final warning, she's large and will love you as much as you allow her to."

"I have girded my loins."

Once through the door, they walked up a few steps into a small, bright kitchen, where they were greeted by a small black, tan, and white horse skidding across the wood floors and scrambling to right itself before careening into the cupboard despite the frantic skittering of claws on a hard surface.

"Oh, sweetie, you okay?" Astra knelt beside the huge dog, running her hands over her legs to check for an injury, but the dog seemed undeterred and commenced licking her. "You're fine, you goof."

She stood and turned to Jack. "This is my Bernie."

Jack crouched to meet Bernie and let her sniff him, her tail at half-staff. Jack loved dogs though they hadn't had one in the Jule-marked since Pinecone wandered in and stayed. That was decades ago. Bernie gave a quick sample lick of his chin, clearly approved, then went in for the full-body affection, knocking him onto his butt and stepping on his lap, forgetting she was more horse than dog. He couldn't help but laugh and felt he'd passed an important test.

"I'm so sorry," Astra said. But the grin on her face said otherwise. It said this couldn't have gone better. "Bernie, come." Astra stepped away and Bernie followed. Astra did a few hand gestures and gave Bernie a treat, keeping her occupied long enough for Jack to get back to his feet. By then Bernie lay on the ground by Astra's side.

"Can I get you some wine?" she asked.

"Yes, please."

As she opened a bottle of something red, he walked through the kitchen to the rest of the house, which was a small living room and a hallway that, he assumed, led to a few bedrooms and a bathroom. It was cozy, with unlit candles, and a fireplace that appeared to be gas. Who was he to judge? On the mantel, his eye was drawn to something red. Many somethings red. He stepped closer. More than a dozen nisser kept vigil. Many of them were ones he had given her over the years, even though she probably didn't remember. She had kept them. Didn't just keep them, but displayed them in a prominent place.

Astra came into the room and handed him the glass of wine.

"I see you're admiring my little army."

Jack pointed to one with a red hat.

"I gave you this when we met, after you gave me a red knit hat."

Astra's mouth opened in surprise.

"I knew it. Well, I didn't know that specifically because I can't remember it, but I knew they were from you." She pointed to the smallest one holding mistletoe. "I had a dream about you giving me this one. In the dream, you showed me the initials on the bottom. When I woke up, I checked and the initials were there."

Jack nodded. "We were at the picnic tables in the Outside Christmas market. I bought you mulled wine while you waited for your friends. You didn't come into the bakery that year."

"When did we meet?"

"Fifteen years ago. I've seen you most of those years. About half of them we had conversations."

"I wish that I remembered."

She stood close and he could smell her perfume—flowers and citrus, he guessed.

Jack wished she did, too. He turned his attention to the rest of the room.

The walls were a soft blue with white trim around the windows and doors, offsetting the dark wood floors, which seemed to run through the house. Two overflowing bookcases flanked the

front door, the top level covered in framed photos, the base surrounded with books that didn't fit. Over the fireplace hung a
modest-size TV, and on the opposite wall, a deep, soft green
couch, with squashy cushions and pillows, sat under a framed
print of sea turtles. He stepped closer. Not a print. It was an
original by Wyland. Astra joined him. He sipped his wine—not
too bad with the lingering ginger taste in his mouth.

"Besides Bernie, that's my pride and joy. My parents gave that
to me as a wedding gift. Sea turtles are my favorite. They're so
awkward on land, moving with their flippers in the sand, but in
water, they can really cruise when they want to, even though their
preferred mode is chill. Get someone in their ideal environment
and they'll exceed expectations. I guess that's life—figuring out
where you're meant to be."

Jack had never seen a sea turtle swim. Living in the Julemarked was all he needed to be happy, to be his best self. At least
that's what he thought. Now a part of him wanted to watch a
sea turtle surf under the waves.

"That must be beautiful to watch."

"We should go sometime. My parents have a place right off
the beach in Florida."

Astra plopped on the couch, tucking one leg under her and
cradling the bowl of her wineglass with one hand. He could
imagine spending a thousand nights like this with her in his cottage and never getting bored. But that didn't involve sea turtles
and sand. He didn't want to risk her closing the door on the way
of life in the Julemarked, but he also knew she needed all the information, even the brutal facts that might be hard to accept. If

this was going to head somewhere, and he really wanted it to, she needed to know everything.

He set his wine down.

"That's not really how it works. Traveling isn't an option. We don't have documents to get on planes, even if we wanted to. We work, then we rest. Repeat."

"You give up the entire world, for what?"

How to explain?

"How did you feel at my cottage?"

"Overwhelmed."

Jack smiled.

"Fair. But besides your entire understanding of reality being overturned. How did you feel?"

Astra sipped her wine and tilted her head. He appreciated that she was taking the question seriously. This was important.

"Peaceful. It was so quiet. There wasn't that constant hum that I always feel but didn't know was there until it was gone. It was like being wrapped in a down comforter. Soft, warm, cozy, calm." She paused. "Safe."

"That's the trade-off. Peace. Satisfaction in simple living, a strong community, and a purpose to make the world a better place one Yule at a time. I can't imagine a more fulfilling life."

"And there's the time thing."

"We're observers of time. We watch the world change and evolve. Sometimes for the better, sometimes not. We see humanity at its best during the Christmas season. We don't have the normal stress of bills, or what you see as traditional jobs. You asked earlier about Santa. While that's not the role we fill, we are a manifestation of Christmas joy. I'm not saying the world would miss us if we ceased to exist, but I do think it would be lesser for it."

"Given most people don't remember you, they couldn't miss you."

Jack picked up his wine and thought about how much he would miss her presence, how her regular appearances in his life were too infrequent.

"Would you miss me?"

He finished his wine in a big gulp as he waited for her response, nervous about what her answer might be. He could feel her eyes on him as she found the words to respond.

"I would. But I remember you, which is why I didn't like being ghosted."

"Ghosted?"

"Disappearing. It means someone who stops responding to your texts and calls, as if they vanished into thin air like a ghost. It's all to avoid having an honest conversation that you are no longer interested in the other person. It's very rude."

Jack was thankful technology was not a part of his life.

"But now that I understand . . ." Astra took his empty glass from his hand and set his glass beside hers on the coffee table. "I think I would miss you. I thought we had a real connection. And that kiss." She smiled and heat flushed through Jack's body. "I've thought a lot about that kiss."

She scooted closer to him on the couch, her knee touching his, her hand resting on his leg, her body leaning toward him, and he could smell her perfume again. This time he picked out the lemon, jasmine, and something he still couldn't recognize but smelled like what he imagined summer would be. Before he could identify it, her lips met his and he no longer cared about the scent; he could only think of her taste. Red wine mingled with coffee and sugar. Intoxicating. Her lips were soft and smooth, and might as well have been electrified with the shocks streaking through his body. She leaned in closer, minimizing the distance between them. He leaned back on the couch, taking her body with him until she was lying on top of him, one knee at his side, preventing her from giving him all her weight, but he wanted it. He wanted gravity to pull them closer together, to feel every inch of her pressing into him, then to flip over and press into her. Heat flooded his body, focusing on where he wanted to feel her the most. Their kiss became more urgent and his hands found the bare skin where her shirt had lifted away from her waistband. His hand slipped under the soft cotton of her top to press into her back. His other hand traced the curve of her hip. He wanted to flip them over, but he also wanted to savor her delicious weight and the tease of where this could lead.

Astra broke off the kiss and sat back on her heels long enough to pull off her shirt and toss it across the room. He froze at the sight of her curves, a simple tan bra skimming her body the way that he wanted to with his hands.

"Is this okay? I wouldn't normally, but . . ." The words came out breathless, and she sucked in deep breaths, her lips now red from their contact with his, her eyes bright and hair slightly mussed. A lock of hair curled onto her cheek. ". . . time is fleeting and all that."

Was this okay? He'd never wanted anything more. His brothers might tease him for his lack of a social life now, but it hadn't always been that way. In recent years, he hadn't wanted the no-strings-attached kind of affection. He craved something deeper, something more meaningful. Something exactly like this.

"More than okay." He finally managed to answer, her mouth crushing his before he had a chance to finish his sentence.

He wanted to touch her everywhere, taste her, hear her respond to his hands, mouth, body. Screw Christmas, she would be his new holiday; worshiping her would be the event that his life would now revolve around. Making her happy, making her life complete, making her breath catch and her muscles tighten, then relax. Over the last fifteen years, he had thought about this moment so many times, envisioning how her skin would feel, the sounds she would make as his fingers discovered a new sensitive spot. But the reality was so much better—and he already sensed he would never have enough time to satisfy all the ways he wanted this woman.

Chapter Twenty-One

Darkness still cloaked her bedroom when Astra felt the bed shift and remembered the events of last night. She rolled over to pull Jack closer and was greeted by a wet, sloppy lick to the face and more hair than she remembered on Jack. And more panting. Another lick. She looked over Bernie's large body to see the other side of the bed empty and a light leaking out from under the door.

"Bernie, what have you done with Jack?" she whispered. The toilet in the bathroom off her bedroom flushed.

Jack came out of the bathroom, pulling a T-shirt over his broad chest, shoulders, and strong arms; the same arms that had managed to carry her to the bedroom like she was no heavier than a tray of pastries. It had been a revelation to not feel big and bulky next to such a fit man; instead, they fit perfectly, in every way. Evidenced by the bonelessness she felt everywhere.

"Sorry to wake you, but my brothers will come looking if I'm not back soon, and the last thing you want is those Neanderthals in your house." He sat on the edge of the bed next to her and she rolled into him. Bernie, not liking the shift away from her, put a paw on Astra's shoulder, a reminder of where her attention should be. "Last night . . ." Even in the dark, she could tell he was searching for the words, cupping a hand on her cheek.

"I know."

Astra put a hand over his and leaned into his touch. She didn't want him to leave, even for a few hours. She needed to know if this was just first-time fireworks, or if this connection went deeper, like an underground lava flow, strong and powerful and ready to break free at any moment. It could destroy everything in its path, or be the beginning of a new paradise, like it had been when the Hawaiian Islands formed.

Everything about their shiny new relationship had a giant clock ticking above their heads. How was she supposed to commit to someone she'd basically just met? Decisions would need to be made, and it wasn't going to be easy, no matter what she chose. Yet, there was something that made it worth thinking about, something intangible like the taste of blue moon ice cream— familiar yet completely unlike anything else. As with all important decisions, she needed as much information as she could acquire. And that's what she'd do. She'd forget about making the decision until they had spent more time together.

"Will you come by later today?" Jack asked.

He felt it, too, the countdown. Twenty-two days until Christmas Eve.

"I wouldn't miss it. Is it okay if I bring Bernie?"

"I would be disappointed if you didn't." Jack reached over and scratched behind Bernie's ears. Bernie rolled onto her back, making her preferred petting zone available. Jack rubbed her belly.

"She's shameless," Astra said.

"I like a girl who knows what she wants and asks for it." Jack's eyes glazed as he remembered last night when Astra had done just that. Her cheeks heated at her boldness, but she maintained eye contact.

"Knowledge is power."

"I'm yours to teach for as long as you'll have me."

Astra took a handful of his shirt and brought his lips to her own, using her other arm to pull him in closer. It didn't take long for the sleepy bonelessness to kindle into flames. She found the edge of his T-shirt and ran her hands along the hard planes of his back, enjoying how they rippled as her fingers met skin. He pulled back long enough to pull off his T-shirt and toss it back on the floor where he'd found it just minutes ago. As he came in for a kiss, Astra's phone rang. They both stopped as Astra considered whether to answer or not. It rang again. In Astra's world, a pre-dawn phone call meant disaster—maybe her parents, maybe something with one of the girls, maybe something with the library. There was no other reason for her phone to ring.

With a deep sigh, she picked it up, noticing it was not a number she recognized.

"Hello."

"Astra, it's Orn, Jack's brother." She shouldn't have answered the phone. In the background, she heard another brother shout, "Tell that dipshit to get back here now. Rolling is his job."

She heard a car in the background. Orn must have left the alley to make the call.

"Sorry about that," Orn continued. "But please let Jack know that we could use his help. Dad is threatening to come into the bakery."

"Of course. I'll bring him."

She set the phone back on the nightstand.

"Your brothers have summoned you. They must really want you if they bothered to call. Orn said your dad was on his way to help."

Jack shook his head and found his T-shirt again.

"Dad ran the bakery for years on his own. He tends to try to take over, and then he and Orn butt heads. Last time he helped, Orn dumped a bowl of flour on him."

"I would have liked to see that."

He leaned in and kissed her forehead. "Stick around long enough and you will."

He turned to look for his shoes and socks and Astra frowned. Nope, she wasn't going to think about it. She would enjoy their time. She flung the sheet off herself and pulled on sweatpants and a sweatshirt, slipping her feet into her wool-lined mules, which were more slippers than shoes, but she liked to push the limit of where it was acceptable to wear them. Driving Jack back to the alley was certainly acceptable.

"You don't have to take me. I can call a cab. I can actually move around in the world even though I don't do it often."

She smiled. His hair was still rumpled from sleep, his lips swollen from their kissing. She could feel the stubble burn on her own face. She never wanted that feeling to go away.

"By the time the cab got here, I could have dropped you off

and returned to bed. I have Steph's car on loan, so I'm happy to take you."

They got in the car, and Bernie tried to join them in the front, but Astra made her get in the back seat. She made up for it by setting her head on Astra's seat back, her chin resting on Astra's shoulder. She gave Bernie's head a little scratch and drove them to the Christmas market. The streets were empty and coated in a light snow falling fast enough to not melt from the salt the plows had scattered. The world was quiet and cheery, with a few houses still glowing from Christmas lights they had left on all night.

While Astra hated getting up this early, once awake she could appreciate the quiet and calm, the chance to find a peaceful place in which to start her day. Astra and Jack didn't speak in the car, and it wasn't awkward, just comfortable. He kept Bernie occupied as they drove through the empty downtown, only delivery trucks and a few cars marring the white roads. She took corners slowly, careful to not slide.

As she pulled up to the Christmas market, Mads waited on the curb holding a to-go cup and bag.

"Looks like you're getting the five-star treatment," Jack said before opening the door and climbing out.

Bernie took advantage of the empty seat and jumped into the front, her large body barely making it through the gap in the seats, then woofed when Mads leaned in the open door. Like a pro, he let her sniff him until she nudged his hand, her way of giving him permission to pat her noggin, which he obliged, then held out the coffee cup and bag for Astra.

"Thanks for returning him in one piece." He smirked and

Jack hit him on the shoulder. "Lots of cream, just how you like your coffee, right?"

"Perfect, thanks." Astra took the cup and sipped while Jack walked around the car to her window, which she rolled down. The coffee was perfect.

"Thanks for driving me so early in the morning," Jack said. He stuck his head through the window and kissed Astra, soft and gentle, a memory of the heat from earlier, but just as wonderful.

"Mmm, I can't even complain, because I get these yummy treats." She patted the bag, which Bernie was sniffing. The sun hadn't risen yet, but the world was turning from black and murky to muffled daylight filtering through the snow clouds. "I'll see you later."

She watched him and Mads walk into the Julemarked as she sipped her coffee. Opening the pastry bag, she pulled out one of several kringle slices and tore off a chunk for Bernie, who gently took it between her teeth, barely making contact with Astra's fingers. Astra's bite was much less ladylike, filling her mouth with the still-warm kringle—cherry almond. They remembered. She hadn't spent much time around Jack's brothers yet, but she already knew she liked them, could see herself enjoying the way they teased one another. Jack's thoughtfulness was clearly a family trait. Maybe this wasn't a ludicrous idea after all.

Astra had Bernie's leash wrapped around her hand as she entered JulBooks, where Jack said they should meet. She didn't remember ever being in the store before, but everything felt so familiar. The yellow wood that made up the floor and bookshelves absorbed the small amount of sunshine that made it through the window, and amplified it, giving the space a warm, sunny glow. A small bell tinkled as she entered the store, causing the old man sitting behind the front desk to look up, raising his abundant eyebrows when he saw her. He had the look of a man who spent his time with books, his skin thin and pale, his shoulders slightly stooped from decades, maybe centuries, of reading, and wisps of white hair that could have been combed neatly earlier in the day but was now trying to touch the ceiling. He wore a white-collared shirt and dark green wool cardigan that could be from any era. His bright blue eyes met hers in acknowledgment, still sharp and youthful despite his age. How old must he really be? How many centuries had he lived in the Julemarked? He must know about her and Jack. She imagined the local gossip didn't take long to hit all the ears.

Another customer approached his counter. Astra gave him a small smile and disappeared into the stacks, Bernie close by her, soon forgetting she was waiting for Jack. She got that way around books; time and purpose disappeared, until it was just her and the pages. She found herself in the fairy-tale section with a few shelves of Hans Christian Andersen tomes, which made perfect sense given the Julemarked's Danish roots. She pulled an old book off the shelf, its linen cover gray with age. She carefully opened the pages and inhaled deeply—every librarian she knew loved that scent. A first edition and it was in the original Danish, so she wasn't entirely sure which stories were in it. She turned another page. It was signed by Hans Christian Andersen. Her heart picked up its pace. She had to know more about it.

The old man behind the counter was now alone. Astra approached and Bernie lay down at her feet when she stopped in front of him.

"Hi, I'm Astra, a friend of Jack's."

"I know who you are." He leaned a little closer. "The whole Julemarked knows who you are. Call me Johan."

Astra could feel her cheeks heat.

"I found this book in the fairy-tale section. Could you tell me more about it?"

He looked down at the book in her hands.

"I wondered if you'd find it again."

"Again?"

He took a moment to study her.

"You don't remember it yet. That you have been here before. But I believe you will—the more time you spend in the Julemarked, the more you'll remember."

She was going to remember her earlier visits to the Julemarked? Jack hadn't mentioned that to her.

The bookstore felt familiar, but she had assumed it was because every bookstore had a similar energy, the same dry, papery scent, the same unspoken invitation to explore—both the stacks and the pages. She looked down at the book in her hands, the worn cloth cover, which may have once been blue but was now a dark gray, the corners fraying a bit. If there had been a paper dust jacket, it was long gone. The pages had yellowed somewhat, but not much. She didn't really understand why it wasn't under lock and key. But something about this interaction, her standing in front of Johan, felt like a dream she'd already had.

"It's there, but not," Astra said. "I've held this book before?"

"It would be about . . ." He paused to count on his fingers. "Six years in your time."

"What did I want to know?"

"If it was real and how much?"

"Same questions today, but I also want to know if you got it signed by him."

The man grinned.

"He came into the shop, a bit drunk from the night before, if I recall correctly. I was a lot younger then. He asked if I wanted to visit the pub. I did. It was a long, chaotic night, and it took me a few days to recover. Hans stayed with me for a few nights. We drank a lot of coffee, spent the nights talking. He was an interesting and unusual person. On Christmas Eve, he left us, and as a parting gift, he gave me that signed copy."

"I can't believe you leave it on the shelves where anyone could take it."

"I hide it in the shelves, and a very small number of people have ever found it, but you've found it twice. Maybe you are meant to be where the book is."

A rush of cold air came into the shop.

"I'm not going to argue with that," Jack said as he closed the door behind him, shutting out the wintery breeze.

Jack and Johan tapped hands in greeting. Jack set a white pastry bag and thermos of coffee on the counter for him, and Johan's eyes sparkled. It appeared he still appreciated the simple things in life, too.

"I hope he's not telling you about his affair with Hans. He can get very graphic."

Johan didn't even blush.

"I would never subject Astra to that. At least not until we know each other better." Johan winked.

Astra ran her hand over the cover, not wanting to leave it behind but also not ready to commit to staying in the Julemarked. She set it on the counter, giving it one last pat of farewell.

"I'd have to learn Danish to read it."

Johan's eyes crinkled with his smile.

"You'll find that you can pick up languages quickly when it's what you hear all day long."

What would it be like hearing a different language every four weeks, and understanding? Making a life in the Julemarked would come with several extra lifetimes to learn, a dream for her. Would she be willing to give up her normal life when it meant rarely if ever seeing her friends and family? All for a man and people she didn't know? If any of her friends came to her with a similar problem, her answer would be obvious. Don't go with the strangers. But when did strangers evolve into acquaintances? Friends? A lover? Love? Could she base her decisions on a man again after things went so badly with Trent? Even if she did fall in love with Jack?

Rather than fight the thoughts, she let them roll through her consciousness to be studied later, discussed later.

Jack looped her arm around his.

"Ready to explore some more?"

Astra nodded, eager to learn what other secrets the Julemarked was hiding.

Chapter Twenty-Two

As Jack and Astra left the bookstore, blue stretched across the sky above the Julemarked, with the faintest hint of purple evening to the east. For now, she took a deep breath to calm all the swirling thoughts, knowing only time would help her sort out the answers. She was still adjusting to the truth she now knew about this tiny place. She studied the skyline where she should have been able to see office buildings and even the top of the Fiserv Forum, but instead it was clear blue sky.

"How does no one notice?" Astra asked.

"A few do, and when they ask, we tell them."

"Then how come everyone doesn't know?"

"Are you going to tell everyone? Announce it from the roof-tops?"

"No."

"Why not?"

"Because I don't want it ruined. And no one would believe me."

"I imagine that the other people feel the same way."

"But . . ."

"The magic protects itself. Trust the magic," Jack said.

"Is it magic? Or something we just don't understand yet?"

"Aren't they the same thing?"

"And you don't have a secret magical ability you haven't told me about?"

Jack laughed.

"I'm totally normal, I promise. If we had superpowers, I'm sure Mads would be using them to pick up dates."

They reached the black wrought-iron arch that marked the entryway to the Julemarked. Astra took off her mitten to run her hand over the cold iron, turning to the brown brick behind it. It all looked normal, like any other alley in downtown Milwaukee. Looking right, she could see a beer garden with a giant television screen, a bar, the Fiserv Forum, and the main Christmas market full of customers buying ornaments, melted raclette on crispy baguettes, and mug after mug of mulled wine. To her left was a cookie bakery, another sports bar, and Old World Third Street. She could even see a glimpse of the Milwaukee River, frozen over except for the very center, where the current was too strong.

When the Julemarked bricked up, she knew it was just a plain expanse of brick wall on the Outside.

"What's it like on the Inside when it bricks up?"

Jack looked up at the arch, his eyes growing distant as he thought about the experience he'd been through hundreds and hundreds of times.

"As midnight approaches, we close up all the shops and herd any lingering people out. One minute before midnight, the clock starts to bong." He pointed to the clock above the candy shop, Jul

Be Sweet, next to the arch. She'd never heard it make a noise while she was there. "The only time it sounds is during that minute. Twelve times. Once every five seconds. On the last bong, the wall appears."

The numbers on the clock didn't make sense.

"Why does it have twenty-five numbers? Do you have an extra hour? And where is the little hand?"

"The clock doesn't tell hourly time; it lets us know the day. See, the hand is halfway past the two because we are halfway through December second."

"That makes sense. Does the wall build magically, like Diagon Alley in *Harry Potter*? Can you still get in and out if you know the right magic words?"

"What's *Harry Potter*?" Jack said, and Astra clutched her heart and gasped. "I'm kidding," Jack continued. "I read them with my nieces and nephews." He paused as she shoved his shoulder. "It's nothing like that. One instant the arch is there; the next instant it's gone and there is a wall of bricks. Faster than a blink. Once it's there, there is no in and out until the next Yule begins."

"What if you're standing where the wall is? Do you get cut in half?"

"That's grim." Jack laughed. "I've never heard of it happening, but I think you'd get kicked out. Everyone in the Julemarked knows to be away from the arch when it disappears."

"What do you do during the week?"

Astra looped her arm through Jack's, holding on to Bernie's leash with her free hand. Jack wore a thick blue wool sweater that brightened the blue in his aqua eyes. His dark blond hair brushed against his eyes like a curtain. She wanted to push it back from his face. His straight nose, high cheekbones, and strong jaw made him look like he belonged on some ancient coin, until he turned his twinkling eyes on her. There was a quiet joy about him, which she read as a love for life and those he shared it with. When she was with him, she never hurried or felt rushed. He had all the time in the world and wanted to enjoy every moment of it. That enjoyment spread to her, letting her slow down and soak up everything around her, too. The family at a nearby picnic table, the mom helping a toddler drink his hot chocolate, holding the cup to his lips, then wiping off the whipped cream from his nose when he was done. A group of twentysomethings stood by a fire, holding mugs of mulled wine and singing "Jingle Bells" as loud as they could. Two older women showed off the pottery they had bought at the store, the hand-painted mugs and plates making a perfect gift for someone (or themselves).

Everywhere around her people were happy. Time did seem to slow in the lead-up to the holidays, begging for the moments to be savored. Astra could see the appeal of living in the Christmas season all the time. Every day filled with anticipation for the holiday, every day a celebration with the visitors to the Julemarked. Because every day was similar, it forced you to really savor the special moments.

Jack opened the door at the end of the alley and they slipped into the back side.

"You asked what we do during the time between Christmas and New Year. We rest, we read, we play games, we eat, do some laundry. But mostly we keep doing the same thing. That's when I play in the kitchen to come up with a new idea or two for the next

Yule, maybe carve a few extra nisser. We make extra stock so we are ready for the next Yule."

"Do you celebrate Christmas?"

Jack led her down a narrow path between two snow-covered evergreens. Astra paused to unleash Bernie, who quickly darted between trees, leaping into the snow, then circling back to make sure Astra was still near. While the Outside didn't have much snow, the Inside had at least two feet covering everything, with stray flakes fluttering to the ground. While cold, it wasn't uncomfortable. Her heavy sweater and mittens kept her warm enough, like being in a hockey rink. Without the wind it wasn't too chilly.

"How do you celebrate something that happens every day?" Jack asked.

"Well, they do celebrate sunsets every day in Key West with a party and applause."

"That sounds amazing." Jack smiled. "But no, we don't celebrate Christmas like you do. Once a month would be a bit much, don't you think? Instead, we celebrate birthdays and anniversaries."

"How do you keep track if you're always in December?"

"We count twelve Yules. Old Johan keeps track of when people are born and has a book so we know when to celebrate important events."

"When's yours?"

"December second in . . ." Jack counted on his fingers. "Six Yules."

They walked in silence for a bit. Occasionally there would be a break in the trees and Astra would see a lot of white snow; then the trees would be back. Bernie bounded through the underbrush and emerged snow covered and smiling. What would it be like to do this with her every day, for so many extra years? Would having all that extra time with Bernie make giving up everything else worth it?

A rabbit hopped across the trail, pausing to watch them as they stepped around it, unafraid of them. Bernie stopped to watch it, unsure what to do with this fearless beast. She stepped toward it and the bunny took a hop toward Bernie. Bernie stepped back, then took another step forward. The bunny hopped closer. They repeated the process until the two were nose to nose, sniffing each other. After a few moments, the rabbit got bored and hopped into the brush. Bernie started to follow, then looked back at Astra and decided to stay in view.

"Does that happen a lot?" Astra asked.

"What?"

She pointed to where the rabbit disappeared. "The rabbit? I've never seen one not scamper away when people came, let alone go nose to nose with a dog ten times its size. It's not afraid."

Jack smiled and nodded.

"We don't have any predators here. Nothing to be afraid of."

"How are you not wall-to-wall rabbits?"

"Magic."

"That doesn't get to be the answer for all my questions. There have to be answers to this."

"How come that's not a good enough answer?"

"Occupational standards. There is always a reason for things, you just have to look hard enough. Dig deeper."

"Okay, smart lady, then how do you explain this?"

They stepped out of the trees, which opened onto a large meadow that appeared to be in the middle of a mountain range, large boulders scattered around like a giant had dropped them like seeds. Bernie dashed between them, kicking up snow and leaving a twisty trail of tracks. The nearest boulder stood right next to them, taller than Jack. Most of the sides were straight, but the one facing the mountains had a seat carved out of it. Astra imagined some ancestor had created it as a convenient place to rest. On the horizon, the sun glowed orange in the space between the low-hanging clouds and the mountaintops, covered in snow-topped pines. Astra was stunned into silence. There was no explanation for this. The faintest breeze kissed her cheek, the air scented with pine and newly fallen snow. Jack set his hands on her shoulders behind her, and she melted into him, sharing this moment. A sight he had surely seen a thousand times, but could it ever get old?

"This is the most beautiful . . ." She couldn't find the words.

"I know."

They stood in silence until the sun completely disappeared and the night sky turned from orange and red to purple to a deep black only broken by more stars than Astra had ever seen.

"I don't normally get to see the sun set because I'm working."

"That's a shame."

"To really blow your mind, this is also where the sun rises."

"You're messing with me now."

She gently elbowed his ribs, then turned to face him.

"Maybe. Stay the night and we can check it out in the morning."

Jack kissed her, a smile on his lips, in a quiet meadow after a literal magical sunset.

As she stared up at the night sky, familiar shapes emerged as she found the brightest constellations: Gemini, Leo, the Ursas. They were familiar, but different. They were all backward. Another sign that she wasn't in downtown Milwaukee anymore. And there, right by the horizon, not far from where the sun had set, was the Unicorn. She found the horn and followed it to the two bright stars that marked the top and bottom of the Christmas Tree Cluster her dad loved so much.

"You can almost see it," Astra said, her voice soft.

"See what?"

Astra took his hand in hers as a guide and pointed to where the constellation was, using the same marking stars that her father had used.

"There's Orion, and find Betelgeuse—that's the bright star on the left shoulder, but it's the right here. Did you know your stars are backward?"

He nodded. "Old Johan has a theory involving science words I don't follow. He and Mads talk about it sometimes."

"My dad would love to get in on that conversation." Astra's heart squeezed at what Jack had proposed—if she were to have a future with him, it might mean not seeing her dad again and never being able to share this with him. As much as she rolled her eyes at how excited he would get about astronomy, she loved him for it. Astra cleared her throat and continued. "Okay, go down and to the right and look for the really bright star." She moved his hand so he could follow. "See it?" She felt his head nod against her hair. "That's the trunk of the Christmas tree. Go up and you'll see another bright star. That's the top." Using their joined hands, she traced the outline of the triangle that made up the tree. "And that's the tree. Do you see it?"

He whispered words in a language she didn't understand, his lips brushing her ear.

"What does that mean?" Astra asked.

"'The Christmas lights rose higher and higher, till they looked to her like the stars in the sky.'"

Astra's heart twisted.

"'The Little Matchgirl.' One of my favorites, but it's so sad."

Jack pulled her tighter.

"I've always thought of it as hopeful. We leave one place to go to another with those we love. They're always waiting when we need them most," Jack said.

Astra leaned into him, reflecting on his interpretation. No matter where she was in the world, even here, when she looked up at the stars, she couldn't help thinking about her parents and friends. They would always be there for her, even if they weren't physically close. With the decision about her future looming over her, that thought offered a lot of comfort.

Astra snuggled in closer to Jack, not because she was cold, but because it was what she wanted—his strong arms around her on this perfect winter night under the beautiful stars. She knew this was a moment she would always remember.

Chapter Twenty-Three

RONNIE SAT AT ASTRA'S KITCHEN TABLE SUCKING THE BEANS out of edamame pods, a mountain of empty shells growing on the table beside her. As the only two single women in their foursome, they often spent more time alone together while Steph and Cassie were spending time with their families. Ronnie had no interest in settling down. She traveled all the time for work selling high-end equipment to medical facilities and schmoozing doctors and hospital executives around the world.

Settling down was what Astra wanted, what Jack was offering her, but the price seemed too high. While the clock ticked down, it was tempting to let the romance sweep her away, but Astra needed a break to recalibrate—thus Ronnie in her kitchen with edamame, with Bernie at her feet hoping for a snack.

"When are you going to steal this dog and stop answering Trent's calls?" Ronnie asked.

"It's not that simple and you know it."

"Stupid lawyers. They ruin everything." She slipped a shelled bean to Bernie, who took it delicately between her teeth, then spit it out, sniffing it suspiciously, finally deciding to eat it. "You should be happy and Trent shouldn't get what he wants. Ever. You were always too good for him."

"You'd say that no matter who I dated. Even Chris Evans and Idris Elba couldn't meet your standards."

"I call 'em like I see 'em."

"This is why I love you." Astra slid onto the bench next to Ronnie.

"That, and my big boobs. They make great pillows." Ronnie put her arm around Astra and pulled her in so Astra's head was resting on Ronnie's right boob.

"Boob pillows are the best pillows," Astra said.

"That's what my lovers keep telling me."

Astra straightened.

"Who's the latest?" Astra asked. Ronnie had always been more comfortable and adventurous with her sexual needs than Astra. She liked hearing about Ronnie's exploits without having to experience them herself. It kept her up on the dating scene for when she was ready to plunge back in.

"A plastic surgeon from Houston. He said he's adding my breasts to the pool of models his patients can use for inspiration." She cupped her chest.

"That sounds like a pickup line."

"One hundred percent, but it made for a fun photo session." Ronnie cackled.

"Are you happy?" Astra asked.

Ronnie smoothed Astra's hair, studying her face, more serious than her usual boisterous self.

"I really am. I'm living a life of no regrets. When you're all surrounding me on my deathbed, I will have a lifetime of adventures to remember. What about you? How goes magical kringle man?"

"Jack goes fine. Speaking of, any chance I can borrow your car?"

"Of course. Anything to help you get some."

Her friends knew all about the Julemarked, even if they still didn't remember it. It had never occurred to her not to tell her friends what she'd learned, just like it never occurred to them not to believe her. Their friendship was about supporting one another, whatever that might entail, so each could become the best version of herself.

"I know what you're thinking. Don't," Ronnie said. "We've all chosen to live our separate lives. If we hadn't, we'd be living *Golden Girls*–style in Boca. If Jack is the guy for you, and that is the life you want, you take it."

Ronnie gave her a stern look.

"I've already chosen a man over my friends once before and it didn't go well."

"Pshh. If we held grudges, we never would have been friends past sophomore year. And Jack might not be 'some man.'" Ronnie continued despite Astra shaking her head. "He's a smart, sexy hunk from a disappearing alley. Sure, it's possibly some weird cult with a brilliant cover story—but maybe not every cult is a bad cult." She paused. "Have you discussed him moving here?"

"No, we agreed to focus on spending time together, then discuss it closer to Christmas Eve. Otherwise, how would we talk about anything else? It's all I seem to think about. How do you ask someone to shorten their life by possibly hundreds of years? He'd be giving up everything he's ever known."

"So would you."

"I know," Astra whispered. "If it were an easy decision, I would have made it already. There's so much on the line."

"Either way, I haven't seen you this happy in a very long time."

"My happiness comes from a lot of sources that don't revolve around romance. Like you, Steph, and Cassie. You three make me happy. My parents make me happy. Bernie makes me happy."

"We both know those are different from finding that one person. That's always been important to you, and you deserve that happiness."

What would Astra regret more? Losing this chance with Jack? Despite not really knowing him, she felt like she did. Maybe he was her person. Would it be worth leaving her family, friends, and work? For love, every risk was worth it, right? Jack noticed things about her, like how she took her coffee and her favorite kringle—small things, but enough small efforts added up. He listened, he made her laugh, he made her swoon. Already, she couldn't wait to see him again. Eager to be swept up in the whirlwind. Without the Julemarked complication, there was nothing to question. She'd be all in.

Being with Jack was like standing in the eye of a tempest. Everything outside their protected circle was gone. It only mattered that they were together.

That terrified her.

Jack's mom had outdone herself. The large family table groaned under all the food. Roast pork with crispy skin, boiled potatoes, caramelized potatoes (Jack's favorite), pickled red cabbage, and gravy covered so much space, the plates and silverware barely fit on the wooden surface. The young nieces and nephews sat around a smaller table in the kitchen where they could be noisy. Candles glowed from every available nook, and the house smelled like home.

His parents' cottage was a larger version of his own, white-washed wood and open spaces, with rooms enough for four sons to grow until they moved into their own cottages.

Astra sat beside him at the table, trying to keep up with the activities around her. Jack's mother and Ani (he would definitely have words with his mom about that later) were still bringing in platters and bowls of food. Astra stood.

"Please, let me help," she said to Jack's mom.

"That's not necessary. You're a guest," his mother said.

It sounded polite enough, but all four sons stopped talking and looked at their mother, who turned and went back into the kitchen for more food. Ani mouthed a "sorry" in Jack's direction and sent Astra a warm smile.

He needed this night to go perfectly, to demonstrate the wonderful life they could have in the Julemarked. For once, time ticked faster than he wanted.

Mads occupied the seat on the other side of Astra, and his brothers and their wives were on the opposite side. His dad sat at the end next to Mads, while his mom took the other end. It was no accident that Ani would have the seat between Jack and his mother.

"Do you eat like this all the time?" Astra asked. "It smells amazing. I don't know where to begin."

"We never eat like this," Mads said. "We're lucky if we get stale bread and water."

The last of the food on the table, his mom swatted Mads's shoulder as she walked past him to her chair.

"We don't normally eat this much while we're open. It's usually a quick fry-up, but Jack wanted a big family meal, even though it had to wait until after the bakery closed. It's something quick while we're open. But he's my son and I like to make him happy."

Astra frowned, but smoothed it out when she saw that Jack had noticed. She gave him a small smile.

"It looks incredible, thank you," Astra said. Jack squeezed her hand.

"You're welcome," his mom said as she slid into her spot, not making eye contact with Astra.

Once she was seated, chaos erupted as children stood by parents to get their plates filled, arms reached for their favorite dishes, and plates crisscrossed the table when requested. Astra scooped a bit of everything onto her plate, but Jack made sure to add some extra caramelized potatoes.

"I'm pacing myself," Astra said, trying to stop him.

"Trust me. They're my favorite and unlike anything you've had before."

Sweet and salty, the sugar-and-butter-cooked potatoes were perfection, especially when eaten with a little bite of pork and cabbage. A special meal wouldn't be complete without them, and he couldn't imagine one more special than this.

Astra speared one of the potatoes with her fork and ate it. Her eyes widened, then closed as she chewed.

"Where have these been all my life?"

"They take a lot of practice to make correctly. You need patience and time to learn the right technique," his mom said, her teeth visible in a smile, or a snarl.

Astra's eyes stayed on her plate.

"Mom," Jack said, his voice sharp. His mom merely smiled. What was with her tonight? She knew how important this was to him.

"Jack, I'm merely telling the truth," Jack's mom said, not talking about potatoes. "Living here is a commitment to a very specific lifestyle. It's not for everyone. Astra needs to know."

Astra blinked at her, visibly surprised by his mom's comments, and Jack didn't blame her. His mom had been pestering him to find someone, and now she was being difficult because she didn't agree with his choice.

His dad cleared his throat.

"Astra, any questions for us?" his dad said. Jack gave him a grateful smile.

Astra finished chewing and took a sip of her water, sitting up straighter as she set her glass down.

"Jack's done a wonderful job of answering my questions and giving me the history. I can see why he loves it so much. And why you might be protective of it." Astra's eyes flicked to his mom. "I understand that people join the Julemarked, but I haven't asked about people moving to the Outside."

Mads's lips formed a silent "oh" and he heard Ani whisper, "Damn," under her breath. Astra kept her body turned toward his dad, but everyone at the table knew who the comment was directed at. Astra was letting his mom know she didn't intimidate her, that she wouldn't meekly disappear when challenged. Up to this point, Jack knew he could fall in love with Astra, that he stood on the peak, where one nudge would send him plunging headfirst to worship at her feet. This was the moment when he tipped over.

When raised by a strong woman, a man can't help but respect and admire other strong women. Astra had proven herself capable of holding her own and now his heart was hers forever.

His mother's eyebrow raised in Astra's direction but she stayed silent while her husband answered.

"It doesn't happen often. Most people come to the Julemarked to get away from something. Old Johan says the original residents were a couple in love but who were betrothed to other people—but that's another tale. To your question, when a person runs from something and they find a place where that something isn't, they tend to stay put. For families like ours that are born and raised residents, well, this is the only life and family we know. There isn't much on the Outside that could tempt us away forever."

Jack could see his mom nodding firmly out of the corner of his eye, but his focus was on Astra, who had set down her fork and was sipping her wine slowly as the conversation moved on around them, not setting the glass down until she emptied the glass.

One of his nieces asked if she could take the caramelized potatoes to their table, and the conversation shifted to community gossip and the children's antics. Jack leaned toward Astra to whisper.

"You're doing great," he said, adding a quick kiss on her cheek.

He couldn't decipher the look Astra gave him in return.

"I know," she said. Before Jack could inquire about how she was doing, Freja snagged Astra's attention.

"Jack says you're a librarian. If you became a resident, is that something you'd want to keep doing? We could certainly use a good library."

"The bookstore is fine," Nora added. "But Old Johan tends to sell books he likes versus books we want to read. The children's section is abysmal."

Astra finally smiled and relaxed a bit. Jack could kiss Freja and Nora for bringing up a topic Astra would love to discuss.

"I can't think of a better use for my talents. Speaking of, I brought some books for the kids. Occupational hazard. I can't help it."

A loud crash came from the kitchen.

"Time to clean up," his mom announced. It was well established that whoever cooked didn't clean, though his mom still oversaw making sure it measured up to her standards. All the men filed into the kitchen, leaving the ladies to drink coffee.

"We'll take care of her," Ani said and shooed Jack into the kitchen, where his mom put him to work drying dishes while Mads washed.

"I think it's going well," Jack said to Mads, making sure his mom was on the other side of the large kitchen.

"It's going great as long as you don't count Mom. I can't believe she invited Ani."

"Ani thinks it's funny." Jack slid a plate into the cupboard. "Do I tell Mom to behave? Let her ride it out? I don't want Astra to get upset."

"Astra seems capable of holding her own. Mom has her butt in a bundle because she's worried Astra will lure you away. Once Astra moves here, they'll figure it out. She didn't love Freja much until the first grandbaby, and now they spend hours every day together."

"*If* Astra moves here. Emphasis on the 'if.' We agreed not to discuss it until closer to Christmas Eve, but it's difficult to not turn every moment into a hard sell."

"Resist. Astra needs to find her own reasons, and telling her what's great isn't going to help your cause."

He nodded as Mads handed him the last dish to dry. He put it away and tidied the area. Just like in the bakery, the brothers seamlessly worked together to finish a task, anticipating where they would be most helpful to each other.

He found Astra in front of the large fireplace in the living room with the children sitting on the floor in front of her, the adults sitting on squashy furniture around the room. He dropped into his favorite armchair, where he could watch Astra in profile as she read the picture books she'd brought for the kids, changing her voice for each character, pausing to ask questions of the kids to make sure they were engaged. He'd never seen her like this, glowing with purpose—her dimple popped to life when his youngest niece, barely able to walk, crawled onto her lap. Astra lifted her arms to accommodate her, but never stopped the story.

How could she not see how effortlessly she would fit in here? He hated that she would have to make sacrifices, but this could be their life. Cozy nights of family, books, and each other. A purpose, a community, and so much time together.

Chapter Twenty-Four

Despite spending as much time in the Julemarked as possible, like the late dinner last night, Astra still had to work. At least today was her last day before taking off. Normally, she'd visit her parents in Florida, but she'd told them she couldn't this year, using work as an excuse. It was easier than explaining she would be speed dating with a handsome man who lived in a magical disappearing Christmas market.

The library board president had just left Astra's office. Some citizens were asking questions about the new children's books, complaining they weren't promoting traditional families. Only a few rumbles, but Astra had seen these sorts of issues explode into a media nightmare. While the board supported her decision to buy books that reflected the world and the wide range of people in it, having these conversations about the importance of representation and fostering empathy in early readers took up time. Preparing her staff to address patron concerns took up time. At least the board agreed she should continue on as she had been, but that was an hour of her day gone for a non-problem.

She and Jack planned to meet up after work—his brothers giving him the time she needed. She checked her calendar, and it was already December 20. Time was running short, but after last night, it seemed even shorter. Even if Astra had no doubts about a future with Jack, she wasn't only committing to him. She was committing to all of them. She understood his mother's concerns, but a difficult mother-in-law could make the shortest moments feel like an eternity. How could she make a decision to leave everything she'd ever known? Trying to cram an entire relationship's worth of activities into twenty-four days seemed ludicrous, especially while still having jobs. How could they create all the small moments that would add up to something meaningful?

She felt like a Hallmark movie on fast-forward, a montage of romantic activities where they got to know each other better, but Astra knew it wasn't enough. There was so much pressure to get to know him. She wished she had the added benefit of their previous meetings, but he refused to tell her anything about them, not wanting to skew her memories when they came back.

As a last-ditch effort, she'd started a "Pro/Con" list.

PROS

Jack
Long life
BERNIE
babies?
No work or house stress
Most of Jack's family
Christmas

No Trent
No bills

CONS
~~~~~~~

Steph
Cassie
Ronnie
My parents
My job
Jack's mom?
No travel
No Wi-Fi
One season

Regret waited for her no matter which she chose, but which would she regret more?

As she pondered, Chloe appeared in her office, holding something glittery in her hands. The glittery object moved.

"Do I want to know?" Astra asked.

"Turtle." Chloe raised it up so she could look more closely. "Sorry, tortoise."

Astra took a deep breath as Chloe set it on her desk.

"Why is there a tortoise in the library? And why has it been bedazzled?"

"That is the mystery of the day. A mom saw it beelining for the container of carrots she had open on the ground for her kid."

Astra pulled out her lunch and opened the container with her salad, then held out a piece of lettuce for the Christmas tortoise.

The little head stretched out to the food and munched, oblivious to the glitter shedding off its shell onto her budget. As it munched, she grabbed a box from under her desk, where she kept spare shoes. She dumped them out into a pile, placed a few more leaves of lettuce in the box, and moved the tortoise into its new temporary home.

Did the Julemarked ever have to deal with glittery reptiles? She doubted it.

"There you go, Sparkles." Chloe tilted her head and Astra smiled. "That will have to work for now. Can I assign you tortoise duty? Do your best to find the owner—maybe send out emails to all our patrons asking if anyone is missing a tortoise. If we don't hear back by Christmas, maybe the zoo will take it? Or the animal shelter? Or a classroom? Make a list of possible places we can follow up with."

"On it."

Chloe disappeared from her doorway and Astra watched Sparkles munch the lettuce in slow, methodical chomps, her to-do list having gained a few more items. She let herself have a moment before diving back in. She wouldn't miss this type of work. One of the items on her to-do list was to look at how she had done with her annual goals, but she knew very little progress had been made. How could it have been? She never did anything but put out fires and balance the budget.

She would be lying if she said losing the worst parts of her job wasn't appealing. Something simple with no people to manage, no budgets to maintain, less smoke, more books.

Maybe there were options. She could try things with Jack for a year. If it didn't suit, she could return to her life. But it might be years before the Julemarked returned to Milwaukee. If she was going to commit, she wanted to do it fully. Vacillating would only lead to unsteady ground—and that was no place to lay their future's foundation.

For now, she needed to get through her to-do list. If she did decide to leave, then she wanted to leave everything in as good shape as possible, because she would be expecting a lot of her staff to pick up the pieces. She stood, stretched a little, gave Sparkles a few more lettuce leaves, then sat back down as her phone rang.

Her cell phone.

It was Trent.

As much as she loved Bernie, she didn't have time to deal with him.

She let the call go to voice mail—something she'd never done before. It felt good. It rang again. She ignored it again.

He texted.

Pick up. I know you're screening.

It rang again.

"What?" Astra said, answering at last.

She had no interest in pleasantries with him. She was ready to get a backhoe and remove him root, stem, and all the dirt around him.

"Is that any way to talk to your former husband?"

"Trent, I'm busy. Now is not a good time for small talk."

"I have a Christmas trip and I need you to watch Bernie."

Astra sat back in her chair and something snapped deep inside, the tremors rippling from her core to her extremities. It had built up since their divorce when it came to Trent—as if each interaction added more tension, more pressure, making her a little less rational whenever he was involved. She knew it was the same for Trent—why else was he using Bernie to make her life more difficult? Despite his flaws, that was never him. He wanted people to adore him, not despise him. Today had been too much.

"If I take Bernie right now, last minute, again, you're never getting her back. She's mine."

She meant it. If he was going to make her take Bernie, then she was really taking her. They'd move into the Julemarked that night if he tried to stop her.

Trent paused.

"Never mind. I'll find someone else."

He hung up.

Victory. It was a small one, if she could even call it that. She hadn't let Trent take advantage of her, but if it was a victory, then why did she feel so empty?

Jack slipped into the car, a different one from the other day—this one was cleaner and didn't have Goldfish crackers on the floor where he set the bag he had with him. It must be a different friend's car. The thought came and went, as the smell of her perfume pushed it from his mind. He'd become sensitive to it and believed he could find her in a dark room by scent alone.

He leaned over for a quick kiss hello and was pleasantly surprised when Astra grabbed onto his scarf when he tried to pull back, but her warm lips were the only encouragement he needed to stay exactly where he was. Her hand moved from his scarf to the back of his neck; she was hungry for more and gave a low groan when he gently bit her lip. If this continued much longer, they wouldn't be going anywhere.

She pulled back, breathless, her eyes sparkling. She was beautiful.

"Hello to you, too," he said at last, his voice rougher than usual. She gave a small smile in response, then caressed his cheek with her warm hand, teasing his nose with the jasmine lemon aroma from her wrist. She studied his face as if searching for something. After a moment, she pulled back her hand and checked the area around the car so she could pull away. What was that about? He wanted to ask her, but it could be only one thing, the same thought that dominated his every waking moment. Would she stay here or come join him in the Julemarked?

"What's the plan for tonight?"

He'd keep the conversation neutral. She'd talk when she was ready. Astra took a deep breath.

"We have options . . . ice-skating, Candy Cane Lane, Zorbing. You can pick."

"Zorbing? Is that what the kids are calling it these days?" Jack said.

Astra gave a low laugh and glanced at him as if wishing that was what Zorbing really was.

"Sadly, no, it's a giant inflatable ball that you roll around in on ice. But maybe we can start a new trend."

"What do you want to do?" Jack asked Astra.

"I don't know. All of them could be fun. Skating—a bit cliché, but classic for a reason. With the Zorbing, that might not be smart with your nausea. The third is Candy Cane Lane. It's several blocks where the neighborhood goes all out with Christmas decorations to raise money for charity. It's very festive."

Jack appreciated that she thought about what might make the spinning sensation he experienced worse. While it had gotten less problematic because he had been leaving the Julemarked so often, he didn't want to risk it.

"You really don't care?" Jack asked. Astra shook her head. "Then I vote lights. We can ice-skate anytime on the pond."

"Candy Cane Lane it is. We should stop for some hot drinks."

"Already prepared," Jack said, pointing to the bag on the floor. "Though you won't be able to drink it and drive."

"My favorite kind. We'll park and walk."

They drove the twenty minutes into nearby West Allis, where Astra got lucky with parking on a side street. Cars formed long lines in every direction, some parking and walking like they were, but most stayed in the car and drove up and down the streets, bumper to bumper. It had snowed last night, leaving a clean blanket over everything. It was too nice to stay cooped up in a car.

While Astra made sure her hat and scarf were secure, her car was locked, and her phone was in her pocket, Jack took a moment to appreciate his surroundings. Every house sparkled with Christmas lights and decorations. Astra herself seemed to glow. Seeing her somewhere other than her house or the Julemarked gave another facet to her, a side she'd be giving up if she moved into the Julemarked. That sacrifice wasn't lost on him. He knew he was asking a lot of her.

"You are beautiful," Jack said, kissing her softly on the cheek.

"That's always nice to hear," Astra said. She stepped closer so she could kiss him on the lips, her cold nose touching his cheek, sending jolts to every part of his body. Would this feeling ever stop? He always wanted to be touching her, kissing her, seeing her, tasting her. It took all he had to pull back. It was either that or get in the car and steam up the windows.

Jack handed her one of the thermoses he had brought, both filled with hot coffee and spiked with a minty alcohol. Astra took a sip, looking at him over the top of her thermos.

"Mmm. Peppermint schnapps?"

"The Pedersens make it, Ani's parents."

"I like the Pedersens."

"So does my mom. She's been trying to push Ani and me together for years."

"I was wondering about that at dinner. Ani seems lovely," Astra said.

"If that was going to happen, it would have a long time ago."

"What didn't work?"

As they walked along the sidewalk, enjoying the lights and Christmas music piping from car windows and hidden speakers, Jack thought about it.

"That's a good question. She's very nice, pretty, but we didn't have that spark when you meet someone and suddenly you have to know more about that person. Maybe it's because we've known each other all our lives."

"Did you have that when we first met?"

Jack smiled as he remembered back to that day, unsure how to answer her. He didn't want to influence her memories when they reemerged, but he also wanted to be completely open with her.

"Not really." Honesty was always the best policy.

"What? It wasn't love at first sight?" Astra's dimple flickered to life as she teased him. Relief washed over him.

"You were very young at the time and called me Santa's younger brother."

"I'm sure I meant to say 'hot younger brother.'"

Astra took another drink of her coffee as she thought of something else to ask. That's how they'd been spending their time, hours-long conversations about everything. Sometimes about his family and growing up in the Julemarked, or about her family and friends and job. Except Trent—but he had to know what went wrong.

"What happened with your marriage?" Jack asked.

Astra rolled her eyes.

"Ugh. The short version is he left me. The longer version is we weren't right for one another and he was the one who had the balls to do something about it."

"If you don't mind me asking, what wasn't right?"

"Probably a million things that added up, but the biggest was I wanted kids and he didn't. It created a cycle where I was angry, he was guilty, but neither of us would change our mind. Now he's like a stone in my shoe that I can't get out."

"Do you still want kids?"

Jack mentally crossed his fingers.

"I do." Astra's eyes became unfocused as she looked into the distance.

"What is it?"

"Would I stop aging if I became a resident?"

Astra looked away and wiped at her eyes. She took a deep breath and an even deeper drink of her coffee. Was wanting children the key to Astra's decision? He felt uncomfortable with how much he wanted to dangle it before her, to nudge her into his arms. Before he could answer, she asked another question.

"What if you left? Would you age faster, or simply age at the same rate as me?"

"I'm not going to leave." He said the words before he even had time to consider them, an instinctual response like yanking your hand away when it touches a hot baking sheet; his body knew how to respond before his brain did.

Astra stopped walking and stared at him, her eyes narrowed and lips pressed into a frown.

"I'm not asking you to, but now I know you won't even consider it. I have been consumed with weighing the pros and cons of moving to the Julemarked, deciding if I can live with abandoning my friends and family, my career, maybe even my dog if I can't sneak her away from Trent, and you won't even pause for half a second to consider doing the same?"

"It's different for me." His nausea surged up and burned his throat. "You're basically asking me to die for you."

"You aren't immortal; it will happen eventually no matter where you live. Maybe knowing you don't have hundreds of years will make the moments you do have more valuable. Like tonight, this might be the last time you'll see me, so you should cherish every damn second."

Astra's eyes sparked with fire and tears. She started walking again, and he moved to keep up with her or risk being separated by the other people on the sidewalk. Watching her walk away from him made him more nauseous than the Outside ever had.

"Astra, you're right. I'm sorry. It's an option and unfair of me to not consider it."

He reached for her elbow, but she stopped again and pulled him out of the flow of people, a few of whom were giving them second and third glances, but he didn't care. There was too much at stake.

"This hasn't been easy for me. I'm trying to understand feelings for you that I have no memory of creating, only some fuzzy dreams and faint memories. Maybe if I remembered everything it would be different, but this is too hard and you're asking too much. I can't do this anymore. I need to move on with my life and stop hoping for a magical solution to my problems. Hope leads to disaster and my life is the evidence."

"Astra, please, no. I'm sorry. You say hope leads to disaster, but I say from disaster comes hope. You were married and I thought I'd never learn your name. Now I know you love sea turtles and snorkeling, you're fiercely devoted to your friends, and you take your coffee with a lot of cream but will add sugar when the mood strikes. Before you, I didn't think life could get better; a great family, the best home, and so much time to enjoy my life. What more could I want? You've upended my world and become woven into every part of it. I can't carve a nisse without thinking about what might amuse you. Every time I make a kringle, I wonder if you'll like it. I never want to look at the stars again without you to guide my gaze. Please, Astra, don't say no. At least give me until Christmas Eve."

Astra's cheeks gleamed with tears. Jack felt a cold trail down his own cheek. He'd never been afraid, and now everything hung in the balance of her next words. Under the glow of a million Christmas lights, he tried to interpret the emotions darting across her face, each disappearing as the next one took its place, until she nodded and wiped away her tears.

"Enough of that for now," Astra said. Jack wasn't sure what decision she had come to, but at least she wasn't trying to leave. "We've come to my favorite house."

She pointed to an enormous oak that towered over the street—every inch of it covered in warm white lights, like stars that had come to earth. Astra took out her phone.

"We need a picture of this," she said.

She held out the phone in front of them and pulled him close so their cheeks touched—hers were still damp—then clicked the button.

"We need more pictures of us," Astra said, holding the phone up for him to see. He couldn't take his eyes off her face in the picture. Her lashes were still a bit dewy, her cheeks flushed. Did she want more pictures because she wanted to cherish this fleeting time with him? She was right; with his long life, he had become complacent, forgetting to treasure important moments, always assuming there would be more. Tonight proved that was no guarantee, and he wouldn't make that mistake again.

Chapter Twenty-Five

WITH ALL THE WILD THOUGHTS WHIRLING IN ASTRA'S HEAD the next day, and still a little angry with Jack—though the man could give a pretty apology—she decided to walk from her house to the Julemarked, about three miles. She needed the time. With only a few days before Christmas Eve, she needed to make a decision. Even without her memories, she couldn't deny her escalating feelings for Jack, much more than mere attraction or even affection. But she wasn't being hyperbolic with what she had said last night. At this stage, he was asking too much of her, especially without even considering doing the same for her. That was all she was asking, to talk about it, discuss the possibilities. Walking through the streets, she passed rows of houses, shops, and restaurants, catching glimpses of familiar faces as she trudged through the wet snow. Christmas trees sparkled through windows, plastic reindeer and inflatable snowmen kept watch over the snowy afternoon, and cars sloppily zoomed past her on the busy street with a whoosh.

Despite her misgivings, the universe had never spoken more

clearly to Astra. Earlier, she had spent an hour yanking a hair clog the size of a gluttonous rat from her tub drain. The bathroom stench was so awful, she had to light candles all over the house to hide the odor. When she brought the garbage out to the garage, she noticed ice building up along her gutters from the thawing and freezing snow. If she didn't get that cleared up soon, it could cause water damage. That was on top of the old furnace and air conditioner, which would need replacing soon. She loved her little house, but something always needed to be fixed or replaced.

So, yes, the idea of leaving all that behind held some appeal in the short term. If she really did go, what happened? Jack assured her they had someone who would handle all her loose ends, but it didn't feel right to leave all that work to this contact. If she was going to leave, she should pack up what she wanted to bring with her; there were things she would want.

She needed Bernie. It wouldn't be her time with Bernie until after Christmas. She'd have to get Trent out of his house so she could sneak in and take her. That was the only thing Astra was certain of. Wherever she was going, Bernie was coming with her.

Astra stepped off the curb and her foot landed on a small patch of snow-covered ice, but instead of slipping, it broke through the ice into the pothole beneath, soaking her foot in icy water up to the ankle. Saturating her sock instantly, the water squished when she took the next step, but she couldn't slow her pace to assess the damage or she risked becoming Milwaukee roadkill.

The universe was telling her to leave.

And would that be so awful? She didn't see her parents all that often, her friends had loving families or were living their best lives, like Ronnie. They'd each given their blessing to her in their own way. The library didn't really need her. A part of her regretted not being there for Steph's and Cassie's families, but if she wanted to have a family of her own, this was probably her best chance. Living in the Julemarked would give her the time she needed. But was she ready to commit to someone after spending so little time together? The potential was definitely there, but her logical, research-oriented brain couldn't accept twenty-four days as enough time to fall in love, to know a person, to make a huge decision.

One way would continue the life she'd become disappointed in. The other seemed greener, well paved, and hung with colorful Christmas lights.

Astra crossed another street, her wet foot becoming more and more uncomfortable with each step. It had started rubbing against the back of her shoe and she knew she'd have a blister by the time she reached the Julemarked. Another blemish on staying.

As she turned a corner, she bumped into a man wearing a red knit hat, exactly like the ones she had bought years earlier at her first Christmas market weekend with the girls. In a rush, she pictured Jack wearing the same hat. But it wasn't just a picture; it was a memory. She leaned up against the building she had been walking past as the forgotten memories slammed into her.

Astra had pointed at the cherry kringle in the case, the one with the thickest layer of glaze. "That one, please," she said. The words came out softer than intended, but the man across the glass pastry case was handsome, even if he was a little old for her. His blue-green eyes twinkled as if he knew what she was thinking; she kept glancing into them as she surveyed the case. When he didn't respond to her right away, Ronnie leaned in and whispered, "Looks like there's more on the menu than just kringle."

"Shut up," Astra said. She turned back to him. His dark blond hair was straight and hung in his eyes, like he'd gone too long between haircuts. Astra pointed again at the cherry slice. "One cherry, please."

Ronnie leaned in again. "Flirt with him. He's clearly into you."

The man had starting packing up their slices.

"Fine," she whispered back, clearly louder than she meant to, because the man's head tilted as if listening.

Looking him in the face—God, those cheekbones would make a sculptor weep—and already cringing at how stupid she was about to sound, she said, "I bought a pack of five hats." She pointed to her head, at the red knit hat perched there. "And I have an extra one. Would you like it?"

On what planet was this flirting? She wanted to push an Undo button and try again. Steph's and Cassie's giggling behind her didn't help.

The man looked down at his hands, which were full of kringle and sticky with frosting, and leaned his head over the bakery case so it was within her reach. Oh my God, she was going to touch him. Her heart beat faster as she slid the hat over his dark blond hair, making sure to pull it down far enough in the back so it wouldn't pop off, careful that it was on securely so it didn't fall into the pastries. When she pulled her hands back, he straightened and smiled.

"How do I look?" he said.

Like a hot Santa.

Astra hoped her smile would cover up her blushing at the thought.

He was older than she'd normally notice, but handsome in a time-less way.

"Like Santa's younger brother."

"If I'm going to accept this, then you need to accept something from me." He looked around the bakery, then grabbed a small gnome from a shelf, its large nose sticking out the bottom of a pointy red hat. "Here's a nisse."

"Knees—oo?" she said, trying to use the same pronunciation he used. He had a slight Scandinavian accent, but it became more obvious when he said the word.

"Yep. Spelled n-i-s-s-e. Or with an R at the end if there are more than one; that's pronounced knees-ah. They are the Danish Christmas elves. We have to give them rice pudding on Christmas Eve or they cause all sorts of mischief."

He gave her a gnome and she gave him a knitted hat. Was this the most ridiculous flirtation ever? She didn't care. She only wished she could spend the rest of the day listening to him talk about Danish Christmas elves in that—she knew now—Danish accent. Swoon.

"Nisse." She said the word with more confidence, holding the small wood figurine in the palm of her hand. The customers behind them were getting antsy and Ronnie was giving them dirty looks. She better get them out of here before Ronnie decided words were needed. "Thank you. I'll make sure he gets his rice pudding." Her eyes sparkled as she smiled at him. She'd have to look up Danish Christmas traditions so she could talk to him about it next year—because they were definitely coming back here.

"Jack," one of the other men growled. Jack. She knew his name. She said it a few times to herself. Jack. Jack. Jack. She didn't want to

forget it. Jack slipped the slices into the bag, then handed it to the other man, whom they needed to pay. She scooted to the register and handed over the cash. Before walking out the door, she looked over her shoulder one last time and Jack gave his head a little nod so the white pom-pom on top bobbled. She couldn't help but be smitten.

Still leaning against the building, Astra struggled to find her breath. The memories kept coming. She remembered the polka with Jack and the way his arms felt as they danced, the year he bought her hot chocolate. She remembered how her heart seemed to recognize him every year even though her brain hadn't—an invisible string that kept tugging her back to the Julemarked, to him. She had known he was the one who gave her the nisser, but now she remembered receiving every single one. She couldn't believe the history they had together, which was all coming to her in one long rush. She hadn't just been falling in love with Jack for the last month; she'd been falling in love with him for fifteen years.

Jack didn't even pause as he stepped under the Julemarked arch, letting the wave of nausea roll through him without slowing his pace. Astra had said she would be visiting today, but she was late. Had she changed her mind after their argument last night? Had she been injured? For once in his life, he wished he had one of those phones so he could talk to her instantly. He had to find her.

He'd made it as far as the Riverwalk along the Milwaukee River when he saw her coming toward him, almost a block away. Relief flooded him. She had decided to walk instead of take a cab or borrow a car. When she saw him, she frowned, but also waved. What did that mean? Was she unhappy to see him? As she took a few more steps in his direction, he noticed a slight limp in her gait. He ran the rest of the way to her.

"How did you get hurt?" Jack said at the same time that Astra said, "What are you doing out here?"

The both started to explain at the same time.

"I'm so sorry. I wasn't being fair. Let's talk about all the options, work this through together. I love you," Jack said.

"I remember. Everything. I remember meeting you, trying to flirt with you, dancing with you. I remember," Astra said.

Jack stopped talking.

"You remember?" he asked, but he didn't need her to answer; he could see it on her face. As if waking up from an enchanted sleep, she was looking at him with knowing eyes.

She remembered.

Astra nodded.

"I'll explain it in detail later, but I have to say something first. Well, two somethings." She took both his hands in hers. "I love you, Jack Clausen. I love that you taught me the proper way to pronounce 'nisse' the first time we met, then kept finding ways to give them to me. I love that you read *Outlander* because we talked about it. I love that you made a kringle for me that combined my two favorite flavors—at least I'm assuming that was for me because I've never seen it in the case."

"It was." Jack grinned.

"Most importantly, I love that you didn't give up on us. Over the years, and last night. Which brings me to the second thing I need to tell you. Yes, Jack, I would love to live in the Julemarked with you. My friends and parents want me to be happy; they'll understand. I'm sure we'll find ways to see them occasionally. It'll be like we're living in Antarctica and connecting is more difficult, but not impossible."

Jack's heart soared, and more than a little comforted that he wouldn't have to live on the Outside, enough that he could ignore the flash of sadness when Astra mentioned leaving her friends and parents, he vowed to make it up to her. He lifted her into his arms, holding her tight against his body, and kissed her, letting the familiar press of her soft lips create more memories for the both of them.

When the kiss slowed, he set her down but didn't let her go.

"I have a favor to ask," Astra said.

"Anything."

"Can I invite the girls to the bakery for some kringle lessons?"

Jack smiled and kissed her again, hoping his answer was clear. He'd give her the stars from the sky if she asked for them.

Chapter Twenty-Six

GATHERED AROUND THE GIANT ISLAND IN THE KITCHEN OF Kringle All the Way stood Astra, Ronnie, Cassie, and Steph, wearing white aprons. All four of them watched Jack, who held a blob of dough in front of him and explained how to roll it out into a kringle shape. Cassie studied the kitchen as if looking for something out of the ordinary. Steph seemed tired, with circles under her eyes. Her in-laws were staying with them before the holidays, adding to the regular stress of this time of year for a mother of three. Astra had begged her to come tonight, even though her husband was on a ski trip. Steph's in-laws could watch the kids so she could have a night out. She wanted one more night with them before she left. She'd let them all know that if she left, she'd leave them letters saying goodbye. Doing it in person would involve too many tears. With choices like this, it was best to look forward and not backward.

"Let's go to the cooler and you can pick out what flavor you want to make," Jack said.

Jack herded them into a large walk-in fridge, where they each found a flavor for their kringle. Jack handed Astra a tub of cherry filling and a can of almond paste, and she loved that he knew her, but maybe she could be unpredictable. She was completely changing her life, so why not be adventurous in her flavors, too? Still holding the tub of cherry and the almond paste, she grabbed the first thing in front of her, a bowl of magenta jelly.

"Really, that's what you're going with? Do you even know what it is?" Jack whispered in her ear, sending a tingle down her spine.

"No, I do not." But she held her head high and walked out of the cooler.

They proceeded to roll out their dough according to Jack's instructions, while Astra kept thinking about Jack's hands and where they had been lately. After yesterday's big decision, she'd spent the night (and most of the morning) in Jack's cozy cottage. He'd promised it could easily be expanded if and when they needed more space, then proceeded to show her why they might need more rooms.

"You're doing it wrong," Jack said to Astra. He wrapped his arms around her to set his hands over hers on the rolling pin, his lips kissing up her neck to her ear. "Like this," he whispered. Astra closed her eyes and leaned into the teasing kisses, a promise of what was to come later.

Across the table, Ronnie started poking holes in her dough with the end of the rolling pin.

"Hey, I think I'm doing it wrong, too," she said, a wolfish grin on her face.

"I've got this, bro." Mads stood in the doorway watching the mayhem. He pulled an apron off a hook and quickly tied it behind his back as he walked to Ronnie. A few inches taller than him, she looked down into his charming smile.

"You'll do."

"How many of you are there?" Cassie said, looking out the door. "Do we each get a brother?"

They all laughed, Mads a little harder than the rest, knowing that Orn and Carl were knee-deep in their wives and kids at the moment.

Mads helped Ronnie fix her dough and they all filled and shaped the kringle.

"What flavor am I using?" Astra whispered to Mads when Jack was busy showing Steph how to transfer her kringle to a baking sheet with a parchment paper sling.

Mads looked in the bowl.

"Guava. Bold choice and one of my favorites. Put some cream cheese in the glaze. Trust me."

"Thanks." She smiled at him.

"You're good for him, you know. He's been lonely for a long time, but he won't admit it."

"I find it hard to believe he would have a hard time finding women who are interested in him."

"You know it can't be just anyone. He had settled into a pretty deep rut without noticing it. You were the change he needed to climb out. But he doesn't really understand what giving up the Outside means." He looked around the island at her friends. "Be sure. Understand?"

Astra watched Jack laugh with Steph and Cassie as they teased Ronnie about her wildly misshapen oval. Somehow it looked more like a fish a child would draw. Joining the Julemarked would mean more than just ignoring her friends like she had when she was married; it would be leaving them. At best seeing them once every few years. At worst, much longer, or maybe never. If no one was sure how the magic worked, it was possible she would become a hazy memory to them. But being with Jack felt more right than ever. She knew her friends would understand if she followed her heart.

"I do," Astra responded. Mads squeezed her shoulder, then walked around the island to help Ronnie. Steph took the chance to walk around the table to stand by Astra. They both had finished their kringle and slid them onto the baking cart, ready for the oven.

"He's lovely," Steph said. "He keeps looking at you when he thinks you won't notice." She paused and Jack looked up in their direction and smiled when he realized he was caught. "Like that."

"It's the swoony phase." Astra shrugged it off, though even Jack's short glance made her heart flutter.

"We both know that's a lie. This is more than that. Change is afoot. I can smell it."

"Are you sure it's not the kringle?"

Steph was always good at knowing when something big was about to happen. She had called Cassie's pregnancy before she had even conceived, taking a glass of wine from her and handing her a glass of water with a simple "trust me." Maybe magic wasn't limited just to the alley.

Steph brushed a stray strand of hair away from Astra's face.

"You have a big decision coming, I think." Steph looked at her more closely. "Or maybe you've already made it. I hope you're following your heart and that you know we will always support you and be there when you need us."

"I know." Astra squeezed Steph's hands, her voice rough as she held back her tears. Steph knew. This was their goodbye. The only goodbye they'd get. "I love you all so much."

That was all she trusted herself to say. She would miss this. Being able to physically touch Steph, see Ronnie's mischievous expressions, watch Cassie master any skill faster than the rest of them. Cassie and Ronnie looked up to see Astra and Steph holding hands, and before Astra could blink, they had both crossed the kitchen and enveloped her in a hug. No words needed to be spoken. They'd never held back their words before, so there was nothing left to be said, only the physical connection needed to convey their love for one another. A circle of friendship that would never break, no matter how far apart they were.

This journey was ending as it had begun, with the smell of pastry and her friends by her side at the Julemarked.

Chapter Twenty-Seven

> On my way to the Julemarked. I put the presents for the
> kiddos under the tree.

Astra texted Steph and Cassie. She'd promised the kids their
presents and she wasn't going to let them down. Steph replied
right away.

> I'm going to miss you.

She would miss Steph and the kids, too, but they'd said their
goodbyes last night and today was all mad-dash preparations.

Earlier in the day, she'd packed a few boxes of things she
wanted to take with her, like her nisser, family photos, and favorite clothes. Jack had assured her that John, their Outside contact, would put everything else in storage until she could go
through her things the next time they showed up in Milwaukee.
She'd written long letters to her parents and the library and left

them in the kitchen. John would deliver them before handling the house. The girls would step in to help with her parents.

Walking into the Julemarked, Bernie pranced by her side. Astra had waited an hour outside Trent's house for him to leave; then she used a spare key she had swiped from Trent to free her beautiful girl. She took deep breaths, letting the scent of cinnamon and pine seep in to ease her tense muscles. The stores stayed open late on Christmas Eve for the last-minute shoppers and people coming by with their families for an extra jolt of holiday cheer.

Outside Kringle All the Way, she tapped on the window to get Jack's attention and waved at the other brothers. Jack took off his apron and grabbed a sweater before leaving the shop and joining her in the alley.

"Please tell me you haven't changed your mind?" he asked.

Astra looked into those sparkling aqua eyes and reached up a hand to push back his hair, which fell over his eyes, something she'd wanted to do that first time they had met. She pulled his mouth down to meet hers, their lips brushing against one another in the faintest of kisses.

"Just try to get rid of me," she said. He pulled her tight against him. Being this close felt so right. This was what the future felt like. Bernie gave a little yip, having been patient enough waiting for his attention. Astra understood.

When Jack pulled back, his eyes gleamed and he cleared his throat, giving Bernie's ears a scratch.

"You'll quickly learn, there are no free rides," he said to Astra. "Time to come help."

Both of them grinning wide, he led her into the bakery, taking her coat and handing her an apron, bringing Bernie to the small office in the back with a bowl of water. Mads and Carl smiled at her; even Orn couldn't hide a small grin.

"Mom is going to freak," Mads said, giving her a quick kiss on the check. "Welcome to the family."

Astra was trying not to think too hard about their mom. Given all the challenges they'd overcome, she was confident she could win her over. She had the time now.

"We aren't married. I'm sure there's more to it than changing my address."

"Not much. Once an Outsider moves in with one of us, a wedding is only a formality."

"There's no pressure," Jack said.

Astra took her place at the counter, grabbing slices and sliding them into bags, only bumping into Jack three times, though she suspected he was doing it on purpose. It was nearing midnight as the crowds thinned and the pastry case emptied. Jack and Astra stayed up front to clean out the pastry case while the brothers scrubbed the kitchen. Bernie had escaped her office jail and was sniffing in the corners for crumbs, her leash dragging behind her. Since it was one of the few nights they didn't need to make giant batches of kringle dough for the next morning, no one was in a rush to finish their chores.

The door jingled open and Astra looked up to tell the customer they were closed, but stopped when she saw who it was. Bernie was already on her way as official greeter.

"Ronnie?"

Ronnie breathed heavily—her face sweaty from exertion.

She held up a finger, letting them know she'd speak in a second. Astra's heart thumped. This couldn't be good. Ronnie never breathed that hard unless there was a man involved.

"This fucking alley and its lack of reception," she finally said. Took one more deep breath. "It's Steph's husband. He's at the hospital, it doesn't look good, a bad accident at the ski hill. She just called me. I'm on my way to her house. Cassie is going to the hospital to see what she can do. That's all I know."

Ronnie's eyes flicked to the clock on the wall. Eleven fifty. She continued.

"Steph didn't want me to come, but I knew you'd want to know. Before you leave. I've never heard her so overwhelmed."

Astra could hear what Ronnie was saying in between the words. Steph needed them. All of them. This was an all-hands-on-deck situation. Just like when Trent left her. Steph, Ronnie, and Cassie had moved in for a week to take care of her. Astra looked from Jack to Ronnie, then back. Her past and future were incompatible because they couldn't exist in the present together. Jack must have seen her decision because he took a step toward her, but she held up a hand to stop him.

"Take Bernie," Astra said to Ronnie.

That was all Ronnie needed to hear. She grabbed Bernie's leash in one hand and pointed to the clock.

"Seven minutes. I'll be waiting in my car. Sorry, Jack."

And she was gone. Astra turned to Jack and they closed the distance to each other.

"No." He whispered as his forehead touched her own. "No. No. No."

She didn't want him to convince her to stay; she didn't even want him to try. Cupping his face in her hands, she sent all her love and wonderment that he existed, hoping he would understand.

Midnight was fast approaching when Jack and Astra left the bakery, Jack not bothering to put on his sweater, choosing to ignore the cold as he walked her to the arch in only a T-shirt and jeans.

The surety of her decision made moments ago had become less so. Did she really want to give up this incredible man who loved her? Who she'd recognized as someone special when they first met?

"Stay," Jack said, his hands holding her face inches from his. "Stay." He pulled her even closer, his sugar-and-coffee-scented breath mingling with her own before touching his forehead to hers, as if willing all his love to pour through that physical connection. "Be with me. Marry me."

Astra's heart thumped with the thrill of those words, the idea of moving here with him. Traitorous heart. The future she'd almost had. Every day would have been perfect. Filled with joy and hope and Christmas cheer. She could envision herself helping out at the bookstore with Old Johan, setting up a library for the residents, having story times to entertain children while their parents shopped. Living a long, happy life with this remarkable man whom she'd fallen in love with over the span of several years, but also all at once. And now he was asking to be hers forever. His love seared her everywhere their skin touched.

She wanted this. She wanted him. Her arms wrapped around him, her lips completing their inevitable connection. He took it as a yes and pulled her in closer, their bodies all but one in the dark archway of the Julemarked. Astra soaked in the sensations, the rightness of his lips on hers, his hands gravitating to where she wanted to be touched. She wanted to let their passion take control, but she wasn't a young woman anymore. She understood there was more to life than passion and living for your one perfect soul mate. She knew wants weren't always what she needed. She needed her friends just like they needed her. She needed the immediacy of a ticking clock that gave life meaning. It took her less than a moment of Steph needing her to change her mind. Three loves of her life outweighed one.

She hoped the remembering would be enough for them both.

She broke off the kiss and nudged him back. In the dark, the Christmas lights reflected off his eyes, stars contained in her entire universe—and she could see the excitement bursting from them. The anticipation of getting everything he ever wanted.

"No," Astra said.

He blinked. Astra watched Jack try to insert that word into what he knew to be true—that they were destined to be together. To live decades, maybe centuries, in the holiday paradise of the Julemarked. Comprehension struggled to take hold. He gave his head a little shake, hoping that would straighten out the facts.

"No?" he finally said.

"No," she repeated. His face crumpled. He couldn't deny that clarity—now Astra needed to make him understand. "I can't leave them again. I can't give up everyone in my life for one person. Steph needs me."

"She has Ronnie and Cassie."

Astra shook her head.

"I need to be there. I can't be there for my friends when I'm lost in time."

"You can still see them . . ."

"It's not the same. Steph has never let me down. I won't let her down. Not this time. I need to be there for them every day. I won't let them down again."

Jack's face turned to stone; shoving aside his feelings, he searched for logic that might work to keep her by his side since emotional pleas had failed.

"Everything is here. What more could you want? We don't get sick, we live long lives with those we love. We could have children."

That pulled at her heart. Above all else, that was something she yearned for.

"This isn't an easy choice for me. I never thought I'd meet someone like you. Staying here would be a dream, but Steph needs me. We can always see each other next Milwaukee Yule." But she knew the words were a lie as they drifted off into the night like a dirty snowflake—pretty but tainted. She couldn't bear to see him again after this. It would be too hard not to fall into his arms and beg to stay, growing old while he basically stayed the same magical age. He knew the truth, too. In unison, their hearts cracked like a frozen river during the spring thaw, seismic shifts pushing and pulling until at last they broke apart and floated down the river. Tears left icy paths down her checks before falling onto her red down coat. It was nearly midnight on Christmas Eve.

"I want more time," Jack said. Pulling her tight, having accepted the truth of what she was saying, though still wishing it weren't so, he clung to the one thing he had left for a few moments—her. The clock hanging above the entrance bonged as the hand finally clicked onto the twenty-five, the first sound it had made all season. It only had one purpose. A final alert to the residents that this Yule was ending and Nulstil was about to begin.

It bonged again.

She kissed him, pouring all the regrets she'd feel for the rest of her life into their embrace. The wish for a different path, the dream of a different future. He kissed her back. Memorizing the way her soft lips yielded to his, then rallied and returned the same. Their salty tears mingled, cold against their cheeks. She was no longer sure who was crying more.

Bong.

Gasps broke the kiss, their sealed lips no longer able to keep the sadness at bay. She needed more air to fight, more air to keep this last sweet connection going as long as possible, searing every sensation into her memory so she'd at least have that during a lifetime of lonely nights.

Bong.

It wasn't too late. She could change her mind. Her friends would know what happened. They'd understand. She could send them a note from wherever the Julemarked was next. She'd be able to sort out her affairs from afar. With gusto, she renewed their kiss, exploring the possibilities of staying by his side. Of not having to end this tonight, or ever.

Bong.

She remembered Steph and her three goofy kids. Steph would need extra hands to alleviate the burden, allow her to support her husband during his recovery, allow her to take care of him without neglecting her kids. Astra was the extra hands. The auntie who could take them for hours to the library for story time and crafts and secret hot chocolate that they promised not to tell their mom about even though they'd arrive home with chocolate mustaches that Steph pretended not to see. The auntie who could move into the spare bedroom in the basement so she could be there when the girls looked for their mom in the middle of the night when she had to take her husband to the hospital for surgeries.

Bong.

Astra broke off the kiss, placing her hands on his face, still inches away from her own. "No regrets. You made me feel like me again. I will never forget you and I will always love you. Always. But . . ."

Jack nodded. "I understand. You love me like I love you, but it isn't meant to be. True love comes in many forms, and there's no denying the love between you and your friends. I wouldn't dream of taking you from that, no matter how much I wish I could. I'll wait, if you want me to. Maybe things will be different in a few years?"

Hope mingled with heartbreak as the idea occurred to them. It didn't have to end forever.

Bong.

Except it did. She knew hope only led to doom. That would just be delaying the heartbreak. Leaving her friends would be even more painful than leaving him. She knew, she'd done it once before, slowly, over time. Each encounter had felt like a fresh knife wound to the barely healing scar. If she wasn't heartbroken over permanently leaving him, she'd be devastated by leaving her friends.

Bong.

No, it was best to rip the bandage now, set the bone, replace the knee. It would be excruciating, but the worst would be over. She didn't want every future encounter with Jack or her friends to be tinged with future doom, knowing one of them would be ending, and never being certain exactly which.

Bong.

Pulling him tighter, she knew this was it. The last kiss, the last touch. The last chime was approaching and then their time would be completely gone. The sand out of the hourglass. There was no more time left to figure out how to stop it. His hands grazed her hips as her lips found his in one last whisper of a kiss, a memory for them both to share, a dream to savor. Sweet like the first bite of kringle, making her want more. But not this time.

Bong.

With strength she didn't know she had, she stepped back away from him, through the archway, leaving the warmth of the Julemarked and his arms, and into the blustery real world. She couldn't keep looking at him, his arms still outstretched because she had been so recently encircled by them. It was too tempting to run back into them. As the snow fell like a gauzy curtain between them, she spun on the icy sidewalk so her back was to him.

Bong.

She took a deep breath. An icy wind tore through her thick coat, finding the gaps in the zipper, and the updraft under the bottom, the cracks at her wrists where her gloves met the sleeves, chilling her. She stared out at the quiet Christmas market, a few vendors finally packing up their shops until next year—ready to go home and celebrate Christmas, the cleaners emptying garbage cans and collecting unwanted mugs, their owners not wanting to take the memories of the market merriment back home. Astra understood. Could she ever come to another Christmas market?

Bong.

She turned for one last look at Jack, at the alternate future she might have had, but the black wrought-iron gate was already gone, replaced by an unbroken brick wall, no evidence that it was anything more, recent visitors already starting to forget about the wonderful shops until next year. But she would never forget, not again. Pulling a glove from her hand, she set her bare skin against the rough brick, a dark gray in the dim light, the rough texture not quite cold, having not been there long enough to soak up a chill. She envisioned Jack on the other side, his hand a mirror of her own. She poured her love into the invisible connection, praying it would see them through this. See them to a different, but happy future.

She looked up at the sky, one star fighting its way through the ambient city light to greet Christmas. She knew it wasn't the official Christmas star, but she'd like to think Jack was looking at it, too, and thinking of her, his Christmas star.

Chapter Twenty-Eight

Astra got into Ronnie's car, heat blasting. Bernie, sensing something wasn't right, tried to weasel her way onto Astra's lap.

"Not now, girl."

Ronnie squeezed Astra's hand.

"Want to talk about it?"

"Nope. Let's get to Steph."

During the twenty-minute drive from downtown to Steph's house, Astra focused on her breathing and what was most important. Steph. By the time they arrived, she had dried her tears and filled her spine with steel. When they rang the doorbell, she heard light footsteps running to the door and saw a tiny face peeking out the window. She waved at Steph's littlest one—five-year-old Annie, in her jammies.

Annie opened the door and squealed, "Bernie."

Bernie reciprocated Annie's enthusiasm with kisses, followed by Annie's giggles. When the greeting was complete, Bernie moved past Annie in search of the other children.

"Mommy said to tell you to go to her bedroom. We get to watch Disney for as long as we want. We're going to catch Santa."

"Lucky," Astra said. Ronnie closed and locked the door behind them. Astra kissed the top of Annie's head before going up the stairs. Ronnie simply patted it. "Thanks, bug." The door to Steph and Rob's room was closed, so she tapped on the wood and opened it slowly.

Inside, Steph's bed was covered with clothes and an open duffel bag, where she put things in and took things out, then put them in again.

"I don't know what to pack for him. Will he need pajamas? A book? Will he need underwear? And for how long? What about shaving?"

Steph turned toward the door, noticed Astra's unexpected presence. She gulped some air and covered her mouth, eyes filling with tears.

"What are you doing here? I told Ronnie not to tell you. You're supposed to be getting your happily ever after." She tried to shove Astra toward the door as if the decision to stay could be undone. Astra took the wadded-up T-shirt out of Steph's hand and wrapped herself around Steph, who finally let her worry and sadness swallow her.

"I couldn't. Not while yours is being threatened," Astra whispered to her.

"I'm not sorry I told her. You would have done the same for Astra," Ronnie said, then wrapped her arms around the both of them.

"What if he doesn't make it? I can't do this without him," Steph said when the tears had slowed enough for her to speak.

"What happened?" Astra said.

"I don't know. His friend used Rob's phone to call. Told me which hospital and that they are prepping him for emergency surgery. I called Cassie and she's doing her thing." They all knew that Cassie was ordering surgeons and nurses around like a general to make sure everything went smoothly. "He said something about dodging a little kid and boxes. That fool was probably on the terrain park. I told him he was too old for that." Steph paused. "What am I going to do?"

Astra took Steph's hands in hers. It was hard to see her ultra-organized dear friend fall apart. Steph was the one who always knew what to do next.

"This is what we're going to do. We're going to pack this bag with a few days' worth of things for both of you. You're going to go to the hospital with Ronnie, and Cassie will get you up to speed on what is happening. I'm going to stay here with Annie, Logan, and Maria. When you know what's happening, call me. Until then, do not worry about the kids, no matter how long it takes."

"I can't ask you to do that."

"You aren't asking. We're telling," Ronnie said.

Astra looked down at the bed, where Steph had laid out some clothes.

"I don't think he'll need his khakis," Astra said.

With Astra and Ronnie's guidance, they got a bag packed with clothes, books, and chargers.

"Do you want me to play Santa?" Astra whispered in case one of the kids had wandered near the door.

"Oh my God, I completely forgot," Steph cried. "I can't believe this is happening. Please. Everything is wrapped in our closet. Everything's labeled."

Astra would expect nothing less from Steph. Steph looked ready to cry again.

"Take pictures," she said.

"I'll do one better—I'll film them opening their stockings and they'll wait to open the presents until you get home."

"We can't make them wait," Steph said.

"You are not missing Christmas morning with your kids, even if it takes place in a few days. I've got this."

After Ronnie bustled Steph into the car, Astra found the kids wide-eyed in front of the television, buried under blankets on the huge L-shaped couch, Bernie nestled between them like a protective mother duck. It was hours past their bedtime, but it was clear they didn't want to miss a second of their unexpected unlimited TV time. They were going to stay up if they needed to prop open their eyes with toothpicks. Astra turned off the lamps. They would all sleep on the couch tonight.

Astra slipped between them, tucking one arm under each girl, and pulled them in close, setting her right hand on Logan's shoulder so she was connected to them all while Bernie curled up in the corner, having passed the caregiver baton to Astra.

"What are we watching?"

"*Frozen.*"

"That's a good one. I like that they're sisters."

The girls nodded and cuddled in closer. She might never have her own family, but this wasn't a bad second.

✦

Astra woke to her nose being pinched closed. She swatted whatever was doing it away. When she opened her eyes, Annie giggled.

"You were snoring," Annie said.

"Yeah, well, you kept kicking me all night like a wiggly worm." Astra tickled her.

"Santa came," Logan shouted and hopped on the couch next to her. Bernie took this as a sign to join in and barked in short, loud yips. Based on the faint light streaming in from the window, it was still early, but it was Christmas morning and children were programed to wake at dawn. Good thing she had gotten all the packages tucked under the tree and stockings stuffed with tiny toys and candy while the kids were conked out. She was worried when Bernie jumped off the couch to sniff at all the wrapped boxes, but none of the children moved.

"Can we open presents?" Annie asked, one arm wrapped around Bernie, the other holding a stuffed otter.

"Not without Mommy and Daddy," Maria said.

Annie and Logan started complaining about waiting while Astra noticed the coffee table in front of them. There was an open box of cereal, a jar of peanut butter, an open package of graham crackers, and a mostly empty container of raspberries. The TV was still on, but now they were watching *Moana*. The princesses had definitely gotten more badass since she was a little girl.

"Having a party?" she interrupted the arguments.

"We were hungry," Logan said. His hair stuck up in all directions. "We made breakfast."

"I see that. Interesting choices. Did you get enough to eat, or should I make some eggs? Then we can discuss present opening." They could use a little protein.

"With cheese?" Maria asked.

"Obviously. What's the point if there isn't cheese on top?"

That seemed to be a sufficient compromise, though Astra noticed Logan trying to peek at the label on the largest box.

Astra went into the kitchen, checking her phone. There was a text from Ronnie left at three thirty.

> Doctors say he should be okay—but plenty can go wrong still. Broke half his body trying to avoid a little kid and smashed into some obstacles on the terrain course. In recovery. Cassie was a rock star. Gonna try to get Steph to sleep. Will call later. ♥♥♥

Holy shit. Even without knowing all the details, recovery was going to be a bitch. Focusing on being there for Steph was keeping the pain of her snap decision to leave Jack in the shadows, but she dreaded how it would jump into the light.

She found everything she needed and whipped up some cheesy scrambled eggs, adding a little hot sauce to hers. She set the plates on the counter and called the kids.

"Breakfast, but let's clear all this up."

Annie grabbed the big box of cereal, and Logan put the lid back on the peanut butter and picked up the heavy tub. Maria carefully wiped up the crumbs and spilled milk. Astra grabbed the rest and put it away while the kids climbed onto their chairs and scooped bites of egg into their mouths.

"When will Mama and Daddy be home?" Maria asked, homing in on the important issue.

All the kids looked up at her—six big, trusting eyes. Steph

had given them the briefest of explanations last night—only that Daddy had fallen on the ski hill and doctors needed to patch him up. Astra didn't want to scare them, but she also didn't want to lie to them. She'd worked with enough kids at the library to know simple and honest was always the best choice.

"Great question," Astra said, sitting at the table with them. "I'm waiting for your mom to call and tell me what is happening. I hope she calls soon, but it could be a while. I do know that Daddy and Mommy will need a lot of help. Maybe we can make a list of ways to do that. Then after, you can see what's in your stockings."

Astra found some paper and a pen and the four of them got to work.

After thirty-six hours with three energetic, scared, and confused children, Astra returned to her home exhausted but relieved to be driving Rob's car, which Steph had loaned to her until Rob could drive it again. Steph had come home that morning and reported that Rob's surgeries went well, but there was a lot of recovery ahead of him. After answering the children's questions and opening the Christmas gifts—leaving a few to bring to the hospital and open with Daddy—Steph had pulled Astra aside.

"It'll be months before he can go back to work," Steph said, "and while his job will take him back when he's ready, they aren't paying for this. I have to keep working full-time. My parents are coming to help, but I don't know how I'm going to do it. He needs help for everything, and I can't leave him alone. He can't use the bathroom by himself. With the kids . . ."

Her eyes started to shine and her lip trembled. Astra wrapped an arm around Steph's shoulders. She didn't need to say the words that were going to be so hard to admit. Steph, the type A leader of their group, always prepared, always with a plan, had been thrown the hugest curveball. This was why Astra had stayed. Looking at her dear friend, she would never regret choosing to be here for her.

"I'll be there. Whatever and whenever. Always."

Steph took a deep breath.

"Thank you." The words were shaky, and she swiped away a tear that escaped. "I know what you gave up. I'll never . . ."

Astra took her friend's hands in her own.

"Shh. Never give it another thought." Astra wanted to say more but couldn't find the words to convince Steph that it was no big deal. They both knew it was, but Astra would make the same choice over and over. "But I need you to know, I will watch your kids, clean your house, cook meals, but under no circumstances am I going to wipe your husband's ass."

Steph smiled, then laughed. That was the result Astra had wanted, because in truth, she'd wipe whatever Steph needed her to. That's what friends were for.

Astra dropped her keys on the kitchen counter and filled Bernie's bowls with food and fresh water. The last time she had left, she didn't think she'd be coming back. Bernie let out a loud woof as a tall, fit man, dressed in slim-cut black pants, black boots, and a well-tailored black wool jacket, complete with elegant cashmere (she would bet money on it) scarf, walked into the kitchen from her living room. His sandy hair, while slightly tousled, looked stylishly cut. More East Coast than midwestern.

Astra screamed, causing Bernie's bark to take a sharper edge.

"Whoa, whoa, whoa," the man said, holding his arms in front of him to indicate he meant no harm.

Astra stopped screaming, but she did grab her chef's knife from the magnetic knife strip above the stove.

"Bernie, come," Astra said. Bernie stopped barking and came to stand by Astra. "Talk." She pointed the knife at the man.

"I'm assuming you're Astra." Astra nodded. "I'm John. The Julemarked's Outside contact. I thought you were gone and came to take care of everything. I was making a list of what I'd need to pack up your house."

"Shit." All the muscles in Astra's body relaxed, all the steel that had been keeping her moving forward since she left the Julemarked evaporated, and she melted to the kitchen floor. Bernie, taking that as an invitation, sat on her lap. Astra let go of the knife and wrapped her arms around Bernie.

"I'm sorry," John said. "I didn't mean to scare you. Had I known you were still here, I never would have come."

Astra looked up at the illogically handsome man in her house and floundered to find the words to explain everything that had happened. Thoughts sputtered and fluttered away.

"Change of plans."

That was the best she could do at the moment.

"No need to explain anything," John said. He stretched out his arm to shake her hand or help her up, she wasn't sure. "It's nice to meet you. Mads said a lot of wonderful things about you."

Still shocked, Astra decided he was looking to help her up. She shoved Bernie off and took the offered hand. John yanked her up.

"Thank you. Mads . . . was lovely. All of it was lovely."

John nodded.

"I can come back at another time," he said.

"No need. I won't be needing your assistance."

John studied her, an understanding in his eyes. He reached in his coat pocket. He set her stack of letters on the counter along with her house key and a business card.

"Here are the letters back, since I no longer need to deliver them. And that's in case you need to contact me."

He walked past her to the door, stopping with one hand on the doorknob. He turned to look at her.

"Not a lot of people will understand or even believe what you experienced." He pointed to the card. "I'm a good listener."

He held her gaze for a moment, then nodded and left.

Astra waited a moment, locked the door, and took off her coat, emptying the pockets out of habit. Her hands froze when her fingers grazed something hard. She pulled it out but knew what it was before she opened her palm. He must have slipped it into her pocket, one last nisse to remember him.

The tiny red-hatted gnome held a stack of books, the titles delicately carved onto the spines and painted in gold. Each book represented a different part of her. *Outlander* for their love across time and because it was one of her favorites. *Fairy Tales by Hans Christian Andersen* because she had found it in the bookstore. *A Christmas Carol* because they both loved Christmas. *Lily and the Octopus*, presumably because of Bernie, and lastly *Circle of Friends*, which seemed self-explanatory. Turning over the nisse, she found Jack's initials, and her heart broke.

She clutched the figure to her chest and went to the living room, where she flopped onto the couch, numb as she took in the bare mantel and shelves, where her favorite objects were missing. Bernie jumped onto the couch next to her, nuzzling under her arm. She'd have a lot to occupy her mind in the next several months as she helped Steph, but right now, alone in her house, she didn't feel a glow of satisfaction at being able to help her friend. Where her little army of nisser had watched the room, emptiness stared back, and she was facing down a gaping hole that threatened to swallow her whole. At least she had this one. She had dared to hope for a family, only to have returned home with a sense of loneliness bigger than she'd ever known. She needed to return to Steph's tomorrow, but for today, she decided she could let it consume her.

Would it be like a wildfire, where once it had burned everything living, it would end?

Chapter Twenty-Nine

ASTRA SETTLED INTO A ROUTINE. SHE'D GO TO WORK, PICK UP food for dinner, then head to Steph's house so she could be with the kids for dinner and bedtime. Then she'd sleep in the spare bedroom and help the kids get off to school in the morning, occasionally picking up or dropping off Bernie. For once, Trent seemed to realize the world didn't revolve around him and was less of a pain in the ass than usual. He didn't even question her when she returned Bernie after the dognapping with the pathetic excuse that she had gotten the dates mixed up. It almost made her feel guilty for what she was planning to do.

Being busy kept her from dwelling on the giant hole in her heart, and the days blended into weeks. Astra was grateful for the lack of downtime. Being needed was a useful Band-Aid for heartache, giving her time to adjust. Now it was time to move on with her life.

The first step was completing Project Save Bernie, and she had three more little accomplices.

She grabbed the tub of peanut butter from Steph's cupboard

as Steph walked into the kitchen. Steph looked from the peanut butter to Astra as Astra slid it into her large purse.

"I don't want to know," Steph said.

"No, you don't. But I expect they won't be able to keep it a secret long. Take comfort that they won't be doing anything you haven't done," Astra said.

Steph laughed. "We both know that's a very short list."

Astra raised her voice so the kids would hear her. "Adventure bus is leaving." She looked back to Steph. "We shouldn't be gone long. With any luck, this will be the final step."

"Like I said, I don't want to know," Steph said, raising her hands and walking out of the kitchen.

Annie, Logan, and Maria thundered in and slipped into their boots and coats and climbed into her car faster than Astra would have thought, eager for their outing with Auntie Astra.

As Astra buckled Annie into her car seat, the at-home rehab therapist walked to the front door. While the kids thought they were helping Astra with a special project, the truth was Steph wanted them out of the house while Rob grunted and groaned through a few hours of physical and occupational therapy.

"Mommy said you have a boyfriend," Annie blurted out as Astra started the car. The unanticipated comment was a pang to her heart, but she couldn't let it show in front of them. She backed out of the driveway, careful not to hit the cars parked in the street, and used the action as a distraction while she came up with an answer. Once she was headed in the right direction, she cleared her throat.

"I had a boyfriend." *Keep it simple, right?*

"Did he die?"

"No, sweetie. He moved away and I couldn't go with him."

"Why not?"

"Because I wanted to stay here where I could be close to your mommy, and Auntie Cassie and Auntie Ronnie and you three."

On their way, they picked up Cassie before heading to their destination.

"I see we have accomplices today," Cassie said as she buckled her seat belt and waved at the three children in the back seat.

"I like to think of them as alibis. Who would do anything illegal with three children?"

"We're going to do something illegal?" Maria said, her eyes wide with alarm. Logan and Annie merely looked excited to break the rules.

"We have to drop off some pants at my ex-husband's house." She stopped the car in Trent's driveway and ushered them all into the house. It was true; she was dropping off the pants she had finally hemmed for him, mainly so she'd have an excuse to enter his house.

With spring on its way, Astra wanted new beginnings in all aspects of her life—starting with Bernie. She hoped this would be the final step.

"Who wants to make a mess?" Astra said, setting the pants in a heap on the kitchen counter. She pulled the large tub of peanut butter from her bag and crawled under Trent's beautiful walnut table, each leg resembling the treelike structures in Singapore's Supertree Grove. It was unique and expensive and Trent's pride and joy.

Logan and Annie clambered under the table with her, while Maria went with Cassie to retrieve Bernie from the bathroom where Trent had been keeping her since the pee incident. Handing each of the kids a plastic spoon, a useful utensil for scooping large globs of peanut butter, she showed them what to do. They slathered several clumps of chunky peanut butter, Bernie's favorite, onto one of the legs.

"Excellent work," Astra said, collecting their spoons and putting them in a plastic bag so she could throw them away when they returned to Steph's house. "Remember, this isn't something you can do anywhere else, okay?"

Cassie held on to Bernie in the nearby kitchen, waiting until Astra was done, her nails skittering on the hard floor. The kids nodded and went to hug Bernie, who quickly licked all the peanut butter they had gotten on their hands.

"I added a few scratches near the handle to make it look like Bernie got herself out," Cassie said.

"She used a fork," Maria said. Astra could only imagine they were blowing little Maria's mind. With the right mix of luck and timing, she supposed it was possible that Bernie could manage to push down the handle to get out—and she hoped Trent believed it, too. If this didn't break him, she wasn't sure what would, but she was sick of waiting for him to cave.

"I almost feel bad about this," Astra said.

"Don't be. He could have avoided all of this if he'd given you full custody instead of taking advantage anytime he didn't want to deal with Bernie," Cassie said. "And everything else you did for him." Cassie pointed to the pants on the counter.

"I'm not sure that warrants what I've been doing. Is this too much?"

"Astra Noel Snow. You love this dog. You've given up a lot to be with this dog. Trent doesn't love her or take care of her the way you do and you know that's the truth."

Astra slid out from under the table, screwing the top on the peanut butter, then crouched down in front of Bernie and let her lick the peanut butter from her fingers. When she stood, she wobbled from a wave of dizziness. Cassie let go of Bernie and grabbed Astra's arm to steady her. Bernie went straight for the table.

"You okay?" She switched into doctor mode in an instant. Cassie's soft hands checked her forehead, then her pulse, looking her over as best she could. "You're a little clammy and your heart rate is up."

"I stood up too quickly. That's all."

Cassie turned her sideways in front of the window, evaluating her profile.

"Are you wearing a different bra? Your boobs look great."

Astra laughed and the kids giggled.

"Same boring tan bras bought on sale from Kohl's. I've lost a little weight, so maybe they look bigger by comparison."

"When does anyone lose weight in their waist before their boobs?"

They looked at each other in the dim room. It had been more than two months since Christmas. The slurping licks of Bernie and giggling children were the only sounds in the silent room.

"No," Astra said, holding up a hand. "I know what you're thinking and no."

"When was your last period?"

"I'm not having this conversation." Astra shoved the peanut butter into her bag and headed to the door. "Come on, crew." She moved her arms to usher the kids before her and out the door.

Cassie followed her and carefully locked the door behind them. When they were all buckled and secured, Cassie stared at her.

"Fine," Astra said. "I stopped birth control with the divorce and my periods have been wacky ever since. But I had one in January. Not pregnant."

"If you think so," Cassie said, but Astra knew this conversation wasn't over.

But she couldn't be pregnant, could she? She and Jack had only been together a handful of times. She was still of childbearing age, but not for long. Women her age struggled to get pregnant, so the odds of it happening were small. Minuscule, right?

Astra ignored Cassie's stares. Until there was some other evidence besides an irregular period and nice-looking boobs, she was going to forget Cassie had even mentioned it. She would forget the tiny flutter of hope in her chest. She would forget the voice telling her it was very possible. She would definitely forget the panic of what it might mean if Cassie was right. Instead, she remembered what mattered—being the friend Steph needed her to be and getting Bernie.

Chapter Thirty

Two days later, Astra stared at her computer screen trying to ignore the fantasy that Cassie's observations had ignited by scrolling through the discussion board topic "Rate the Jule-marked Hotties." She was trying to free Jack from her mind, but ignoring any thoughts about him wasn't working. Maybe inundating herself would slake her preoccupation, like crashing a computer by overloading it with data.

OnTheOtherSide42: 8/10 the amazon in the knitting shop.

whodoes#2workfor: Not enuf babes.

AlienzRHere420: 20/10 the bakery boys.

SillyString137: This whole thread is repugnant.

AlienzRHere420: Lighten up SillyString137.

Mads4Kringle: I couldn't agree more with AlienzRHere420, on all counts.

Mads4Kringle? Could that be Mads? It would be like him to trawl discussion boards and chime in. He seemed to live with one foot in each world. Jack would never do such a thing. She respected his steadfastness in regard to the Julemarked. How could she not? It was her own loyalty to her friends that had galvanized her decision. Acknowledging it didn't help. Reading this feed didn't help. Remembering Jack's turquoise eyes and strong hands definitely didn't help. For once, she wished she could go back to forgetting the Julemarked and all its residents. The knowledge was too much for her. If only there was some way to write over it, replace the data with something new.

She closed the window and opened the budget.

Astra sighed.

The budget was definitely not an effective replacement for Jack's calming presence.

Chloe knocked on the door.

"Hey, boss. Doing okay?"

Astra waved her in.

"Working on the budget." Chloe sat down. She was young and in the middle of her library science degree. Astra spent a lot of time crunching numbers, but what if she could share the work? Maybe free up some time for the projects that excited her. She was looking for something to occupy her mind, and mentoring Chloe might be the distraction she needed. "How would you like to assist me with budgets?"

Chloe smiled.

"Really? I'd love that." Bless her, the innocent dear. "But I can't start today. I'm about to leave. My brother is here to get me."

She gestured over her shoulder to where a very attractive

dark-haired man stood next to a bookshelf thumbing through a graphic novel. He looked to be in his late twenties and a firm believer in well-groomed facial hair. His lush, immaculately trimmed beard would make a hipster weep with jealousy.

"Nice gene pool," Astra blurted out. "Sorry, that's not appropriate."

"I get that a lot. It's truly okay." Chloe tilted her head and studied Astra. "He's single. I can introduce you."

Astra looked up at him again and tried to imagine going on a date with someone so young. She snorted. When had late twenties become someone young? Probably when she fell in love with a centenarian.

"No, but I appreciate the vote of confidence."

Chloe shrugged and stood to leave.

"If you change your mind, I'm happy to set it up," Chloe said.

"Let's focus on budgets and go from there." Astra waved. "Have a good weekend."

Chloe and her brother left and Astra stared after them. That answered one question. Two years ago, she would have happily taken the introduction. Romance would be last on her list.

She'd focus her attention on teaching Chloe about budgets and started to make a list of topics to cover. Once she had Chloe up to speed, she would have more time for programs.

Astra's phone rang. Her cell phone. It was Trent. Finally.

Before she could even speak her greeting, Trent's clipped voice interrupted her.

"She's yours. I'm done."

They were the sweetest words she'd ever heard. She closed her eyes and leaned back in her office chair. She couldn't let him know she knew what he was talking about.

"What do you mean?"

"I'm done. I give up. Bernie is yours."

"Is everything okay? Did she pee again?"

"She chewed on my table. She's never chewed on anything before."

"You let her have free rein of the house after she peed on your bed?" Astra might as well lay it on.

"No. She got out of the bathroom."

"How did she turn the knob?" Astra asked, knowing full well that it was a handle, not a knob, on the bathroom door. "Is Bernie a genius?"

"It's a handle, so she must have gotten a lucky swipe. Between needing to repaint the bathroom door, the mattress, the table . . . It's either this or the pound. At least you don't have any nice furniture."

"Of course I want her, but I can't afford to pay for an attorney to redo the agreement."

"I've already called him and he's writing an addendum."

"I won't be able to get her until next week, unless you can get the documents done today. Then I could swing by after work."

"They'll be done. Just come get her."

Astra hung up the phone, and for the first time in months, she wanted to celebrate.

She sent a text to the girls:

Project Rescue Bernie Complete! Bring your party hats!

✦

By the time she arrived at Trent's, he had packed up Bernie's toys, bedding, food, and medicines, with Bernie already leashed sitting next to the pile like an orphan about to get kicked to the curb. Astra gave her a kiss on her head and Trent pointed to the table where the documents were. Astra could see the leg that Bernie had chewed. It wasn't too bad, just a few bite marks and not a single smudge of peanut butter. Good girl.

"I can see what she did. Naughty Bernie." She wagged her finger at Bernie and Trent squinted at her. That might be too far. "If you turn the table, no one will notice. I'm sorry it happened. I know how much you love this table." She slid into a chair and pulled the paperwork toward her. It was only one page. "I need to read."

"I need to go." Trent checked his watch.

"If you're in a rush, take Bernie's things out to the car. It's open."

She turned back to the document and slowly read it, not waiting for Trent to respond. After a moment, he picked up all the items and carried them outside. This Trent wasn't so bad, the one who wanted something from her. The addendum was simple and to the point. It relinquished all of Trent's rights to Bernie and gave full ownership to Astra.

She signed it, and by the time Trent came back in the house, she had Bernie's leash in hand.

"Thanks, Trent. Good luck with your life."

She walked out the door. Bernie hopped into the car and sat on the front seat looking at Astra as if to say, "Let's blow this joint."

They did.

Cassie arrived first, a full hour before Ronnie and Steph were expected to join them to celebrate Bernie Custody Day at Astra's house. Rob was getting more self-sufficient with the help of his skiing buddies—a huge relief to Steph. Cassie came in through the side door and unpacked her bag on the kitchen table. A bottle of Moscato, a tub of hummus, a container of carrot sticks, a bag of pita chips, and one pregnancy test.

She held it out to Astra and Astra shook her head.

"You peed in a water bottle to get Bernie. You can pee on a stick to see if Bernie gets a sibling," Cassie said.

"This isn't necessary."

"Did you get your period?"

"No."

"Then it's necessary. If not for your peace of mind, do it for mine. I cannot have a friend of mine not knowing if she's pregnant. I'm not letting you have wine until you do."

"No need to use the big guns. You can be very bossy."

Astra joked but her hands shook as she took the box with a nod and went to the bathroom. Cassie followed.

"I can actually pee by myself."

"I'm just going to wait outside until you're done, and then we can watch the time together."

Astra closed the door, tearing open the box and unfolding the instructions.

"Just make sure to get enough urine on the stick that it's soaked through."

"I can read."

"Don't bother with the reading, just pee."

Astra ignored her. If Cassie thought she was pregnant, she probably was. But Astra didn't want to hope that she might have this last piece of Jack to hold on to, that he'd given her one last gift, even if the thought of raising the baby alone terrified her. With a quick glance at the four pages of instructions with very tiny print, Astra chose to ignore them and listen to Cassie. Finding that awkward hovering position that allowed her to relax enough to pee while giving her enough room to hold the stick beneath her, Astra sent a thought into the ether that she would embrace whatever future was approaching and find peace with it. If she'd learned one thing during her time with Jack in the Julemarked, it was that life was lived best in the moments spent with loved ones.

She set the stick on the counter. As soon as she flushed, Cassie was through the door and had picked it up.

"Dude. Gross," Astra said.

"You really have no idea what I went through to become a doctor, do you? On the scale of gross things, this doesn't even get a fraction."

"A fraction. Quit showing off your fancy STEM education."

"That's second-grade math." Cassie rolled her eyes.

They both looked at the stick. It was one of the fancy digital ones, so there was no deciphering of pink lines. Astra was surprised Cassie hadn't dragged her into her office for an official one.

"How long do we have to wait?"

"A few more minutes." Cassie paused and sniffed. "You need to drink more water."

"Are you going to bill me for this, too? Should I bend over and cough?"

"The bend-over-and-cough thing is for men. If your doctor is doing that, you need a new doctor." Cassie looked at Astra, who was picking at her fingernails. "You're nervous?"

Astra nodded. Taking the test made the possibility real.

Cassie hugged her with the non-pee-stick-holding arm.

"I know, but no matter what, we're all here for you. And the kiddos will be over the moon to have another cousin."

It beeped and Cassie moved it behind her back.

"Do you want me to look and tell you? Do you want to look? Or should we both look at the same time?"

Astra thought through the scenarios.

"Me. I want to see it first."

Cassie held the stick up to her with the display facing Astra.

PREGNANT 3+

Astra covered her mouth and her vision blurred. She tried to swallow but couldn't.

"You're killing me," Cassie said.

Astra wiped away some tears and cleared her throat.

"What does the 'three-plus' mean?"

Cassie whipped it around to see and let out a whoop. Then stopped and looked at Astra.

"This is a celebration, right?"

Astra nodded and tiny Cassie pulled her into a fierce hug that let her know everything was going to be wonderful. She was old. Well, not old, just old for a pregnancy. Or maybe older than she thought she'd be when she got pregnant. She'd be AARP-aged when her kid graduated high school. Women all over the world had babies well into their forties. She wasn't even forty.

Astra felt old and young all at once. Light and weighted down, happy and sad. This was a moment she'd given up on during her marriage to Trent, settling for being the cool aunt to her friends' children.

Overwhelmed and immediately exhausted, either from relief or from the excuse that a human was growing inside her, she wasn't sure. She squeezed Cassie to her, grateful that she'd be there to guide her, help her find the right doctor, because her current gynecologist didn't deliver babies. As she released Cassie, a million questions bubbled out of her.

"I need a doctor. I've drunk more than I should since Jack left—have I ruined her? Or him? What if she's a he? I don't know what to do with a boy! And what about . . ."

Cassie took her face in her confident and capable hands.

"Breathe. It's all going to be fine. Your body is made to do this. Thirty-eight is not even close to being too old, but there are more risks and I have a handful of doctors to recommend who will be perfect for you. We're going to be here with you every step of the way."

Astra nodded as she took in a deep breath, her belly pushing out as the air filled her lungs, then let it out slowly. She could do this. Women did this every day. And she had a literal library at her disposal for information. She'd yet to meet a problem that couldn't be solved with some diligent research. She looked at Cassie, at last letting herself enjoy the moment. She put her hand on her belly, not that there was anything to feel. She'd always had an extra-soft stomach, so any baby growth would be impossible to notice at this point.

"I'm going to have a baby." Her voice came out a whisper.

Relief and wonder spread, the kind she felt looking up at a Christmas tree on December 25 in the predawn light surrounded by presents. So much possibility with a future she never thought she'd have. Fear crept in at the edges, but she had months to address that. Right now was for happiness.

The front door opened as Ronnie and Steph arrived. Bernie barked her greeting as her nails tippy-tapped on the wood floors. Astra's stomach flipped in anticipation of sharing the news with her dearest friends. Cassie and Astra found them in the kitchen, where all the snacks were safely on the counters, away from Bernie's very eager snout. Ronnie set out two bottles of champagne and immediately began opening one. Steph set down a bottle of nonalcoholic sparkling cider, shooting a quick glance at Astra.

"Who's ready to celebrate the return of our favorite fur baby?" Ronnie shouted, opening a bottle of champagne with too much enthusiasm, causing a small fountain to splash out. Astra tossed a kitchen towel over it before Bernie could lap it up, while Ronnie poured four bubbling glasses, handing one to each of the ladies. Cassie promptly took Astra's, even though she had no intention of sipping it, and set it on the counter, making a show of pouring Astra a glass of nonalcoholic sparkling cider and putting it in Astra's hand. Steph and Ronnie didn't miss a move.

"I knew it," Steph said, wrapping her arms around Astra. How did she always know?

"I owe you twenty bucks," Ronnie grumbled to Steph. "It's all she could talk about on the way over here. How she had a feeling you were pregnant. I told her if you were, you would have told us because you'd be . . ." Ronnie paused to do the math on her fingers. "Almost twelve weeks."

Ronnie shoved Steph away from Astra so she could have her turn squishing the air from her lungs.

"Unless she didn't know until ten minutes ago," Cassie said.

Free from the aggressive hugging, Astra held out her glass, and her beautiful, strong, fabulous friends did the same.

"To the dearest friends, you are better than any warrior, lover, or family. You are my hope, my happiness, my heart."

Glasses clinked, bubbly was sipped, and the women circled up in a group hug. With these three women by her side, Astra felt invincible.

Chapter Thirty-One

IT WAS ONE OF THOSE DREARY MARCH DAYS IN MILWAUKEE when everything was gray and dingy and made you question if spring would ever truly arrive in Wisconsin. A few grimy snow piles clung to the curbs and the corners of buildings, more dirt and garbage than snow. Icy and shiny from melting and re-freezing, the bright white flakes were a long-gone memory, just like the magical Christmas season. Astra tucked her chin into the scarf around her neck, hiding it from the biting wind, her pace brisk to stay warm enough that the cold wouldn't seep too deeply into her bones despite her thick layers and years of experience walking in all types of weather. While the temperature wasn't below freezing, the damp, harsh wind cut to the core.

After last night's revelation, she hadn't been able to sleep.

A baby.

A baby without a dad.

How would she tell Jack? She missed him and it hurt every day that they weren't together. She knew she'd given up the love of her life to keep the life she had. While she didn't regret it, it didn't mean she mourned his absence any less. The baby would be here before she could see him next, and given what she knew about him, should she even tell him? Why let him know about a baby he would hardly see? He had made his opinions about leaving the Julemarked clear. Would they change for a baby? Or would he try to convince her to move with him again?

She wasn't going to change her mind. Being with her friends and family was where she needed to be. Out in the world, living all the seasons and the challenges that came with them, regardless of how ephemeral it seemed to him.

As she turned the corner into the empty alley near the Deer District, the alley where the Julemarked might appear in eight more months, the wind abated, providing respite from the brutal chill. Standing in front of the blank brick wall, Astra almost doubted any of it had happened. It was a normal span of brick wall, the same as the ones in the rest of the alley. There was nothing special, nothing to mark that it would be an entrance to a magical place. Not a chip in the mortar or color variation in the bricks.

Astra pulled off her mitten and set her hand on the rough surface, the brick cold like it should be. She had hoped coming here would help her feel closer to Jack, give her some comfort, but there was nothing. He wasn't dead, so this wasn't like visiting a grave where she could talk to his bones. He was out there in the universe somewhere, with no idea he would be a father. She had to tell him.

But how?

How did one get a message to a place that didn't exist eleven months of the year?

She had one idea.

Standing alone in the alley, the loneliness and loss threatened to swallow her. Even before she remembered all their encounters over the years, on some level, she had known those moments existed. Her heart had recognized him even when her brain hadn't. She had come here hoping it would help clear her mind, give her strength to raise a baby on her own.

She leaned her head against the cold brick and let the hot tears fall.

"Hey, you okay?" a man's voice said from behind her.

She turned and saw John, right on time. She wiped at her tears.

"I'll be fine. Feelings and all that—they can catch up with a person when you least expect it."

"Why don't we step inside somewhere. I'll buy you a coffee," John said.

He pointed around the corner to where there was a coffee shop. She followed him to it, and into the warm, richly scented store.

"What can I get you? I'll order and bring it to you."

"Tea, please. Something herbal. No ginger."

John nodded and Astra chose a table that was the farthest away from anyone who might overhear. As she waited for John to return, she thought about what to say to him.

He returned with their drinks.

"I'd ask how you've been, but I think I have an idea," he said. He grinned and it was a lovely smile that would dazzle any person whose heart wasn't already given to someone else. "Do you want to tell me why you called me?"

"How much do you know about me?" Astra asked.

She sipped her tea and let the warm drink soothe her. Giving up coffee wasn't as difficult as she had thought, mostly because it reminded her of Jack.

"Enough that I was very surprised when I saw you in your house. Why didn't you take the plunge?"

"Sometimes you have to choose between great loves. I could have had one great love with Jack, or three with my friends. Three is greater than one. That's the very simple and short version."

John nodded.

"And today?"

Without even thinking, she laid her hand on her belly, and John tracked the move, his mouth dropping open.

"I need to tell him something." Astra wrapped her hands around her teacup, the heat taking the last of the chill from her fingers. "I'm pregnant."

"I didn't see that one coming," John said.

Astra couldn't help but chuckle, and it felt good, a release of energy she'd been hoarding.

"Neither did I. I'm not sure I can see him again, but he should know that he has a child in the world. Right? Or is it crueler to know you have a child you can't be with every day?"

"He needs to know. I would want to know." He took out a small pad of paper to jot down some notes. "I can help. As soon as the Julemarked opens on December 1, a contact like me will be there to help with whatever they need. I can send the same message to all the contacts so he'll get it as soon as the Julemarked opens, no matter where they are in the world. I can send a letter, a video, photos. Whatever you need. He'll know as soon as possible."

A weight lifted. John was going above and beyond by reaching out to his network. Maybe in time she would be ready to see Jack in person, but this was the right first step.

"Thank you, John. I hope I can repay the favor someday."

"Well, John is an excellent name for a boy. Or you could start a trend by making it a girl's name, too."

Astra smiled.

"I'll take that into consideration."

They finished their drinks and made small talk. She was surprised to learn he worked as the style editor for the paper—he certainly looked the part. When she started the walk back to her house, the day warmer and less grim than when she had left, she felt more at peace with her uncertain future. She'd taken action and now it was up to Jack to decide what to do when he learned about their baby. Wispy wishes sparked that maybe he would choose to stay with her, but she blocked them out. She would only focus on what she could make decisions about with the information she had, and right now, she needed a lot more information about having a baby. As she formulated a research plan involving internet searches, catalog deep dives, and maybe some medical journals, her hands went to her stomach as she walked.

Chapter Thirty-Two

GIVEN HOW LITTLE TIME ASTRA HAD SPENT AT HOME SINCE Christmas, her Christmas lights and decorations were still up, though the tree had lost most of its needles. Well, that was part of it. The other part was she hadn't been ready to let Christmas go, because admitting it had ended meant admitting her chance with Jack was truly over, and she hadn't been ready to do that. She had too much to do, like continuing to help Steph, and now training Chloe and developing new initiatives for the library. As she waited for her tea to finish steeping, she walked through the house straightening pillows and folding a blanket she had left on the couch from last night's *Downton Abbey* binge with Bernie. Bernie followed behind her, neither of them quite believing that they got to stay with each other. She'd only heard from Trent once since the final Bernie exchange. It was a few days ago. She'd answered the phone reluctantly but knew she could hang up. Her curiosity had won out.

"Hi, Trent," she said.

"Hi, Astra. How's Bernie?"

"Doing great. We both are. Is there something you needed?" Why beat around the bush?

He paused.

"I've been seeing . . ." He paused again. Was he literally calling to brag about a date? Her finger hovered over the End Call button. ". . . a therapist." Astra sat up straighter. That was a surprise.

"Good for you." And she meant it.

"I didn't handle our divorce well. I wanted to say I'm sorry. Divorce can make a person do crazy things. You should have always had Bernie. That's it. I just wanted to let you know that I regret the way I treated you. You deserved better and I hope you find it."

They ended the call. *Huh.* She should feel jubilant, vindicated, but she didn't feel much. A part of her was happy for him in the same way she'd be happy anyone had improved themselves, but she didn't really care. She understood his needing to make the apology, but she hadn't needed it. She had moved on, and the heartbreak he had caused her was nothing compared to the emptiness she felt when she thought of Jack somewhere with her collection of nisser that had once been displayed on the empty mantel in front of her. Both lost in time. All she had was the tiny nisse he had snuck into her pocket as they said goodbye.

She had to move on. Especially after her talk with John. She needed closure, and that started with Christmas decorations finally going back in their boxes. Already in her work clothes, she pulled out the boxes from the basement and started packing up. It might take a few years before she could put them out again. She needed a long break from the holiday spirit. Would Christmas ever bring her the joy and comfort it used to?

Even though she moved quickly, she'd be late for work, but

that was one perk of being the boss. As she slid the last boxes away, a little more of the weight lifted off her shoulders. She'd find her way back to loving Christmas again, but it would take time to dull the edge of the sharp pain that lanced through her every time she thought of the future she'd given up. She would make the same choices again, but that didn't lessen the razor edge.

She added hot tea to her large stainless-steel mug, and the herbal scent of lemon and chamomile rose in steamy wafts that calmed her further. Would she ever be able to drink coffee again? Walking past coffee shops with the bitter roasted scent was enough to make her catch her breath. She'd just have to learn to live with it.

At the library, Astra dropped her things in the office and grabbed an empty library cart, heading to the 600s, where the books on pregnancy were located. She'd start there.

Taking a book off the shelf, Astra would read a few pages, then add it to the cart if it seemed like a useful reference. If not, it went back on the shelf where she'd found it. Surrounded by the smell of paper and a hint of the cleaning solution used to get stains out of carpets, Astra found her Zen. Taking action, developing a plan, asking questions, researching answers. These were all skills that brought her comfort.

Astra picked up a book about what fathers should expect during a mother's pregnancy and how they could help. Jack would have been an amazing partner, attentive to her needs, striving to ease her worries, helping her before she even needed help. She could even smell him—coffee, sugar, and a hint of almond. Her imagination was getting the better of her. She took another deep breath, but the scent was still there. Pregnancy could mess with the sense of smell, but this was too much. She clutched the book tighter, willing her brain to shove away the memory. It was too real, too painful to remember. She thought she'd been making progress, and now her mind played tricks on her.

"Astra," a voice whispered, so similar to Jack's it sent goose bumps down her spine.

Astra's breath stopped. It couldn't be. Hope surged faster than she could turn around, her brain stomping on it like a firework that exploded too close to the ground. She needed to put it out. Her imagination had gone rogue, and when she turned around, it would be some person with a similar voice saying her name, not Jack.

She took a deep breath, ignored the almost overpoweringly familiar scent, and set the pregnancy book on the cart. She forced a smile on her face as she turned to the patron, already starting her response.

"Yes, how can I . . ."

Astra stuttered off into silence. How was this possible? In front of her stood Jack, his eyes sparkling like a South Pacific lagoon at midday, his bangs flopping over one eye, wearing a thick green sweater, and carrying a bag that he dropped to the floor when their eyes met.

"Is this real?" Astra whispered, not daring to move or blink.

She doubted every one of her senses; her brain worked to convince her that this was all in her head. It couldn't be. It was March, almost April. She'd have to check to see if hallucinations were a side effect of pregnancy. It would be in one of the books.

Jack stepped toward her and Astra stepped back. Whatever this was, she didn't want it to end, and it would end if she reached for him—when her hand went through the mirage of him.

He paused, his hands up as if she were a frightened animal.

"Astra." He smiled, just a little, enough to show a small chip in his front tooth that hadn't been there before. Why would she invent something like that? "It's real."

If this was a hallucination, it was a damn good one. He reached for her hand, which still rested on the book cart. The warmth of his skin on hers made her knees buckle, and the distance between them closed immediately as he caught her, keeping her from falling to the floor, their bodies pressed close against each other, her brain finally conceding defeat to her senses.

He was here.

He was really here.

"Jack."

He was exactly as she remembered, yet so much more wonderful. His body firmer, his scent sweeter, his arms stronger.

"You need to stop swooning over me. You're going to hurt yourself."

Astra stared into those turquoise eyes, losing herself in the wonder as if she were diving deeper and deeper into the wells of blue. She stopped his lips from completing their smile by gently pulling his face toward her, giving his lips something else to do, the only response her body could manage. She needed to taste him, feel him, before she could formulate more words, more questions.

When their lips touched, the distance between them disappeared, each touch twining them tighter together, erasing the time they had lost, making it meaningless, each caress blending into the next, an infinite kiss.

His response matched hers; he pulled her against him, her feet no longer on the ground so it didn't matter that her knees had melted to butter, or that she couldn't draw a breath because he was all the air she needed. Her fingers buried themselves in his hair.

A minute, five minutes, an hour, time lost meaning—only that when they broke off the kiss it was too soon, but words needed to be said, answers needed to be given for this miraculous moment.

"How?"

Jack took a deep breath, slowing down his rising and falling chest, proof the kiss had affected him as much as it had Astra.

"Short version, it turns out you can leave the Julemarked even when it's after midnight. The longer version involves a sledge-hammer, a blizzard outside of Moscow, and some creative paper-work."

Chapter Thirty-Three

Holding Astra in his arms, Jack couldn't believe he had finally made it, that he could touch her at last. Jack needed to kiss her again, he needed to hold her tight, he needed to tell her so much. He wanted to do it all but couldn't decide which he wanted most.

Astra looked around them and seemed to realize they had drawn a bit of attention with all the kissing. She straightened and smoothed her skirt.

"Let's go to my office." He picked up his bag as she took his hand and led him to a small and cozy office, full of stacks of paper and pictures of her friends and family. It even smelled like her, citrus and jasmine and summer (now he couldn't wait to find out if that's what summer smelled like).

Astra turned the two chairs in front of her desk toward each other and gestured for him to take a seat. They sat, and she took his hands in hers.

"Tell me everything," she said.

"I knew the instant the wall appeared I had made a mistake. I punched at the bricks." Astra winced at the thought. "Not my brightest moment, but a tiny chip of mortar came out, then immediately filled in. I knew the wall could be broken. I knew it."

He held up his hand where the bleeding knuckles had given way to scabs and now were puckered pink scars.

He remembered the terror of that night, knowing he didn't want to spend another minute in the Julemarked. He had rushed to the storage shed containing tools and grabbed a sledgehammer, not even acknowledging his brothers as he passed through the bakery, where they had finished the cleaning that he and Astra had abandoned minutes before.

The first whack against the wall sounded like a dull thud, followed by the clatter of small brick chunks to the pavement below. He swung again before the wall could heal itself completely, scattering more chunks. With a grunt, he swung again. His progress was slowed by the self-healing wall, but he wouldn't quit until he was through. He remembered the story his dad had told of Gunter—his motives needed to be pure. What was more pure than love? His jaw tightened as he swung again, but this time there was a second thud. Mads had joined him with another sledgehammer. To his left stood Orn and Carl, each holding pickaxes, and they took turns hammering in the same area, not letting the wall gain on their progress.

Jack gave them a wide smile; no words were needed—they knew. The dull thuds were followed by more clatters, and larger chunks of wall. Jack had no idea how thick it was, or if there even was another side. He only knew he had to keep going.

"Do you have a plan?" Mads asked, breaking the silence. Some of the Julemarked residents had gathered to watch, one running off to find his parents, he presumed.

"Get through."

"That's the plan?" Mads stopped hammering to stare at him.

Jack swung with all his strength and a chunk flew back and hit him in the mouth; he barely felt it, but when he ran his tongue over his teeth, he felt a jagged edge where he had chipped a tooth.

Jack swung again and grunted a response. "Yes."

"You don't even know where you'll be. You could land in the middle of the ocean."

"I'll figure it out."

Mads picked up his sledgehammer again and, between blows, gave him all the brotherly advice he could.

"Assuming you don't get eaten by wild animals or shot in a war zone, get to the nearest city with a Christmas market and look for the contact." Mads paused to look at the hole. It was getting bigger. Soon he'd be able to get through, so there wasn't much time. "Your best bet is to go to where the Julemarked appears. They usually keep an eye on the area. Once you find the contact, they'll get you the paperwork and money you'll need to find her."

Jack nodded. He could do that. He had to do that. The hole was almost big enough for him to jump through. It was dark on the other side, so there was no way of knowing where he'd land. It could be Singapore or Antarctica. For all he knew, he could end up on the other side of the universe. No matter what, he'd find a way back to Astra. She was his Christmas star, leading him home.

Another swing, and he felt a hand on his shoulder. His father held out a bag with a long strap that bulged, his eyes filled with understanding.

"Let us know you made it."

His mom hugged him tight. "I knew she'd take you from me."

"Mom," Jack said.

"Shh." She cut him off. "Tell her I'm sorry."

She kissed his cheek and let him go.

Pausing long enough to slip the bag across his body, briefly noting it was heavier than he had expected, Jack squeezed his father's shoulder and caught a glimpse of Ani. She gave him a nod, which was all the goodbye he had time for.

He returned to the wall, hammering with more intensity now that they were so close to breaking through. He gave each of his brothers a nod and one last swing. Without looking back, he dropped the hammer and dove through the hole into a pile of snow. He looked over his shoulder in time to see Mads's face before it was covered by bricks that disappeared into nothing, leaving him alone.

Around him was snow, miles of it. The sweat he'd worked up from the hammering quickly froze and he dug into the bag his dad had given him before he got too cold. His father had packed for all occasions but included extra sweaters, a coat, mittens and a hat, extra food, and some water and ginger. He layered on everything and looked around him. Snow swirled, but it was more from the wind than weather. White surrounded him, and stars twinkled above, the same stars he'd seen all his life, but reversed. High in the sky he found Orion, and followed the path to the Christmas Tree Cluster, his eyes filling in the shape once he'd spotted the trunk and top star. Seeing it above was like a sign that he was on the right path, following the stars back to his own. With one last glance above, he started walking toward the nearest lights.

While cold, it wasn't unbearably so. As he approached the remote farm that was the first sign of habitation he saw, he looked for clues to where he might be. He could rule out most warm countries.

A truck stood outside with a Russian license plate. At least he spoke the language. He knocked on the door. A tall bearded man in a plaid shirt and jeans answered it.

It took Jack a few moments to explain he was lost and to learn that they were four hours from Moscow, the closest Christmas market town. And it was already mid-January. He'd jumped almost three weeks forward in time. In the bottom of his bag, Jack found gold rectangles, each about the size of a pack of cards, which his father had added in for just this type of circumstance. They didn't know where he would land, but most places valued gold enough that he could barter with it. The man agreed to let him sleep on the couch and to take him to the nearest village in exchange for one of the gold rectangles.

The next day, the farmer dropped him off in the village, where he found a bank to cash in another gold rectangle. Using the money, he made his way to Moscow, where it took him a few weeks to connect with the Julemarked contact near Red Square. From there, it took almost two months and the rest of his gold bars to get a passport and the necessary paperwork to leave Russia and fly to the United States. Jack had focused on only the next step, not knowing when he'd actually find his way back to Astra.

It wasn't until he found her at her library (after going to two different locations) that he had let himself believe it was real. He knew her instantly even though her back was to him, the way her auburn hair grazed her shoulders, a little longer than the last time he'd seen her, the way she held a book like she was cradling a treasure—her fingers trailing over the cover.

His heart had hammered with disbelief that he was actually here. His arm reached for the nearest bookshelf for support as he took a few deep breaths to calm his trembling. It had been a gamble coming here instead of to her house. He'd thought about waiting at her home, or leaving her a message on her door, but once he'd landed in Milwaukee, he knew he had to see her as quickly as possible.

Now that he was here, doubt crept in. Would she be happy to see him? What if she had moved on? What if she never wanted to see him again? He'd been such a fool to not go with her that night. He'd anticipated this reunion from the moment he'd jumped through the brick wall, and it hadn't occurred to him that she might not feel the same. She hadn't spent months thinking about their reunion. She'd spent months moving on with her life. Maybe this wasn't the best thing for her. Was he being selfish? She had a life, and how would he fit into it—and why hadn't he thought of any of this before now?

The doubt threatened to overwhelm him. Maybe he should leave—reach out to her another way that was less confrontational. He didn't want her to feel uncomfortable or put on the spot.

An older man sat at a computer not far from Jack, and he was watching him—his white hair unruly. Their eyes met and he nodded, as if to say, "Now's your chance—take it."

With that tiny nod of encouragement, Jack found the courage he needed. He'd come too far to not see it through. They both deserved to know what could happen, whether it ended five minutes from now with a brutal rejection, or fifty years from now after a long life together. They deserved that.

Now, what to do?

Jack wanted to say something romantic, something memorable, something that would convey how important she was to him. If this went well, this would be a story they told their children, grandchildren, and friends for the rest of their lives. It needed to be something that made her knees weak and her heart flutter. But in the end, he could only say the word that was in his heart.

"Astra."

As she had turned, his anxiety over his word choice had evaporated when he saw her face for the first time in months, more beautiful than he had remembered.

And now they sat in her office, fingers intertwined, and he planned to never stop touching her.

"I can't believe you're here," Astra said. Wonder shone from her eyes as she trailed her hand down his arm, touching her forehead to his. "I have so many questions and want everything in greater detail, but there's one important thing I need you to answer."

"Anything."

"Why didn't you call? I could have helped."

Jack looked embarrassed.

"I didn't know how long it would take and I didn't know if you'd even want me. I guess I figured it would be harder to send me back if you saw me in person."

Astra shook her head and smiled.

"You fool, of course I want you." Astra looked down at the ground. "I do have to tell you something," Astra said, struggling to find the words. "I never thought I'd see you again."

Jack tamped down the dread that surged. That was never a good way to start a conversation. Was she with someone? Married again? That wasn't logical, but nothing about this was.

"Please just blurt it out. I can take it."

Astra squeezed his hands.

"It's not bad news, at least I don't think so." She took a deep breath. "I'm pregnant." Jack didn't move. He was pretty sure his eyes were still blinking, but that was it. That wasn't what he'd expected. He did the math. She'd be three, maybe four months pregnant. Assuming it was his. Please let it be his. His glance shifted to her stomach.

"It's definitely yours," Astra said, seeming to know what he was thinking.

His mind raced ahead to teaching their little one how to bake, decorate a Christmas tree, build a snowman, sled down a hill. Everything he'd always dreamed of was happening; he just hadn't expected it to happen on the Outside.

"How?" he finally said.

"The usual way." Astra laughed. "We were stupid."

"No, that's not what I meant. Or maybe it was. I just never thought, it never occurred to me." He finally took a deep breath and let the wonderful news sink in. "I'm so happy."

He was. Jack had left everything he thought he wanted, the Julemarked, his family, that quiet, simple life. He'd left it all, and had never been happier.

"Let's get out of here," Astra said.

Before they left the library, Astra sent her friends a text.

> To Ronnie, Cassie, Steph: My house ASAP. Be ready to
> celebrate. Bring husbands and kids.

"I hope you're ready for this," Astra said.

"Before they get here, I have something for you," Jack said, reaching into his bag and pulling out a grayish book—the book of Hans Christian Andersen fairy tales. "I found this in the bag after I left, so I assume Old Johan put it in there. He did say it was meant to be with you."

Astra clasped it to her chest.

"Thank you. I can't believe he gave this to me."

She set the book next to her only remaining nisse.

They'd been home for only a few minutes and Cassie was already pulling into the driveway, her husband and kids emerging from the car. Ronnie was right behind them with a bag. Before they all got to the door, Steph arrived. Cassie's husband went to help Rob out of the car while Cassie and Ronnie helped free Steph's kids. The entire crowd entered the house through the side door that led into the kitchen. Astra and Jack waited for them by the fireplace.

Before coming into view, Ronnie shouted, "We're here, what's the news? Are you . . . ?" She stopped mid-sentence when she saw Jack standing next to Astra with his arm around her. Steph held her hand out to Ronnie. "Dammit." Ronnie dug in her pocket and handed Steph a crumpled bill. "She always fucking knows."

The kids gasped, then giggled at the language, and the room erupted in squeals of joy, back slapping, exuberant hugs, and Bernie tippy-tapping among everyone, assuming she was the cause of the excitement. Someone opened a bottle of champagne for the adults and passed out glasses. Someone else opened sparkling nonalcoholic cider for the kids and Astra.

"I ordered the good Indian takeout. It should be here in thirty," Steph said. "I got extra tikka masala for the picky eaters." She looked down at her kids.

In the corner, Rob settled into an armchair with one arm still in a cast, but he managed to hold a glass of champagne just fine. The men were laughing at something. They would never replace Jack's brothers, but he would fit in well with the gentle fathers and generous husbands.

She had given up on hope so many times, given up on the idea that she could have the future she had always wished for. That's the funny thing about wishes: they don't disappear when you give up on them—especially when they were wished upon a star.

Chapter Thirty-Four

"How does anyone not remember this place? It's like the North Pole on steroids," Ronnie said. Astra and Ronnie had come to help Jack move the belongings he wanted into her house and get the boxes she had left last Yule. They sat at a picnic table outside Kringle All the Way, sipping hot coffee that Jack had brought out to them. His kringle were fantastic, but his coffee was the true miracle, the perfect balance between smooth and bitter to wake her up. She had missed it while pregnant, and now that she was nursing, she still needed to be careful, but with little Lisbet keeping them both up most nights, coffee had become a necessity. At the moment, Lisbet was getting shown off to all the Julemarked residents by Jack's parents. His mom was so thrilled to meet her new granddaughter, she didn't even seem upset that Jack had left, though they had to promise to spend any Yule in Milwaukee at the Julemarked. That was more than fair.

"Only people who make a personal connection with someone who lives here remember. No one really knows why. My theory is you remember because of me and Jack. That's your personal connection," Astra said, covering a yawn with her mittened hand.

"So if I start kissing people, will they remember it?"

"I don't think it works that way, but feel free to give it a go," Astra said.

"What about him?" Ronnie said, nodding toward Jack and the man he was walking with. It was John.

John's brown hair was effortlessly perfect, like he'd stepped out of a Versace ad, especially coupled with his dark wool coat, cashmere scarf, and slim dark pants. He didn't seem to notice that every woman in a twenty-foot radius checked him out. Now that she knew John better, she couldn't wait to see how he reacted to Ronnie.

"What are you lovely ladies discussing?" Jack said as he and John joined them at the table. He set a box down next to Astra.

"Ronnie wondered if she should start kissing random people in the Julemarked. You know . . ." Astra looked at John. "So they would remember the Julemarked after it disappeared."

"Well, not random. I did have someone specific in mind." She gave John a long look up and down. "I don't think he'd forget anything about kissing me."

Jack laughed and John grinned back.

"I'm in if you are," John said.

"Ronnie, this is John," Jack explained. "He's a local who helps the Julemarked when it shows up here." Jack lowered his voice. "So he already remembers it."

"I'm their fixer," John said.

Jack sat next to Astra and she leaned into his warmth, even though it wasn't that cold. Being near him warmed her from the inside.

"So you're local," Ronnie said, eyeing him up and down.

"Born-and-bred Stallis boy."

Ronnie held out her hand to him.

"Pleasure to meet you, John."

Something occurred to Astra.

"How do you remember the Julemarked?" Astra asked.

"Mads and I had a fun Yule several years ago," John said.

"And Heidi from the glassblower the next Yule," Jack said.

"I certainly didn't forget her. There are websites for the things we . . ." John said.

"That's enough, I don't need to know any more about the websites." Astra laughed.

"I do," Ronnie said. "I love a good website. The internet is full of all sorts of fun nooks and crannies about nooks and crannies." She tapped the bench next to her for John to sit down and they began talking between them about things that made Astra blush.

Astra leaned her head onto Jack's shoulder.

"I think Ronnie has found her soul mate."

"I know the feeling," Jack said, kissing the top of her head.

"What was John fixing for you today? I thought you already had the paperwork you needed."

"That just got me here. John is creating a history of me in the world including better identification, bank accounts, a job history. I think I even have a tweeters."

"Twitter?" Astra chuckled.

"Yes, that's the one. I'm a real boy now."

"How does he get all that? Is he a criminal?" Ronnie said, overhearing their conversation, and examined John with new, intrigued eyes.

Jack laughed.

"While not entirely legal, he's not a criminal in the sense you mean. He's made some connections on where to get things through his job. He's surprisingly inventive and resourceful."

"It appears there was no consequence from your dramatic escape," Astra said. Jack had told her the story about Gunter and how his escape attempt had caused the Julemarked to jump ahead five years.

"Dad said there wasn't even a blip. I guess that proves Old Johan's theory right. For the right reasons, the Julemarked will change the rules." Jack pulled her tighter. Jack had changed his rules for love, too. Astra was grateful every day for it.

"Did you get everything?" she asked.

"Almost. When the bakery closes, the boys will help me load up the truck." He nudged the box. "But I thought you'd like to be in charge of this one."

Astra sat up and pulled the box closer.

"Is it . . ." She didn't finish her sentence, instead opening the box to see several pointy red hats nestled into newspaper. She hugged the box to her. "I have missed my nisser." Astra looked around the alley. "Are you sure you want to give this up? I know it comes with a cost."

"A life without you and Lisbet in it is not a life. There isn't even a question, I'm just sorry I didn't realize it a few seconds sooner. At least I didn't wait until the next Yule."

"Year. We say 'year' on the Outside."

"Year," Jack repeated.

"And there will be many more." Astra kissed his cheek. "But first, Florida."

Chapter Thirty-Five

BERNIE DASHED THROUGH THE WAVES, CHASING A SEAGULL into the sky with a woof. When it came to water, the Lab part of her won out over the mountain dog.

It had taken them three full days to drive down, partly because she was teaching Jack how to drive, partly because they had to stop to feed Lisbet and let Bernie run around. When they had pulled into the parking spot the night before, the sun had already set, so they couldn't see the water, only hear the waves hitting the sand in a rhythmic pattern with the warm breeze against their skin. Her parents promptly relieved them of Lisbet and sent them to bed.

Next week, Ronnie, Steph, Cassie, and their families would join them for a week of chaos and loud laughter and so much food. Her parents had started making daily excursions to stock up on everything from diapers to alcohol.

Right now, Jack stood ankle-deep in the water as the waves washed around him and Bernie chased each one back into the Gulf of Mexico. He stared at the vast expanse of dark blue that was growing lighter as the sun rose higher in the sky. In his arms, he held Lisbet close to his bare chest and whispered stories in her tiny ears.

"He's been out there since the sun started to rise," her dad said as he joined her on the beach, a steaming cup of coffee in his hand. "He makes a mean cup. No matter what, hang on to that one."

"There's more to a good man than his ability to make coffee."

"True, he made some kringle, too. Best I've ever had."

Jack still woke up hours before her, unable to break a lifetime of habit. He had even made kringle dough before they went to bed the night before, saying it was part of his nightly wind-down and he couldn't sleep until he'd made some. His hands started rolling kringle dough before he was fully awake. Back in Milwaukee, John was helping Jack find a place to work and had already connected him with a chef who would be interested in some unique dinner kringle. Things were coming together like the pieces of a puzzle.

That sense of peace she had felt in the Julemarked came with Jack when he left it. Anytime they were together, she felt it.

"Are you ready to see what's under the waves?" Astra walked to stand next to the two loves of her life, taking Lisbet from his arms when she reached out for her mama. Holding Lisbet brought Astra an entirely different kind of joy and completeness. Every day she discovered her love ran deeper than the day before.

"I've seen seas before, but I've never been in it," Jack said. "The water is so warm and clear." He whispered the words as if he were in a church, with reverence and awe. Astra tickled Lisbet's toes, then handed her to her waiting mom, whose patience had been tested while waiting her turn.

"Finally," she mumbled, and carried Lisbet off to the tent they had set up for her now that the sun was starting to rise.

Astra had on her UV swim shirt and shorts, perfect for snorkeling because she didn't need as much sunscreen. She handed a similar swim shirt to Jack and a tube of reef-safe sunscreen for any skin left exposed.

"We need to protect your pale skin. You do not want to start out with a sunburn."

"I've never had a sunburn."

He pulled the shirt over his head.

"Today's not the day."

"Is it weird that I kind of want one? Just to say that I have."

"Yes, it is. But if you really want one, try it later in the trip."

She helped him apply sunscreen to his exposed skin, enjoying the excuse to let her fingers caress his neck. They waded into the water up to their waists and she showed him how to put on the face mask and snorkel.

"Your brain is going to tell you to take your face out of the water to breathe. You need to ignore it. Let's practice here before we put on our fins."

Jack put his face in the water.

"Now breathe. Slowly. In and out."

It didn't take him long to get the hang of it. As they wrangled on their flippers, it occurred to her that he might not know how to swim. She looked over at him, but he was already gently kicking himself forward—a natural.

She caught up with him and he gave her a thumbs-up. As they went toward the reef, she pointed out a starfish hiding in the sea grass, a lobster's antennae poking out from some rocks, and tiny blue fish darting between small swaying sea fans.

It was Christmas morning without a snowflake in sight, only blue water as far as they could see. As they approached the small reef, Jack tapped her arm and pointed to a medium-size turtle coasting ahead of them, pausing to nibble on some sea grass. They floated in the water, just the two of them. Jack reached over and grabbed her hand, and they shared this moment together.

When they returned to the knee-deep water an hour later, she pulled off her flippers and looped them over her hand so she could walk to shore, leaving her mask in place. She turned to see if Jack needed help removing his own awkward footwear, but he was kneeling in the water beside her, his mask pushed back onto his forehead and his hands fumbling at the waist of his shorts. Water dripped from his hair, his swim shirt clinging to his defined torso.

"Do you need help?" Astra asked. He'd been doing so well, she'd forgotten that this was his first time snorkeling.

His hand curved around something and he looked up. His eyes matched the color of the water he knelt in, sparkling as much as the waves at sunset.

"Astra," Jack said, a faint tremor to his voice. "Before you, I thought my life was perfect. I had family, community, a long life in a literal magical land, but I wasn't living—not really. I had abundant time, so it had no value. When I almost lost you, I realized how meaningless time was when I couldn't be with you. You've shown me that a second lived with the right person is better than one hundred years alone. Now every moment is precious because I know its worth."

He opened his hand to reveal a sparkling diamond ring that resembled a star or maybe even a snowflake—she loved that it could be either. Set in white gold, a round center stone was surrounded by smaller pear-shaped diamonds that formed the points.

"Will you do me the honor of making every second of my life priceless?"

The last year had been full of change for both of them, but through it, Astra never doubted they belonged together.

"Yes!" Astra said, unable to find any other words.

He slid the ring onto her still-dripping finger. Once it was secure, she couldn't wait for him to stand. She pulled off her mask, tossing it to the beach, and sat on his bent knee, sealing their love with a salty kiss as the waves dared to knock them over.

Growing up, Christmas had been crisp snow, cold wind, and fresh-cut evergreen trees. Astra had always assumed that without all those things, Christmas would feel like any other plain day of the year. But with Jack in her life, that wasn't true, and never had been. Surrounded by a salty breeze, swaying palm trees, and brilliant blue water, she realized Christmas wasn't a place or a season or a time. Christmas was a state of mind—one she would never forget.

Acknowledgments

Nathaniel Hawthorne said, "Easy reading is damn hard writing." While I don't know if you'll find *Once Upon a December* easy reading or fun reading or even enjoyable reading (though I certainly hope you do), I do know it was a doozy to write (pandemics, computer crashes, and more!). To all those authors who wrote books during a pandemic—I see you, I know what you did, and you are all rock stars.

On to the amazing people who helped make this book possible.

Karma Brown, Colleen Oakley, and Heather Webb—my debt of gratitude for your time, wisdom, and unflinching feedback can never be repaid. Every writer should have friends like you, I hope I did you proud.

Nicole Blades, Sarah Cannon, Carla Cullen, Melissa Marino, the Tall Poppy Writers, and all the fabulous women writers who support one another behind the scenes. We are stronger together.

Laura Gest—thank you for reading and lending your experience to help me bring Astra's work world to life. And an enormous THANK-YOU to librarians everywhere. You are the story walkers, the empathy masters, the wisdom keepers. You are the first line of defense against ignorance and hate, and welcome everyone with open doors and pages. If there was a place where time worked differently, it would be a library.

"There was nothing quite like the friendships forged in close living quarters, then tempered with copious amounts of bad pizza and cheap booze." Kate Clausen, Anne Siess, Lynette Skidmore, Lorelie Parolin, Maria Cancino, and Kara Patterson—you inspired my badass quartet of women (and don't waste time trying to figure out who is who—they are an amalgam of us all). I love you all!

Rachel Ekstrom Courage. You've been by my side since the beginning, and I am so very grateful for your guidance, business savvy, and enthusiasm. I'm so excited for what comes next.

Kerry Donovan—thank you for your excellent editorial comments and flexibility. You have a wonderful talent for asking the right questions that sends me down exciting new paths. Thank you to the Berkley family, including Tina Joell, Jessica Mangicaro, and Mary Baker. Also, Vikki Chu for the flawless cover (I'm obsessed with the snowflakes), Stacy Edwards, Eileen Chetti, Craig Burke, Jeanne-Marie Hudson, and Claire Zion.

Try as I might to keep my writing during normal daytime hours, I inevitably end up crabby, rushed, and stressed when a deadline approaches. My supportive and loving family takes it all in stride. John, Ainsley, Sam, Mom, Sandy, Pam—I'm so lucky to have you!

Lastly, a giant hug to all my readers. Thank you for continuing to read, share, and recommend my books. XO!

Once Upon a December

Amy E. Reichert

Questions for Discussion

1. In *Once Upon a December*, Christmas traditions, like Astra's annual trip to the Milwaukee Christmas market, play an important role. What are some of your favorite Christmas traditions?

2. Christmas means something different for different people. For Jack, it's his everyday experience. For Astra, it's snow and sparkling Christmas trees. Over the course of the novel, do these meanings change or evolve? How so? What does Christmas mean to you?

3. Astra's group of friends is clearly supportive of one another and represents a celebration of female friendship. Over the course of the novel, what are some examples of their bond? Why do you think female friendship is so important to Astra? Do you agree or disagree? Why?

4. In the novel, Astra initially chooses to leave her friends, job, and family to join Jack in the Julemarked, but changes her mind at the last minute. What do you think of her flip-flopping? Given a similar choice, would you choose to live with your true love in a magical place where you would age slowly and your dog would live much longer or stay with your sometimes frustrating job, annoying ex-husband, and fantastic friends and family?

5.   It isn't until Astra remembers all of her past encounters with Jack and the Julemarked that she decides (at least for a while) that she is going to leave with him. What about her remembering pushed her to that decision? Do you think those memories were crucial, or should she have been able to make a decision without them?

6.   Nowadays, libraries are so much more than a place to check out books. Many have unexpected items in their circulation, like paintings, portable Wi-Fi, zoo passes, and even kayaks. In addition, they offer programs for all ages of patrons, story hours, after-school programs, and so much more. A librarian is trained to help patrons find the resources they need, whether in a book or on the internet, and offer services that will best support their community. (Visit your local library to find out about their offerings.) How do you think Astra's work as a library director reflects her character?

7.   In *Once Upon a December*, you see Astra and Jack's love story unfold in two timelines. How did learning about their past encounters affect your understanding of the present-day meetings? Did it change your understanding of events?

8.   How does the title, *Once Upon a December*, reflect the story and themes?

9.   Why are all dogs perfect?

Keep reading for an excerpt from
Amy E. Reichert's novel . . .

THE KINDRED SPIRITS
SUPPER CLUB

Available in paperback from Berkley!

TWO DAYS, TWENTY-THREE HOURS, AND THIRTY-TWO MIN-utes. Almost three full days since Sabrina Monroe had last spoken to someone who wasn't a relative. Her record was seven days, four hours, and fifty-five minutes, but still, almost three days was impressive. In her ideal world, she could continue the trend indefinitely, a sweet happily ever after of telecommuting and food delivery.

She sat in the center of a large indoor waterpark, the WWW (Wild World of Waterparks)—or Three Dub, as people had started calling it—the latest addition to the Waterpark Capital of the World. The fake boulders hadn't yet acquired the usual dust and stuck gum, the colors still popped on the waterslides, and the painted murals were not yet dimmed by years of exposure to eye-burning levels of chlorine. With her feet propped on a white plastic chair, identical to the one she sat in, Sabrina stopped scrolling through the news app on her phone when a stack of towels toppled off a neighboring table into a puddle. She scooped them up, draping the wet towels over chairbacks and setting the still-dry towels at the center of the table, then returned to her lounging position before anyone noticed. Her nieces and nephew, Arabella, Lilly, and Oscar, frolicked in the kiddie area, a three-tiered structure of rope bridges, water cannons, and small slides for the little ones not quite ready to brave the twisty four-story flumes. An enormous bucket dropped one thousand gallons of water every fifteen minutes with a clang, a roar, and a rush of wind that blew over a lazy river circling the entire room, where tubes bobbed like Froot Loops and tweens raced around floating adults, who scowled at their rambunctiousness.

It should have been difficult to take her nieces and nephew to a waterpark without speaking to other people, but she had bought the tickets online, then took refuge among the crowded tables while the kids played. Being alone was always easiest in a crowded, noisy location, and no room was louder or more crowded than an indoor waterpark on a rainy holiday weekend.

Within the confines of this humid, echoing warehouse, Sabrina avoided interacting with people by scrolling through the news on her phone. She didn't notice the people who stood up with meerkat attentiveness. She didn't notice the people swiping chairs from other tables. She didn't notice a nearby angry, tattooed chair-swiping victim returning from the snack bar with a giant fully loaded margarita.

Dumb luck had her looking up from her phone at exactly the wrong moment.

She watched as the Refill-A-Rita catapulted out of the tattooed man's hand, centrifugal force and a red plastic lid keeping most of the fire-engine-red contents inside until they collided with the bridge of her nose. Tequila-laden pseudo-strawberry slush exploded onto her hair down to her flip-flopped feet, staining her yellow swimsuit a sunset orange and obscuring her vision with kaleidoscoping stars from the surprising pain. Bent over in agony, Sabrina avoided the unexpectedly aerodynamic white plastic chair that followed the margarita as it arced over her head toward the chair swipers.

A man wearing colorful swim trunks emblazoned with red crustaceans fought back a smile as his eyes inspected the substance dripping from her head, confirming Sabrina's ridiculous appearance. What right did he have to judge her? He had crabs on his pants. As he took a breath to speak, Sabrina broke her no-talking streak.

"Duck," she said, pointing to his white plastic table as a cup of soda soared over them. Caught in food-fight cross fire, the man crouched under it and out of the fray. Now she could do the same.

Sabrina dropped to the ground and scooted to safety, wiping the worst of the overly sweet slop off her face, the alcohol and red dye stinging her eyes. The warring people around her shouted, more food and plastic water bottles skittered across the wet concrete, and soon tables stuttered as bodies shoved against them. The man huddled under his table an aisle over from her. Around them, the babble of water rushing, children screaming, and parents yelling echoed off the walls and windows, amplifying the noise.

From her location under the table, she could spot her charges scampering in the spraying water, oblivious to the commotion at the nearby tables.

Two beefy men shoved at each other like Greco-Roman wrestlers, hairy bellies bumping against each other. Feet stumbled past her table, knocking her phone into a waiting puddle. She snatched it out of the water as her heart raced. Not her phone. She didn't have the money to replace it. She dried it off the best she could on a small, still-clean section of her swimsuit.

A pair of delicate feet stopped beside her table, followed by a cheerful face framed by chin-length bouncing blond curls. The woman's edges blurred into a soft glow as if she stood in front of a lamp. With Ghost Molly, it was barely noticeable. More recently deceased spirits had a blur that made it obvious they were new to the afterlife, helping Sabrina and her mom recognize them.

"Whatcha doing, honey?"

"Hey, Molly." Sabrina wasn't surprised to see her here, in the middle of the brouhaha and unconcerned for her safety as a tray of nachos splattered through her toes—the perks of being ethereal. She'd known Ghost Molly all her life, and she often appeared when Sabrina least expected her. Sabrina scooted over to make room. Between one blink and the next, Molly situated herself next to Sabrina under the table, her arms wrapped around her bent knees, excitement sparkling in her eyes. Sabrina checked her phone, making sure it still worked. So far, so good. She clutched it to her chest, careful to keep it out of the sticky margarita.

"This is bananas. What happened?" Molly said.

"Chair swipers. It escalated quickly." Sabrina's nose throbbed, the pain seeping across her face like water into dry ground. "Why can't people use their words?"

"Look at that cutie-patootie." Molly pointed to the judgmental crustacean-clad man between the chairs and table legs. "Let's scooch over to his table."

Sabrina shook her head. Molly loved shoving her toward men. A rush of warm air hit her face from the giant water bucket, drying the melted margarita coating her face and chest. Her skin started to itch.

"This will probably be all over the internet later," Sabrina said, ignoring Molly's comment. A nearby table was jostled.

Molly smiled. "Will you show me the videos?"

"Yeah."

"Pinky promise?" Molly held up her hand with the pinky extended. Sabrina matched the gesture. When their pinkies touched, it was like sticking her finger in a snowbank. Molly beamed. She loved internet videos.

Khaki-encased legs and sturdy shoes walked by the table.

"Security's here," Sabrina said.

As Sabrina leaned forward to get onto her hands and knees, a glop of slush fell onto her wrist. Gross. By the time she straightened on her feet, Molly stood next to her, too. She wore high-waisted turquoise swim bottoms that cut in a straight line over her belly button and a matching thick-strapped bikini top that ended under her rib cage, leaving only a couple inches of exposed skin between the top and bottom, so much cuter than the margarita-splotched yellow tankini Sabrina wore. It was infinitely easier to wear cute clothes when you could conjure them with a thought. Molly bounced on the balls of her feet while watching the hubbub around her. Some of the nearby people still shouted as the security team separated the warring families.

"This is so exciting," Molly said. "Oh, here comes the cutie." She pointed.

The dark-haired man approached her table with a stack of towels, weaving between the crowded plastic tables and gawking patrons. She wanted to crawl under the table and dig a pit she could disappear into, hiding the melting slush and blossoming black eyes of her embarrassing situation.

"He's the cat's pajamas," Molly said, waggling her eyebrows. "Just how I like 'em."

Sabrina wanted to agree, but her mind threw up every defense. He was going to talk to her, and she would only be able to stare back at him. She started cataloging facts to distract herself. He had thick, wavy hair flopping in different directions, longer on top and shorter on the sides, and a few days' scruff defining his jaw and framing his full lips. Small red patches flanked the bridge of his nose where glasses must usually perch. Later, when she replayed this moment over in excruciating detail, she'd realize he was exactly her type, but for now she ignored it and moved on. He stopped in front of her.

"They take their seating seriously here," he said with a smile.

Sabrina blinked. He'd made a joke about the asinine situation. She wanted to respond with something clever, or at least something not idiotic. Instead, her mouth went dry and she focused on the pulsating pain increasing across her head—anything to distract from her racing heart.

When she didn't speak, he continued. "I thought you might need these." His voice was low and smooth, yet with a touch of roughness, like he had been out too late at a concert the night before or spent the day in the chemical-laden air of WWW. Blue eyes took in her sloppy appearance and stopped on her nose—ground zero of her misery. She pulled her eyes from the wet concrete floor to look over his right ear, close enough that he might think she was making eye contact.

"Thank you." There, that was a perfectly normal response. Sabrina grabbed the top towel and wrapped it around her shoulders to stop more slush from sliding down her swimsuit. Molly stood behind him, signaling that Sabrina should smile by pointing at her own dimpled grin. Sure, smiling like a fool was exactly what this moment needed.

Sabrina ignored her and grabbed another towel to wipe off her face. Not being able to see him gave her time to take a calming breath—in through the nose, out through the mouth.

"Are you okay? I saw that giant margarita hit your face," he said. "I can't believe the distance that flew. I think we have a new Olympic event."

More jokes she'd ignore. Witty banter rarely worked for her; instead it came out as awkward. Even through the terry cloth, his attention burned on her face, adding to the stuffy heat in the waterpark.

"Not great." Sabrina patted the towel carefully around her nose. It hurt to touch the skin. She hoped to hide any bruising, which would be difficult to explain at work, in addition to her Kool-Aid-stained skin. It would take forever to scrub off. There was only one way to handle this. She gulped in some air so she could keep talking. Thinking about it only made it worse. She blurted the first comeback that came to her. "Red's my color."

He laughed at her joke.

He laughed. At her joke.

But was he laughing at her because what she said was funny? Or because she looked funny? Or because she was being so bumbling it was funny? Either way, it was a good laugh that came from his belly, where all real laughs were born. It wasn't a cruel laugh. Those she could recognize.

Molly gave Sabrina two thumbs up. Sabrina struggled to stop a scowl from forming in response. It had been too long since she'd had to ignore a ghost while talking to a non–family member.

"I'm Ray." His lips curved up at the corners, and their fullness didn't flatten when he smiled. She didn't want to be thinking about his lips. She wanted him to go away. She bowed her head, and he kept talking. "Do you want to shower off?"

Shit. He wasn't going away. Sabrina tried to relax the muscles in her body, the ones that wanted her to remain stiff and alert to all potential danger. Peak flight mode.

"I'm going to grab the kids and head out." She pointed in the direction of the giant bucket as it dropped the water, and a wave of air blew a loose strand of hair into the sticky residue on her nose. She wanted to say something clever, maybe hear him laugh again, but the words melted on her tongue. Her conflicted body and brain exhausted her.

"You have kids?" Ray said, searching the play area. Good, he wasn't looking at her anymore.

"No." Sabrina said. Molly crossed her forearms to form an X behind Ray's back, making it clear she didn't want Ray thinking Sabrina had kids. Molly liked to worry about things that didn't matter. She gave Molly a quick frown while Ray still looked toward the splash zone. "My brothers' kids," Sabrina continued. "I'm the cool aunt."

There, that was better. She could have normal interactions, even when covered in margarita.

"I bet you are." Ray reached out to pull the hair off her nose. Sabrina winced as even that small touch hurt. "That's not going to look great tomorrow. You should really get ice on it. I'll get some."

Before she could call him off, he headed toward the bar. Sabrina turned to Molly.

"You need to knock it off. I'm trying to have a conversation, and you're being very distracting."

"I'm *helping*."

"You think you're helping, but you're not. He may not be able to see you, but he can see my reactions. Just shush."

If Sabrina hurried, she could be gone before he returned, ending this awkward encounter. Ray seemed like a nice enough guy, but why bother getting to know someone well enough to get over the Awkwards when she'd be gone in a few months?

Amy E. Reichert is an author, wife, mom, Wisconsinite, amateur chef, and cider enthusiast. She earned her MA in English literature and serves on her library's board of directors. She is a member of Tall Poppy Writers.

Ready to find
your next great read?

Let us help.

Visit prh.com/nextread

Penguin
Random
House